No Serenity

Alex Campbell Real Estate Mystery Novel

Volume Two

By Charles Chaplin
(no kidding)

Binx
Publishing

Seattle, WA

Published by Binx Publishing Seattle, WA

ISBN: 978-0-9852103-1-1

Books by Charles Chaplin

WARNING:

Hopefully as your flight continues you have found some amusement with the first Alex Campbell Real Estate Mystery Novel, No-List Alex. It's not necessary to read that one first but it does help the writer's meager bank account. This second installment will hopefully see you through your connecting flight. You have re-boarded your delayed connection, the blob with dandruff and Doritos breath is still hanging over in your narrow seat, the woman who insisted on bringing on board a kitchen sink for her mother in Omaha has now been shut up and reconciled to the fact that the sink has to be checked. The flight attendants are doing their cabin check, still smiling in spite of it all. It's a wonder they don't use electric cattle prods to herd us on and off the planes (there's a marketing idea, tough love airlines). What a horrific job, dealing with folks like you and me every day in crammed, recycled air filled tubes! Hopefully, this airplane read will be a nice diversion and you will have a laugh or two. It is not a politically correct novel. Please do not bother turning the pages or scrolling down if your fragile ego can't handle poking fun at the collective insanity of our species. Enjoy your flight and cheers!

One

"You know your dog has absolutely wonderful hip subluxion. Sort of like my little Hadley over there. See him? The Pembroke Welsh Corgi, next to that substandard poodle-- the one Barbara Moxler owns that she claims is purebred but we do have our doubts! Hadley is from the dam Montsford and sire of Pembroke, straight from the Isle of Brit pedigree. You know the line that shows at Westminster every year? Anyway, what is your adorable dog's name and isn't he an Otterhound?"

Oh god, a stuffy Capitol Heights queen on the loose at the dog park. And this one is one of the roly-poly, velvet loafer wearing, over middle age, variety. Complete with pinky signet ring and a violet cashmere sweater tied oh-so-casually over his plump shoulders. Eeeww! I knew we should not have stopped by the Capitol Heights Dog Park.

"Ahh, yes my dog over there is named Clyde. He's actually not a pure---,"

"Yes, he is just too cute! I'm Percival Emerson, Percy to my friends. No, I am not related to *the* Emerson but on my mother's side I am a direct descendant of Woodrow Wilson. Ahh, I know a purebred when I see one and your Clyde is one! Is his pedigree from a show Otterhound pairing?"

Is there anything more nauseating than a purebred, dog park, Nazi? "Well Percival, Clyde over there is a rare Scottish Lowland Terrier. Not to be confused with the common Scottish Terrier. You may not have heard of the breed, not too many have. It's all very in-house as we say. The breed is not often shown; we don't want just *anyone* getting a Lowland. Makes the breed so *common* when they become so well known, don't you think? I mean really, look what happened with the Bichon Frise, practically on cans of Alpo." I tried to get Clyde's attention, so we could hopefully beat a hasty retreat. Clyde is actually a pure bred mutt who happens to look a lot like Benji from the late 1970s movies. I made the whole Scottish Lowland Terrier breed up. I love to use it when I encounter the Percys of the dog world. And true to form, old Percy bit.

"Oh goodness, yes! You know, I am familiar with Scottish Lowland Terriers. I think my cousin may have had one years back. The whole dog world has become so common and commercialized. Why I can remember when hardly anyone knew what a Bichon was, much less could own one! Did you say your dog's name is Clyde? Now that *is* original. And stop this Percival bit, I told you I am Percy to my friends and I can just tell we are going to be great friends! Where did you say you lived in the Heights? It is simply amazing to me how Clinton has grown. I didn't grow up here. I'm originally from Marblehead, did the whole Exeter and Crimson routine, true blue, northeastern stock. And now all these years later, I've ended up here in Clinton. It's such a cozy place to live, don't you agree? I've got my investments to keep me busy and I occasionally do an interior or two. Just the stereotypical homosexual bachelor I suppose. And you?"

Oh shit. The full tilt third degree from a pretentious aging queen on the make no less. Why me? Always, me.

2

"Ahh, I'm Alex Campbell. I don't live in the Heights. I just stopped by to let Clyde have a quick run. I'm a real estate agent and Clyde is along with me today while I preview houses. In fact, I've got to get Clyde back on the leash; we have got to get moving. Lots of houses we still need to see on our preview list."

"Ohh, so nice to meet you Alex. Here let me give you my card. You never know when one of your listings or clients is going to need some interior design help." Percy pushed his business card in my hand, his pinky ringed, meaty little paw lingering a bit too long in my palm. Gross.

"Ahh, thank you Percy. Yes, you never know when a decorator may come in handy."

"Interior designer. Decorator sounds like someone who puts icing on cakes or a simpleton mother-in-law who thinks buying silk flowers at the local crafts store for the living room is creative. And yours, Alex? Your card? I run across all kinds of people. I would like your contact information. I think we have so much in common and need to get together, don't you?"

Not in this lifetime or the next you snobby, fruit cake. "Well, ahh, sure here is my card Percy. But you know I have to be blunt with you. I'm bisexual and currently very celibate, so I really don't think there is chance of a connection if you know what I mean?"

Percy leered, "Ohhh, one that plays hard to get! Now I do like a challenge. And you are bi to boot! That *is* so trendy these days. Well, that gives me a fifty percent chance. Anyway, we will simply have to set up a play date for my Hadley and your Clyde."

A dog play date, my ass. I managed to catch Clyde's eye and gave him a significant look. Miracle of miracles, he actually dropped the stick that was in his mouth and walked right over to me. Never, has Clyde willingly come over to be put back on his leash. He must have picked up on my desperate psychic plea to help me flee from this snotty, would-be suitor.

"Ohhh, I can see you and smoochy-pooch are going to go bye-bye. Time for you and daddy to get back to work my new doggy friend?" Percy said while leaning his face down and cupping Clyde's shaggy muzzle in his fat hands. "Tell Uncle Percy bye-bye Clyde. We'll have to set up a date for you and Hadley to play, huh?" Clyde answered by giving Percy a nice sloppy lick; right up the center of his pudgy face, from the bottom of his fat chin to the top of his poorly dyed, receding hair line. Percy leapt back, gave a sputtered gasp, while vigorously wiping his face on his pink, overly starched, shirt sleeve. When he looked up and saw us staring at him, Percy regained his composure and pretended to not be bothered by dog slobber.

"Ohh, I see our little Clyde here is a kisser! Why you little devil you." I'm sure Percy was jones-ing to whip out the bottle of hand sanitizer which he no doubt had stashed in his monogrammed leather fanny pack. "Ha, dogs, they can be just, so loving. Anyhow, Alex you *do* give me a call and we will have to set up the play date. I know Hadley would just adore it!" Yeah, sure. So far, Hadley had not given Clyde a second look. Currently his snout was busy scouring the bushes at the edge of the dog park.

4

"Yes, well nice to meet you Percy. You and Hadley enjoy the park." With that I snapped Clyde's leash on his collar and quickly took off for the street, where my old two-door, fading blue, Volvo was parked.

Clyde and I made a hasty retreat down the hill from Capitol Heights. It was true, I had been previewing a couple of houses. Now that the real estate market was slowing in Clinton, old habits such as previewing listings appeared to be making a comeback. I have been selling real estate in Clinton going on four years now and it is always something new. Talk about a sleaze filled industry. I sometimes feel as if I am the only agent who actually just tells it like it is and let the chips fall where they may. Maybe that is not the best way to handle things in terms of my bottom line, but quite frankly I don't have the energy or interest to constantly create and work on a good "sales" public persona. At least I am no longer known at my company, Winterfrost Real Estate, as "No-List Alex." My first listing turned into a family murder saga and the drama involved was not something I relished (see Volume One). Since then I have had more sedate listings.

I was done with previewing for the day but it sounded like the perfect white lie to get us away from the clutches of the pudgy queen on the make. I had Clyde safely belted in the passenger seat and he was sitting up very straight looking out as we wound our way through the mid-size city of Clinton. The sparkling water of Warner Sound glistened below, the summer heat making it sparkle even more. As we got into the aging downtown corridor, the water disappeared and assorted office towers, older white stone 1920s office buildings, rotting piers, and railroad tracks appeared. My neighborhood lies just south of downtown and is wedged in between a greenbelt. It is the old waterfront factory section and another set of railroad tracks boxes it in. Thus far, my hood has stayed off all gentrification radars. In fact, it does not even have an official name. It falls right between two city council districts, so it is almost officially no man's land. I like it that way. It keeps it undiscovered and hey, it was affordable when I purchased my small house a couple of years ago.

There are modest bungalows which were constructed for the factory workers in the early 1900s to1920s, Clinton's boom era. My 800 square foot bungalow sits on a dead end street and was built in 1919. When I purchased, it was essentially a tear down. I tried to keep as much of the "old world charm" (as we say in the real estate agent business) but there was not too much to salvage. If in fact, there had been much "charm" when it was constructed in 1919. I gutted most of it, made it into a two room house; open living room and kitchen and then there's the bedroom and a small bath. The entire back side of the house is now glass or rather two thirds of it is comprised of two glass and steel garage door panels. Then glass floor to ceiling windows with glass paned french doors in my bedroom. My lot backs right up to a greenbelt and has a large, ancient oak tree at the back of the lot. There is also a small stream that goes through the back yard.

I put Clyde in the back yard and he promptly took off to survey the grounds, make sure no squirrels had invaded his turf. I hit the switches and the two glass garage doors went up. I like fresh air and in the summer putting the two doors up usually keeps my house fairly cool. The water front is not too far from my lot, so I do get cool water breezes (even if my part of the waterfront is rotting, undesirable piers and abandoned factories). I was pouring kibble in Clyde's food dish when my cell phone began to ring. I didn't recognize the number, so I let it go to voice mail. I do not like a lot of the technological "advances" but screening calls is one feature I am all in favor of. If I do not recognize a number, I do not answer. If it is a sales call, they will move on and if it is someone (a potential client maybe?) I need to hear from, they will leave a message. I loathe sales people of all kinds, which is ironic considering the business I am in. But I do not see myself as a sales person. What kind of ego does someone have to have to think they can "sell" a client a house? I see my role as a guide, advocate, and organizer, someone who educates my clients about the home buying or selling process. I will give my honest opinion about a property and then let the client make up their own mind if they want to buy or sell. Maybe that's why I am not a millionaire agent? But my approach keeps my life simple and my clients seem to appreciate it. I was filling Clyde's water bowl when Wanda's voice rang out.

"Hey Alex! So where's my baby at? Here honey, take this bottle and bag of fruit and give me that kibble bowl. Oh, you got them windows up and I see my little furry baby is outside protecting his turf. Here baby, come on over here to mama and get some real loving!" Wanda took the stainless bowl of kibble and let herself out on the stone patio, cackling her loud, infectious laugh while Clyde took off like a bullet for her. Clyde came crashing onto the patio; up on two legs into Wanda's arms and they immediately began their usual tango dance greeting ritual. Somewhat sickening, in my humble opinion. I do not allow Clyde to jump up on people, but over the years with Wanda and Clyde I have given up.

Wanda Billings is a mortgage loan officer with Safety Mortgage and she also owns and manages Salon Wanda. It is a well known hair salon, she founded almost twenty years ago and worked in and ran on a daily basis until she realized her skills with money could be translated into the mortgage business. She began doing loans about eleven years ago. Unlike many mortgage people, Wanda is organized and has ethics. She has not done any of the slimy subprime loans and in fact, she's saved many a buyer/seller from the far too prevalent subprime and negative amortized lenders (predators) out there. Wanda is a real force and her clothes are on the wild side, especially for the staid, buttoned downed banking/loan world. Today's summer ensemble did not disappoint. Wanda wore bright orange slacks with a swirly magenta patterned, billowing top. Her hair piece was blond-ish today and piled fairly high on her head, pushed up with an orange headband that matched her slacks. Gold, chandelier earrings fell to her broad shoulders and she was hoofing around in a pair of aqua blue mule style shoes with little spiky heels. Something I have never been able to figure out is how she (or any woman or drag queen) can walk in such shoes much less wear them all day. The feminine mystique—boy would Betty Friedan not like that spin on things. Wanda is on the latter side of forty-five and she is single, enjoys having serial boyfriends, and proud to be a woman of size, as she refers to herself.

NO SERENITY

"Hey, quit dawdling in there Alex and get our slushies made. It's too hot not be having us a slushy. Get that bag of fruit into that blender I gave you. The rum is on the counter too, I was guessing that you might be low, so there's a fresh bottle, no need to skimp."

I promptly pulled out the stainless steel, god knows how expensive, blender Wanda gave me as a birthday present and proceeded to start dumping in ice and pieces of fruit. Wanda has a real fetish for slushy drinks. It's as if she is stuck in 1970s Pina Colada time warp. "Slushy drink" in Wanda's world, means lots of rum. I was just finishing the last phase of blending when Wanda completed her greeting dance with Clyde and walked back into the kitchen, tapping her magenta talons on the polished concrete counter top. "Ohh, look, you got a message on your phone." Wanda said while picking up my aging flip top cell phone. "Maybe someday you gonna get with it and get yourself an up-to-date phone, start texting? Oh, the lady is asking for your message code, what is it again, your birthday?" Before I could respond, "Yep, that'll do it. Oh, honey take down them big green glasses I gave you, we need us some serious slushy with this heat." Wanda said pointing to the glasses on my open kitchen shelves. I was pouring when Wanda began to relay the phone message, "Ohh, baby this is a man, say his name is Percy. Who the hell is Percy? What kind a name is—oh never mind. Oh, he say he loved meeting you and Clyde at the park today—does this mean you finally got yourself something going on Mr. Fudge Royal? Ohh, now he saying he has a friend who needs to sell her house! Oh Alex, this could be some serious dick and money for you."

I handed Wanda her glass, grabbed my cell phone and hit nine for save. "Boundaries, Wanda. We've spoken about you listening in on my messages. Aupt---," I said putting my hand out to stop her from speaking, "Let me finish. And I do not care for the Fudge Royal reference. As you know, I am a bisexual, not an ice cream flavor." Wanda muttered something about how any sex would do me wonders these days or some such sarcastic remark. "And, if you would let me finish Wanda, this Percy is nothing to be remotely excited about. He's a snotty, pudgy, over middle aged, screaming queen who has a yippy Corgi, a decorating business and naturally he lives in Capitol Heights. He accosted Clyde and me at the dog park today. It was all I could do to get us out of there without being molested. Why is it always the ones like Percy who are hot on my case? Don't answer that! Here, let's sit on the patio, I'll light the tiki torches and see if that will keep the mosquitoes away. You can rummage around in there and whip up some chips and salsa for us. I will now listen to my message, thank you very much. Aupt, now drink your slushy and be quiet."

Damn if the assertiveness and boundaries pop-shrink book I recently read, <u>Step On My *ick And I'll Slug You</u> wasn't working wonders with Wanda. I went out to the patio table, picked up my notebook and pen and proceeded to listen to Percy's message. Wanda looked at me bug eyed, then picked her drink up and dumped some corn chips in a bowl, all the while muttering not so quietly to herself. In fact, her mutters were quite similar to the growling grumbles Clyde is so fond of giving me when he is none too pleased with one of my human decisions.

10

Two

Percy's message indicated that his neighbor needed a real estate agent and wanted to sell her house. After a slushy, and much prodding from Wanda, I decided to return Percy's call. Despite all my derogatory comments to the contrary, she seemed to still think that Percy and I could become an item. Bottom line was, my bottom line needed more funds. So, I dialed up Percy. Half a ring later he picked up.

"Ohhh, Alex I just *knew* that was you calling back!" Gee, I guess the phone i.d. or the fact you left me a voice message thirty minutes ago have nothing to do with your psychic powers? "Ahhh, yes Percy. I am returning your call. It sounds as if one of your neighbors would like to list their house for sale?"

"Yes, the woman to my left wants to put her place on the market. She is divorced and she and boy-toy are ready to move on. Between you and me, it is just as well because I really do not think she is Capitol Heights people if you know what I mean? Now her ex, he is already missed. God that man's chest is just something else. Not that the boy-toy is any strain on the eyes. But you know, I find more mature men to be so much more exciting and developed. Don't you, Alex?"

Oh god! "Ahh, yeah, well Percy what is your neighbor's name and contact information? I will be happy to get in touch with her and see what I can do."

"My you are a sly little fox, aren't you Alex? I am not letting you off that easy! I insist we get together for a drink tonight and I can fill you in on all the pertinent details and give you her information. So where shall we meet? We could just meet at my house. I do have a very well stocked bar, if you know what I mean?"

A fucking, innuendo queen as well, barf. "Look Percy, I've already had enough to drink with my friend Wanda here and really it's almost 8:00 p.m. and I have an early day tomorrow and…"

"You know Alex, I just won't take no for an answer. After all, I have a fifty percent chance with you, now don't I? Say, if you have already had drinks, why don't we get together and have a little nosh. You haven't eaten dinner yet, have you?"

"Ahh, no Wanda and I have not eaten dinner yet but Percy---," Wanda gave me a wide eyed look and snatched the phone out of my hand.

"Hey, this is Wanda Billings from Safety Mortgage, who am I talking with?" From there, Wanda took over. So much for the "Don't Step On My Dick" book. Sure enough, in no time, she and Percy were chatting away talking about food and where to meet. I did manage to call upon the powers of my pop-shrink book and I snatched the phone away from Wanda, her magenta talons scratching me in the process.

"Percy, no it's Alex. If we are all going to have dinner then I want us to meet at a place called Mama Honey's. Do you know where it is? No, it's a Cajun place downtown."

"Ohh, Alex. Cajun is a bit spicy, don't you think? I mean spicy is something else in the *boudoir* but at the table, I really prefer something a bit more sophisticated. And downtown? Really. I don't think downtown is very safe after work hours, now do you?"

"Well, you know Percy maybe dinner isn't such a good idea. If you want to give me your neighbor's information now, we could all meet up for coffee sometime." Unfortunately, Percy did not fall for my ploy and he took down the address of Mama Honey's and said he would be there in a half hour.

We closed up the ranch, put Clyde inside, and off to Mama Honey's we went. Wanda was still under the illusion that Percy was a good potential for me and she tried, unsuccessfully, to get me to change my clothes. As if dressing up for Mama Honey's is even in the cards.

Mama Honey's sits on the edge of downtown with the Highmont neighborhood above it. It is located in a 1920s yellow brick front, former hardware store building. It is always humid inside, due to the open kitchen that sits in the middle of the restaurant. Mama Honey is the owner and she is a woman somewhere in her sixties of Creole origin. She makes the best seafood jambalaya and coconut cream pie around. The place is very popular with the lunch time crowd and has scattered regulars for dinner. Mama was happy to see Wanda and me. "It's good to see da two of ya again, Miz Wanda and Mister Alex, my dears. Where be our Mister Clyde this fine evening, at home I am supposing? I'll make sure you be takin' him a bit of my gumbo wid ya. I gots da beers on da way and your jambalaya be a coming. Let me put you two over here by da big window, it's near da conditioner for the cool." The window was fogged up and tearing, due to the humidity. The air conditioning units in the window transoms were straining to keep things semi cool inside. We let Mama know Percy was coming and to bring him what we were having. I told Wanda that I picked Mama Honey's because I thought the downtown location and the ethnic aspect would keep Percy from coming.

"Well, I guess that shows you about making judgments about folks now don't it Alex? You know you really should give people more of a chan---,"

With that Percy appeared at the door and Mama Honey led him over to our table. All the while, he was busy fanning the air with his fat little hands. He had changed into a large short sleeved tropical shirt, which all pot bellied men of a certain age seem to buy. It must be the generous cut of the fabric, because in my opinion it sure isn't the predictable kitschy fabric patterns and blah colors. Percy wore his mu-mu shirt un-tucked, over stone colored chinos, pressed as rigid as a board. His shirt sported a print of olive green palm fronds on a mustard yellow fabric. The shirt too was starched and pressed within an inch of its life.

"Oh mercy, it is just so humid in here! Alex you didn't say we would be having dinner at the bath house. Not that I am opposed to bath houses Alex, but really not for dinner. That's more for dessert, if you know what I mean? Oh and lordy, you must be Miss Wanda? Nice to meet you. I feel like we are already best friends! And you are so colorful, not that I mind black people mind you. I meant your clothing, such interesting color choices and patterns. I am Percival Emerson." He said holding his pudgy pinky ringed hand out limply for Wanda to, what kiss? Meanwhile his other pudgy paw was unlocking his leather monogrammed fanny pack, which he unceremoniously plopped down on the table. "Not to be confused with *the* Emerson but my mother's side does descend directly from Woodrow Wilson. Oh my, I am so hot I can hardly breathe. Have that lady bring me a glass of ice and I'd love a voddy-tonny. Oh, you two are having beer? And in the bottle I see?"

"Mama's only serves four kinds of bottled beer and one red, one white house wine Percy." I said while smiling broadly at Wanda.

"How, quaint. Well, when in Rome I always say!" Percy unzipped his man purse (fanny pack) and pulled out a blue atomizer and proceeded to spritz himself with some strong sandalwood and lilac combination. He also extracted a pale blue, monogrammed, handkerchief and blotted his sweaty brow. "Whew, I just don't know how I am ever going to eat in such heat."

Wanda was now purposely avoiding making eye contact with me. "Well Percy, no one says we have to eat you know." I said. "Oh here is your beer and we always get the jambalaya so we took the liberty of ordering it for you as well. It's what Mama Honey's is known for. So tell me about your neighbor who wants to list her house." Damn if my assertiveness book wasn't helping out yet again. No more waiting around for the information I wanted, just outright ask for it!

"Ughh, jambalaya? Doesn't that have shell fish in it? You do know that shell fish can give you hepatitis don't you? I mean we must watch ourselves you know? Oh, I see the jambalaya is here, well..."

"When in Rome! Right Percy?" I replied.

"Ohh, you are a little devil aren't you, Alex?" Percy said while pulling out his bottle of hand sanitizer and wiping down his spoon with it. Then he rinsed the spoon off in his water glass and asked Mama Honey for a fresh glass of water, another glass of ice, and a chilled glass for his beer.

Wanda cut in, "So Percy, Alex tells me you got a neighbor that is divorced and wants to sell her house up in Capitol Heights?"

"Why that's right Miss Wanda, I sure do. You may even have heard of her, she's a minor celebrity of sorts." Percy demurred, while wiping his thin lips with his napkin. "You know for Clinton, she really *is* a celebrity. She's done all the local station morning spots and she keeps saying her book is going to be published soon. Now there are some things I do question about her. Her taste in décor for one, but far be it for me to judge her success. I personally think it was her success that drove her golden pec'd husband away. But that's a whole other topic now isn't it? Oh! This jambalaya is certainly spicy. I don't know how you two can eat this so quickly. It is just burning my tongue right off."

Not as fast as I am going to burn it off if you don't cut to the chase and give me the pertinent details. "So Percy, who exactly is this minor celebrity neighbor and what are the details regarding her house?" I asked.

"My, Miss Wanda, he sure is an impatient little real estate agent, now isn't he? Although, I do suppose that impatience has its place, if you know what I mean? Well, I certainly don't want to keep you two in suspense for too long. My neighbor just so happens to be the one and only Serenity! I mean can you imagine that? Living right next door to me and little Hadley? Now as I said, she sure is up and coming

16

but the décor of that house is just simply atrocious! I tried in vain, to help her out. You know Adele Cory who owned the house before her, oh she had a front hall and living room to die for. It was yummy rose tones and chintz for miles! Anyway, as I mentioned, Serenity is divorced and she and her workout "business partner" and note my wink-wink here folks, well they are on a tear to move on to life in the big city and big time celebrity. I do hope the new owners will let me get my hands on that interior. I mean Adele would just turn over in her grave, god rest her soul, if she saw how awful her house looks now. And that dog of Serenity's is just a nuisance plain and simple. You know Adele had those adorable Pekinese? Anyhow, Serenity has the most annoying Weimaraner you have ever met. That poor dog is named Kali! Can you imagine naming your poor child or dog after some heathen god? Really! Oh, I am just going on now, aren't I?" He said while simultaneously chortling and emptying his beer glass; which he promptly held up to catch Mama Honey's eye. "Just put a drop of booze in me and off I go! So I saw Serenity after we met at the dog park this afternoon Alex and I told her I had the perfect real estate agent for her. I said I would have you give her jingle if that was okay with her. She agreed, naturally. You know most celebrities are just plain insecure underneath it all. And when you live next door to someone as well established as I am, oh I am sure she appreciates all the help I provide. We'll just leave it at that."

"Well alright then Percy." Wanda interjected. "Sounds like you da man of Cap. Heights. Got it all going on with them celebrity peeps, now don'tcha? Now I know our completely out of touch with anything Hollywood, Alex, has no idea who this Serenity is. So why don't you just fill him in, give him the real 4-1-1 on this woman." Wanda took a pull on her beer bottle and quickly glanced at me. I for one was a bit perturbed, because I could tell Wanda had no clue who this Serenity was either.

"Ohh, well we all can't keep up with our *Clinton Entertainment Tonight* now can we Wanda? Serenity is only *the* number one Lifestyle Diet and Wellness Coach. Voted number one in Clinton just last month in fact. Can you beat that? I mean just because she can't figure out her house décor does not mean she is not one hot and awesome lady. She has even got me considering some of her custom protein shake diet plans. That is what Serenity specializes in; her protein meal plans. They are her own proprietary blend, powder shakes. She and that boyfriend, Javier, are just the toast of Clinton with them. You know he is the head workout coach at TOTAL. She owns that place, started it with her ex's money several years ago and she ended up with it in the settlement I suppose. You know Serenity is so much more than just a diet coach. She sees the complete picture. She offers complete wellness coaching. In fact, I think she might have even pioneered that concept. With her it is all about the total quality of life, not just a diet. And don't even say the "d" word around her unless you want a lecture! She doesn't believe in diets, just total wellness. As I said, I am thinking about signing on as one of her clients. Not that I have an issue with my weight. I just think Serenity can take me to the next level."

Oh god. What level would that be, the seventh circle of fire in purgatory Percy? I tried to look sincerely interested and said, "Ahh, yes. Serenity is a coach and her boyfriend, Javier, is a personal trainer. I can see the connection they have. So her ex husband, what did he do and is he out of the picture now? Do you have any clue when she wants to sell and where she intends to go?"

"See there Miss Wanda, our little Johnny-on-the-spot real estate agent is asking all the right questions to get his listing! Her ex does some kind of foreign investment/consultant work. Clearly, he made quite a sum. It's just too bad they never had the sense to invest it in that house's interior. Now that may just be your listing's stumbling block Alex, that interior! Well you'll see when she shows you the house. Anyhow, her ex has been out of that house for at least the last nine months. I have not seen him in a while, not that I would mind as I may have mentioned that man is not hard on the eyes. Of course, replacement boy-toy is no strain on the eyes either. Oh dear lord, you should just see that Javier in his spandex work out shorts. He just puts online porn to shame! You know if you sign up for Serenity's total program, it includes one-on-one training with Javier. I for one, am seriously considering it. I mean if you have to be tortured at some dirty gym, might as well be some hunk like her Javier to torture you. But now mind you, I am still not too sure weight is one of my top issues. What do you think?"

What do I think? Yes you are at least sixty pounds overweight. "Ahh, well you know Percy I am not a good one to judge with health and weight issues. You'd best leave that to people like Serenity and her trainer. So any idea, when she wants to sell and where she intends to go?"

"Ohh, and a diplomat to boot! Why I am sure those diplomatic skills help out enormously in your real estate game." Percy replied while swabbing at his forehead again with his monogrammed handkerchief. "Well it is not public knowledge, so you did not hear this from me because I am not one to gossip. Serenity and Javier are planning to open a big franchise, once Serenity rolls out her protein drink nationally and her total wellness book/dvd and PR blitz. I believe they are planning to head to LA and in fact I know she's been there twice scoping things out. She told me she has an agent there who is doing some product endorsement leg work for her. I know for a fact, she wants to be out of Clinton soon. I am sure she would prefer that house be sold before she leaves. That is one of my hesitations with signing on to her lifestyle diet and wellness coach program. I mean, I want to have Javier personally helping me with those weight machines. If they relocate, I don't know how she'd find as hunky a replacement to run the gym part of things here. Oh well, we will just have to see how things all play out now won't we?"

With that said, Percy proceeded to eat two slices of Mama Honey's coconut cream pie and dinner slowly wrapped up. When the bill arrived, Percy pulled a pocket sized leather notebook out of his man purse. He scribbled a phone number down, ripping off the little sheet as he stood up, "Alex, this is Serenity's personal cell number. This is not to be given out or shared mind you. It is her personal line, not the public number. I told her you would be giving her a jingle this evening or tomorrow morning. Now, I'd love to stay and chat some more with you two, but I do have to run. I can't keep Hadley alone at home too long you know! It was divine meeting you Miss Wanda. And Alex, I expect to see you very soon, putting your sign in the neighbor's yard no less. Next time, we'll dine at a place I suggest. We won't have to suffer from such humidity while eating! Tootles, to you both, my new best friends!"

Wanda was quietly chuckling to herself as Percy bustled out the entry door. He paused briefly at the entrance to give his forehead one more quick swab with his hanky. "Well looks like you got yourself a good listing lead Alex. Now that dinner wasn't too bad, was it baby? Maybe he's not your next Romeo but he's a start, ain't he?"

I glared at Wanda and picked up the bill. "Ohh, yes Wanda. He's quite the start. Gosh, I *am* aiming high aren't I? And look, Mr. Everything there just left YOU and me with the bill for his little *nosh*!"

Three

I left a voice mail for Serenity and called it a night. The next morning after taking Clyde for a long walk, we stopped by Sasser's Bakery. Sasser's is a wholesale shop that does breads and pastries for Clinton's Italian restaurants and assorted coffee shops. That they have an actual store front open to the public is a little known fact. The store front sits on an unmarked cobblestone street, the bakery and warehouse directly behind it. The small shop front is frequented by regulars from my neighborhood, truck drivers and freight men who service the warehouses and waterfront freight businesses in Clinton. Daynia runs the shop and immediately scolded me for not bringing in Clyde more often. She gave him some treats she had set aside and brought me a steaming cup of perfectly brewed drip coffee and cherry danish.

"You look too much work, not enough danish, eat. Dog needs more walks, thiz things I know." Daynia said as way of hello and reprimand. I learned long ago the best thing to do with Daynia is just smile and nod your head, which I promptly did. I sat down at one of the small blue topped aluminum tables and was savoring the fresh bakery smells and brewing coffee when my phone began to ring. I did not recognize the phone number but sighed and forced myself to answer. It was Serenity and she gave me her address and asked me to meet her at her house at 2:00 p.m. That got my blood flowing and I quickly finished up my breakfast and went back to my ranch so I could put together my listing packet, and pull up some comps for her neighborhood. Normally, I like to have a day or so before going on a listing appointment. I can do more research and better prepare myself but Serenity was insistent that we meet today, so today it would be.

I had on my real estate presentation garb, meaning I brushed my hair, put on khaki pants that were not too wrinkled and actually had somewhat of a crease left in the legs. I wore a short sleeve green and blue checked button down shirt tucked in (which is an effort on my part) and sported a brown belt to match my brown agent shoes (meaning they slip on and do not lace up) which were a bit muddy and scuffed but hey, at least I remembered to put on socks (even if they did have holes in the heels). I was not wearing my "Jesus sandals" as Wanda refers to my aging Birkenstocks. I left the house at 1:15. It would most likely take me only twenty minutes max to get to Serenity's house but I don't like to leave anything to chance, especially when first impressions are important, I did not want to risk being caught in traffic and late.

Capitol Heights is a neighborhood that lies north of downtown to the west of the Lee District and just south of the Bluffs. The Bluffs is Clinton's old money neighborhood and where my last listing was. The Lee is a neighborhood of freshly minted doctors and lawyers and young on-the-rise "professionals." Capitol Heights is where some of the Lee District aspires to move when they move up. Capitol Heights has always been the Bluff's odd-girl-out cousin. It was constructed a couple of decades after the Bluffs was built, mostly in between 1915 and 1935. It does have some water front view properties but none of the grand estates the Bluffs offers. At one point in the 1950s, Capitol Heights tried to become a part of the Bluffs (this was prior to the city

23

of Clinton annexing both of them) but that would not do. The Bluffs people would have nothing to do with Capitol Heights. In fact, during that time period the Bluff estates that bordered Capitol Heights erected a tall fence, effectively shutting them out and drawing the line in the sand. The inherent friction between the Bluffs and Capitol Heights is still evident today as most residents of Capitol Heights have a chip on their collective shoulder. Most Heights residents pride themselves in being more "down with the people" than the Bluffs residents. The typical Capitol Heights resident is a successful professional or an old money trust fund baby who "rebels" by living with common rich people. I find the typical Capitol Heights person to be wealthy and almost more snobby or upside down snobby than a Bluffs' baby. Capitol Heights is a pretentious neighborhood that professes to be nothing of the sort. Since it was its own unincorporated town for many years, more than half of the houses are still operating on septic systems, and most of the quarter acre lots were legally subdivided, so on quite a few blocks there are large houses built very close together.

Serenity's house is on Fenton Place and the large houses there are on subdivided lots, so the houses almost touch one another. Fenton Place has a mix of Victorian clapboards, some 1920s stuccos, a few neo-Georgians, a couple of narrow Tudors and one or two custom designed, modern houses. Serenity's house is pale yellow, 1926 stucco and the curb appeal is quite nice. The lot is narrow, as is the house's footprint. That is not atypical for houses in Capitol Heights so I did not think that would negatively impact the listing price too much. A postage stamp sized front yard with raised flower beds and a couple of squares of grass held a small stone walkway that went from the sidewalk to the oak front door. A newer white Range Rover was parked in a small cobblestone paved parking pad in front of the house. I parked on the street. Most parking in Capitol Heights is street parking so the fact this house has a parking pad that can hold two cars is a great selling feature.

The house definitely has curb appeal and as I rang the bell and waited I was mentally comparing it with other listed properties of similar size and vintage. The honey stained oak door with its large wrought iron knocker, opened. A thin, tanned, woman with straight, shoulder length, expensively dyed blonde hair who stood approximately five foot seven held up her hand and motioned me in while gabbing away on the bright pink cell phone pressed against her ear. She turned and walked to the rear of the house. She was barefoot, her toenails painted a pale pink and two toes had rings on them. She also had on an ankle bracelet with bells that jingled as she walked. Serenity was dressed in blue Lycra shorts with a magenta thong peeking out the back and a barely there green tank top with the peace symbol and "TOTAL" printed below. The tank top amply showed off her large-size, obviously surgically enhanced, breasts. The floors were vintage red clay tiles, an original wrought iron railing lined the curving stairwell. The entry hall, stairwell and back living room were all painted dark mustard yellow in a sponge effect (straight out of a 1990 do it yourself crafting video). We arrived at the back room which was two steps lower and consisted of red clay tile floors, an open kitchen and living area complete with a vintage oversized stucco fireplace and two sets of french glass doors looking out on the narrow rectangular back yard. Serenity pointed to an enormous overstuffed burgundy, velvet, sofa next to the fireplace. She walked over to the kitchen counter, shuffling papers there and checking her laptop while still gabbing away on her cell. I waited patiently while she continued babbling, "Ohhh, it is sooo important that you honor that feeling and align yourself with your personal commitment for your body wellness and…."

This went on for at least fifteen minutes, so I spent the time taking in the kitchen/living room. Above the oversized fireplace was a large airbrushed painting. It was some kind of phoenix from the fire mythical creature and what looked like Mt. Olympus in the background, complete with some maidens dressed in Roman era togas. It was framed in an overpowering gold gilt, elaborately carved frame. The more I looked, I realized the painting actually had some kind of metallic sparkling material applied to its surface, to add a mystical shimmering effect I suppose. Next to the fireplace on the floor, sat three, two foot tall and one foot wide white candles which judging from the fresh wicks had never been lit. Off to the side of the fireplace a wooden shelf bracket had been tacked to the wall and it held three black, wood carved, word sculptures, "Live, Laugh, Love," complete with a few votive candle holders which were made of assorted burgundy glass and mirror pieces. On the other side of the fireplace was an identical wooden shelf bracket and it held a half foot tall clown with a red balloon riding a vintage bicycle and another wooden word sculpture, "Dream." Across from the enormous sofa on either side of the fireplace were oversized floor pillows, in a gold metallic, pumpkin and burgundy fabric. Inside the fireplace, which was almost big enough to stand up in, sat a minute Dura-flame log in its wrapper, perched on an iron log holder. Placed around this were several pots of silk flowers in assorted colors of burgundy, dusty rose and white. In the middle of this fetching seating tableau was an oversized cedar plank coffee table. The table contained a stack of colorful inspiration coasters (be merry, bottoms up, live life, etc…), and a large coffee table photography book (which looked like it had never even been opened). The book's topic appeared to be about images of personal recovery or some kind of esoteric art school thesis bullshit. Massed produced, remainder-bend, picture book blather that nobody reads or looks at unless they are in a doctor's waiting room. An opened bottle of merlot wine sat in the middle of the plank coffee table. Perched on the far edge of the table, was one clear, oversized, lipstick stained, wine glass, complete with a starfish icon identifier charm on its stem with a resin of merlot in its small goldfish bowl sized bottom. A medium sized wall screen TV was tuned into a shopping channel, the sound muted.

On the wall next to the french doors, which led out to a nice looking patio and grassed in back yard, was a five foot tall, poster reproduction of a late 1800s French advertisement. A generic harlequin, spouting French huckster words was boxed in a mass produced black frame. In between the two sets of french doors was a tall narrow curio cabinet which contained various photos of Serenity. On top sat a small burgundy shaded lamp with beaded fringe. Next to it, was a color photo of Serenity in a wooden frame with inspiration words printed around its edges, and a wilting yellow Dahlia blossom sat

27

in front of her picture. Wooden curtain rods ran across the tops of the french doors. To the sides hung metallic grey and burgundy colored fabric which was about a foot short of hitting the floor and held up to the wall in wooden flower swag holders. It was clear they were for decoration only as there was not enough fabric to reach across half of one of the doors. In the corner nearest the kitchen area were boxes which contained a protein drink called "Power Up Serenity." A long kitchen bar with four cushioned swivel stools faced the kitchen. The brown and grey granite counter tops and stainless appliances would be nice selling features. However, the kitchen cabinets were all painted in a sponge effect burgundy and had knobs which were iron cone spirals, oddly similar to some kind of kinky bra Madonna would wear. The kitchen walls were painted a mid tone grey and the whole ambiance was dark. Stuck to the front of the refrigerator were photos of Serenity and some had a Latin man with her who I assumed was Javier. In the middle of the door panel was a laminated sheet of paper which read in cursive print, "You Are Beautiful."

I was beginning to get a bit annoyed sitting there waiting for Serenity to end her call. Serenity looked up over at me and gave me a wide smile, all her bleached teeth gleaming a bit too bright in the dark living room. She put her hand over her cell and said to me in sotto voice, "This might take a while, so why don't you take a tour of the house and then we can talk." So off I went, along with my clipboard for notes. In the hallway I passed a dining room which was very dark. The same burgundy velvet material that covered the gigantic sofa was pulled across the two narrow floor-to-ceiling side windows. A huge rectangular table made of what appeared to be polished concrete with very uncomfortable looking wooden benches along its sides, sat in the middle of the room. A gold gilded, Louis XIV crystal style chandelier practically touched the middle of the dining table's top. Down the center of the concrete table was a cheap piece of gold silk fabric with maroon fringe on the sides. On top of it were hundreds of used wine corks, mixed in were silk burgundy rose buds and a few tea lite candles. The walls were sponge painted in a burgundy color and the ceiling was black. From here I noted the half bath located under the curving entry stairwell. Its walls and ceiling were covered in a gold foil with burgundy accents wall paper. The half bath sported a black toilet and sink. The handles to the black sink were gold gilded swans and a little cherub pedestal dish held several small bars of black and burgundy soaps. I was beginning to see that Percy may have a valid point about this home's décor. Up the stairs I proceeded. Along the custom wrought iron railing, someone had interlaced a sheer burgundy fabric with occasional frilly ribbon/bow accents. It looked like Stevie Nicks might have dropped by sometime in the late 1980s and forgotten her wrap.

Upstairs were four bedrooms and three baths. The entire second floor, bathrooms included, was covered in plush, burgundy, wall-to-wall carpeting. I have never understood the concept of wall-to-wall carpeting in a bathroom, around a toilet, really?! The two smaller bedrooms shared a Jack and Jill style bathroom (thankfully with white fixtures) and were clearly meant for children. One of them, painted light brown with mustard trim, contained a treadmill and other assorted exercise machines. The other bedroom, a light Pepto-Bismol color, had been converted into a whole-room closet. Metal racks of women's clothing were arranged in rows across the room and one whole wall had a makeshift built-in shoe rack which contained what appeared to be at least one hundred pairs of assorted of women's shoes. I suppose Imelda Marcos would be proud. The other bedroom with its own bath, what was supposed to be a guest bedroom, was set up as a home office. A white IKEA dining room table with two computers and a massive printer fax machine occupied one half of the room and a green exercise ball sat in front of the computer, usurping the role of the brown leatherette chair on wheels that was shoved off into a corner and held boxes of some kind of promotional post cards. Honey colored particle board bookshelves took up one whole wall and they appeared to hold every single For Dummies book ever written. The subjects ranged from yoga and spiritual fads to finance and marketing. You name it, the For Dummies book was there. The walls were painted a pale mossy green and someone had attended a (mid-1990s crafting craze this time) stenciling seminar. All over the walls were randomly painted (in burgundy naturally) inspirational phrases. It appeared as if an inspirational guru had projectile vomited phrases of happy-goo all over the walls.

The rear of the second floor was the master suite. Double doors led in to a good sized room which was painted a pale icy grey blue with some kind of gold shiny accents. A king size bed with a black, faux fur, bedspread and a padded headboard of gold gilt that Liberace himself would have been proud of dominated the room.

French doors opened up onto a small Juliette balcony which overlooked the back yard. Across from the bed, hanging on the wall was a very large plasma screen TV set with surround sound speakers installed. A large walk-through closet led to the master bath. The closet had a few men's clothes hanging up, which I guessed were the boyfriend's or leftovers from the ex-husband. Surprisingly, two thirds of the entire closet was filled with yet more of Serenity's clothing. The master bathroom was large with a jetted soaking tub and multi headed shower stall and here again, thankfully, all of the fixtures were white. Assuming real flooring lay beneath the burgundy carpeting, with that ripped out and the whole house repainted inside and out, this could be a really charming house. So how to market and sell this place? Look for Goth buyers who like burgundy, or neurotic, new-agers who want a house with readymade inspirational quotes, or what? Hopefully, Serenity might be able to move out of the house and I could sell it empty and encourage buyers to *Bring your own style and vision to this Capitol Heights classic!*—oh god this business really seeps into your mind after a while.

Four

I went back downstairs and parked myself on the gigantic sofa. Finally Serenity finished her call. "Hi, I am Serenity and you must be Andy. So how much money are you going to make for me?" she said while literally flopping herself down the other end of the ocean liner sized sofa. No, gee I'm sorry I kept you waiting for forty-two minutes (but who's counting?). Nope, just right for the bottom line. Before I could answer, her bright pink cell phone began to ring and vibrate, her custom Miley Cyrus "Party in the U.S.A." ring tone blaring loudly. She held up her hand to signal for me not talk, "Ohh, it's a call I really should take but I'll have to let this one go to voice mail. It's important for me to honor myself and value my own time and space, right? Anyhow, what did you say you could get me for this house?"

"Ahh, actually I didn't say. I did have a chance to look around your vintage home and what I usually like to do is learn more about my clients, go over our work philosophies to see if we are a good match. Then I like to schedule my sellers for a tour so we can go look at comparable properties that are actively listed and assess their price points firsthand. After that, we sit down and review the active and sold statistics, and finally arrive at a list price that you think is good and I think will work in the current market."

Serenity did not look up; instead she appeared to be reading a text message on her phone. "Oh, well I am a very busy woman and I am sure you are familiar with who I am. I'll have to text her back later. Speaking of me, would you like a protein shake Andy because I feel my body telling me now is definitely the time for me to Power Up

Serenity!" With that Serenity hopped up and took off for the kitchen area. I got up and followed her to the kitchen bar. Serenity plopped a stainless steel blender on the counter top which appeared to require a rocket manual to operate. She opened a large white plastic container, which once I looked more closely had a full color mug shot of Serenity on the label manically grinning on some Hawaiian beach. In bright green lettering the label read, "Power Up Serenity! The high protein energy drink of the 21st century!"

Serenity began scooping out white powder into the blender. "This is our new banana, nutmeg, almond, carob chip flavor. It's my personal new favorite. Which one of my line is your favorite Andy?"

"It's Alex. I, ahh, well I like your vanilla flavor?" God could only hope she had a vanilla flavor as I had never heard of nor tried hers, nor any other protein powder drink.

"Ahhh, yes," Serenity replied with her back to me as she filled a pitcher of water and added that to the powder in the blender. "Why the mocha, hazelnut vanilla bean was our first flavor. You must be a long time Power Up Serenity-er, eh Andy? You see what differentiates my unique protein powder blends, from others is, the added spiritual element of making sure our drinks align with your body's natural abilities in order to metabolically balance out and bring your state of awareness into the realm of serenity. So you can see, the protein drinks are an achievable state of being." With that she punched some touch pad screen on the blender and the motor fired up. Serenity quickly shot over to the refrigerator, put the pitcher under the in-door ice dispenser and filled half of the pitcher with ice cubes, which she

33

promptly added through some kind of hatch at the top of the blender's lid. The ice cubes were decimated in no time and Serenity shut off the blender. She began to pour the mixture into two small goldfish bowl sized, wine glasses. These wine glasses were thankfully free of lipstick stains or merlot resin at the bottom. "Sooo important to maintain your protein levels throughout each and every day. We simply must take time each and every hour to honor our bodies with the bounties of mother earth and the fruits of our twenty-first century food advances.

So you saw the house and I am sure you can see its value, what with it being an original Capitol Heights property. And then of course there is my own personal unique style that I have added. I am sure the décor adds to the overall value if not the good energy that I strive to maintain at all times in my temple. I refer to my living space as my temple Andy, second only to our bodies which are our living temples. Your living temple seems to be well maintained Andy and that's important to me when I select anyone to represent anything related to me or my Serenity line. You could however benefit from our muscle buffing treatment machine at TOTAL but your body is not fat, you are thin. I definitely can only interact with those who respect their living temples and do not allow extra baggage to cling to their being."

Wait, did this woman just string together "my own personal unique" isn't that some kind of grammar violation? Wouldn't one dip in the narcissist's possessive word pond suffice? "Ahh, well again my name is Alex and yes I agree maintaining good body weight and looking after your health is important." I took the glass from Serenity and managed a small sip. The powder drink wasn't as awful as I had anticipated but it was sickeningly sweet for my palette and the lingering banana and bitter medicinal aftertaste was not to my liking either. "I did look through your unique home. Before you list your home, there are some things I like to have my clients do first in order to neutralize the space so that prospective buyers can visualize themselves living in the home when they tour it." Neutralize as in completely move all of your crap out of here and repaint in light colors from top to bottom.

Serenity took a long pull on her protein drink, toasting me in the process so I too had to have another gulp of my protein drink, taste buds be damned. "You are right the buyer needs to feel that they can make this their personal temple too, of course for the right price. And price is really what I am reflecting on at this moment Andy. I am happily divorced and the settlement from that was nice. My gym and rejuvenation spa, TOTAL, and my serenity product lines are doing well but still I must consider and honor my wealth well-being in this process. So, I have had one agent give me a listing price over the phone and another one is scheduled to come by later today. My neighbor Percy was so insistent that you are an awesome agent, so I thought I would give you a chance as well. I mean listing a home of this caliber along with my prestige in the local community and well, not to brag, but all too soon I am going to be a worldwide lifestyle diet and wellness coach phenomenon. My vision board says it is so and so it is, *Namaste*. So I am sure you can appreciate the honor it will be for an agent to list my space, my temple and bring top dollar to me for it. In fact, you should pay me for the honor to list this property, ha, ha, ha."

Ahhum, and you are thinking your home is what going to appear on *Lifestyles of the Rich and Famous*? It should be my HONOR, did she say that, to list your dark turd decorated house? "Well Serenity, you do have options and you should choose the real estate agent who will best meet all of your needs. I have tried to explain how I work with listings. Providing you a bottom line list price right now is not how I work. Nor do I think it is ultimately in your best interest for me to just pull a figure out of the air without doing a bit of research and showing you firsthand the competitive properties that are on the market at this time. And our market has started to drop a bit, just like the rest of the country. How an agent could give you a list price over the phone without even visiting your home is beyond me. Some may show up here and then give you a list price before they leave but again that is not how I do business. From what I have heard you say, you are looking to maximize your profit on the sale of this house. To accomplish that, we have to treat this like the business proposition that it is. That means I may provide staging tips that are not exactly flattering or I may give you a list price that is somewhat below your expectation but backed up by statistics and based on firsthand knowledge of the applicable competitive properties. By doing things this way, ultimately your home will take less time to sell and you will not be given false expectations that in the short run may appease your ego but ultimately do not serve your bank account. I am sure as the evolved lifestyle coach and businesswoman that you are, you can appreciate this approach to selling your home? I know it is not always easy to separate your ego and feelings from your home--temple-- and see it as the market commodity that it has to be in order to sell. And that is precisely why a good real estate agent will not always tell you what you want to hear and will not be quick to price something just so he or she can stick their sign in your yard as fast as possible."

Serenity stood there with her mouth a bit open, staring at me. Her cell started ringing and vibrating on the counter again but she ignored it. She picked up her glass and said, "Well I guess you have a personal and unique way of working, bottoms up." She toasted me and we both finished off our nasty tasting banana what-the-fuck protein drinks.

I put my client presentation folder on the kitchen counter along with my empty fish bowl, I mean glass. "Yes, well thank you for inviting me to see your home Serenity. I know your time is valuable and you are obviously very busy right now, so I will leave you with this packet of information that I typically go over with prospective clients. If you have any questions please feel free to contact me. I can see someone is trying to reach you, so you better take that call, I'll see my way out." With that I headed out of the kitchen, down the hall and out of her temple.

Five

O nce out on the front stoop I took a deep breath and let out an audible exhale. Humans. I suddenly caught a strong whiff of something repulsive yet all too familiar, Stinky! Sure enough the strong sickeningly sweet odor of freesia, rose, musk and some kind of spice, assaulted my nostrils. I looked across the street and there she was, Winterfrost's one and only Share Shelton, complete with her black Mercedes SUV with "SOLD" vanity plates. Share is pronounced "Sharee" and the spelling of her first name has zero to do with what she is about as a person. Share is the type of woman who would eat her young if it meant she could claw her way into another listing. She is Winterfrost Real Estate's premier agent and she knows it. I refer to her in my private Alex world as Stinky because she wears the most obnoxious perfume known to man or woman. The nauseating odor lingers for at least a half hour after Share vacates any room or sidewalk for that matter. At any rate, her infamous odor announced her arrival. Today Share's hair was its usual bright red hue with lots of orange streaks and it was moderately spiky. Her hooker heels were only about a foot tall. As a short woman, Share compensates by wearing stilettos that only Tina Turner or Clinton's best drag queen could get around in. She spikes up her hair for a light and fun touch, I'm sure. In reality, it is spiked to gain more height. Without heels and hair, Share probably stands no taller than five feet. With her bitch boots and spiked up hair she clears five foot ten, sometimes more. It never ceases to amaze me how she manages to have her pointy drag queen bitch boots or shoes exactly match her outfits. Same goes for her stick on talons; they always match some portion of her outfit to a tee and her color palette changes daily. I have often wondered if she has some third world refugee chained up in her no doubt thousand square foot bathroom, who does nothing but mix custom nail colors for each day's outfit and attaches fresh talons to her master.

Today Share's ensemble was its usual color coordinated clown show. She had on a burnt sienna pant suit; the coat top portion of which was low cut and peaking through was a shiny, deep orange, silk blouse. Naturally, it was almost completely unbuttoned in order to show off her D cup inflatable friends. Nestled in her freckled tit valley today, was a thick gold chain necklace with a chunky clump of what appeared to be citrine parked right in between her girls. She is somewhere in her sixties but claims mid forties. Share was cackling away on her cell and had just finished her call, looking both ways before crossing the street when she caught sight of me. Let's just say Share does not particularly care for me (see Volume One). In fact, I doubt Share likes anyone unless they are paying her big bucks. When she saw me she wrinkled her nose, forced her painted on and surgically inflated burnt sienna slathered lips to arch up into a semblance of a smile. Or was that upward lip arch merely her way of advertising her incisors like wolves do in the wild to potential enemies? Share gives the title of the famous book, Women Who Run With Wolves a whole new meaning. She slipped her cell phone in her suit coat pocket and click clacked and jangled her way across the street. The clicking from her super pointy bitch boots, the jangling from the array of chunky gold bracelets she wore. Share is probably the sponsor of the jewelry collection offered on QVC. She might even be a paid advertisement she wears so much costume jewelry. To her credit, I have never heard Share tell anyone that any of her bling is real; she's quite proud to find bargains and loves to brag about them.

"Well, well, if it isn't our own little Alex Campbell out on another listing appointment." Share said as she reached me on the side walk. "Been inside wowing Clinton's most famous lifestyle, diet and wellness coach with your selling abilities? Hey, you know competition is good, in fact it is patriotic," she said while tapping one of her deep orange colored talons against her gem stone American flag lapel pin. "I suppose it is good that Serenity is shopping around and that we are both with Winterfrost. We wouldn't want one of those low end companies getting a listing in a neighborhood as prestigious as Capitol Heights now would we? I mean it really doesn't matter if I or you get the listing, right Alex? The important issue here is the corporate brand and maintaining our market share, right? I'm sure you gave it your best and that is good for Winterfrost but really when it comes to prestige and someone as famous as Serenity, it is probably in everyone's best interest to leave this listing to Winterfrost's premier agent. And who could that person be, why oh-h of course that premier agent is me!"

Okay, so could I slug her now or would it be better to hold off until I was in my car and I could run her down? "Yes, nice to see you too Share. Serenity is inside on a phone call and best of luck with all of that." Now take your smelly vapor cloud and get the fuck out of my way. With that said Share gave me another tight grimace that passed for a smile and clicked and clanked her way up to the front door. Just then a white van with "Doggy Day Care" scripted in red on the side, pulled into the other space in Serenity's parking pad. A twenty-something guy got out and opened the van's side door and called out, "Here Kali." As he was attempting to snap a lead on the Weimaraner's collar, the dog jumped out of the van, doing a happy circle dance in the small grass patch. Just then the front door opened and Serenity stood at the entrance yakking on her cell. Share, smiling big and wide, was just stepping inside the door when the dog bolted and ran up the small walk and through the front door. Kali body slammed Share flat onto the entry's floor, while squeezing past Serenity. Share let out a loud shocked scream and began to spew a string of expletives about out of control dogs. Serenity dropped her cell and began to yell, "Bad Kali, bad dog, no! You sit! You stupid shit dog!" Chaos then ensued as Serenity started yelling for Kali to halt and sit. The doggy day care guy headed off to the front door to try and help out. Meanwhile Stinky was picking herself up, her crunchy spiked hair somewhat flat on one side now, looking madder than hell. Then, catching herself, she started to affect an aura of joviality and all is okay.

I decided that was an appropriate end to this listing appointment interview and quickly made my way down the sidewalk to my aging two door sedan.

Six

Just as I was about to unlock my car, whose voice should I hear calling out my name but Percy. "Yoo-hoo, Alex! Wait right there. I want to hear all about everything! You know there seems to be some kind of commotion going on at Serenity's front door. Hard for me not to notice, as I am in that stunning white contemporary to the immediate left of Serenity." Percy was huffing and puffing his way towards my car.

"Ugh, hi there Percy. Yes, well I met with Serenity and I doubt we'll be doing business together. Thank you again for thinking of me and providing me with the lead. My colleague Share Shelton is there now. There was a problem with Serenity's dog, caused a bit of front door commotion." With that I turned the key in my door's lock and was hoping to jump in the driver's seat and speed off. Not so fast.

"Ohhh, do tell me everything. Just everything! I am dying to hear it all. Not that I am one to gossip but hey a girl's gotta have some news you know." Percy then clamped a meaty paw on my arm and pulled. "Why here you silly man, just come right on over to my house and fill me in on it all." Percy was surprisingly strong and before I had time to formulate any kind of white lie escape response, I was being pulled and walking in the direction of his white, contemporary, two story house. Percy's house sits on an identically narrow lot as Serenity's house. However, Percy's front door is on the side of the house, down a narrow path. On the right is a dense laurel hedge and Serenity's house. Percy's front door is on the side at the very back of his house. The narrow path ends in a circular stone entry way, complete with a midsized, slate, water fountain. Off to the right and over a black granite container wall filled with flowers and carefully maintained trailing greenery is Serenity's back yard. To the left, an opaque glass front door stood half way open. "Oh, follow me, dear," Percy said, "and please leave your shoes by the door. Of course you are welcome to leave your clothes there as well if you prefer. We can just go *au natural* here and have our own nudist retreat in the heart of Clinton. Ha, ha you know I am teasing that is unless the idea strikes your wild side?"

"Not in this lifetime or the next ten Percy," I answered as I followed Percy inside. Percy slipped his hooves into bedroom slippers that had his monogram in needlepoint on the front. I stayed in sock feet, the cool slate flooring a relief after hot shoes. I followed Percy up a few slate steps into a large, open, white living room and kitchen combo. The floors were black polished marble; all of the furnishings were covered in white fabric and accented with custom brightly colored needlepoint pillows. The needlepoint rug in his seating area was royal blue and white and it looked like it belonged on a museum wall not the floor. Percy had mirrored end tables and a large mirrored coffee table, all obviously custom designed. Over the fireplace was a large Frank Stella painting which actually took up the entire fireplace wall, extending on both sides beyond the mantel. A very expensive Hepplewhite sideboard chest was on the wall next to the fireplace, the other side had a glass table which was filled with silver framed photos and crystal candlesticks with white candles, all candles burned just so, to give the impression that Percy regularly used them. The open kitchen was shiny lacquered white cabinetry, stainless appliances, and spotless countertops of an unknown stone looking material that was the same royal blue hue as the rug in the living room. Percy was definitely a decorator and not one to sneeze at. His pad could easily grace the covers of any high end home magazine. The entire place gleamed; you could see yourself in any surface, so shiny perfect I began to wonder if in fact Percy actually lived here. Large custom glass sliding doors were open and on a polished concrete patio sat Hadley basking in the sun, panting (probably the only place he was allowed to let his tongue hang out and pant).

"Follow me Alex, and we'll sit out here on the terrace, I have some iced tea, would you care for a glass?" He said while bustling out the door over to a custom bronze, glass topped patio table which held a crystal pitcher of iced tea and a mirrored tray of pale blue milk glass goblets with his monogram etched in them. The terrace was a rectangular area just off the living room and its backdrop was a concrete wall with a water fall that stretched completely across the entire terrace. It was approximately twelve feet tall and the water continually streamed into a narrow rectangular strip of water below. To the left were stone steps that appeared to lead up to the top of the waterfall. To the right were dense tall laurel hedges and a modernist sculpture inset in the hedge. Above the terrace was a small balcony that went across the rear of the house and on the right was a suspended, bronze railed walkway from the bedroom's balcony to the top of the waterfall area.

"Sure iced tea sounds nice Percy, thank you. Wow, your house is really beautiful. I am assuming you designed it yourself, must be a great tool to show prospective clients? Your house is so clean it is almost hard to believe you and Hadley live here." I took the goblet he handed me.

"Oh my, you are just too kind, isn't he Hadley? Here come sit on the sofa and just tell me everything about your meeting with Miss Serenity. Isn't she a star? I just know she is going to make it internationally." With one meaty paw, Percy swooped Hadley off of the bronze, white cushioned outdoor sofa while perching his plump body on the sofa's edge and setting his goblet of iced tea down on a matching bronze coffee table. He patted the sofa's canvas cushion, signaling me to come sit next to him while picking up a pale blue china plate which had thin cookies and offering them to me.

"Go on now and take one. They are my old aunt Isabel's almond lemon biscuit recipe, one that has been handed down for at least four generations. You just help yourself, as thin as you are you should just eat the whole plate."

I took one of the proffered cookies and took a bite; they were not bad for a three hundred year old recipe. Percy set the plate down, tossed a cookie towards Hadley without looking and Hadley caught it in mid air and looked back at Percy expectantly. Percy proceeded to devour several cookies. I remained standing and proceeded to tell Percy how the listing appointment went and that I did not think Serenity and I would be working together. I told him how I tried to diplomatically state that our approaches to listing her property were too divergent. I let Percy know that Share was now next door for a listing interview. I just gave her name and stated she was with my company; I did not say another word regarding my opinion of Stinky.

Percy promptly wrinkled up his pug nose, "Ohh you must be joking! Why surely I would have smelled that Winterfrost whore a mile away. Oh the repugnant odor of *that* woman. Ugh, you know Share Shelton is one of the most reprehensible real estate agents in Clinton. All that new money just eats her trashy act right up. Why you just would not believe the things that bitch has done. One of my interior clients listed their house with her. She thinks she has design abilities. Really! Her, I mean just look at those hooker outfits she parades around in, nothing short of Tammy Faye Bakker, except none of Tammy's fun humor, may she rest in peace. I mean just do not get me started on my Share Shelton stories, why we'll just be here all the way until breakfast. Really, Serenity had that woman over for an interview? Oh, I have just got to have a word with Serenity. You know most celebrities are just so busy and ungrounded, I mean they can't help it really but that's where good neighbors, such as me, come in handy. I will just have to march over there later on and set Miss Serenity straight, now won't I Hadley?" He said as he tossed another cookie Hadley's way and Hadley hopped up and caught this one again in mid air. "Really, I can't believe Share could even show that clown face of hers in Capitol Heights after the con job she pulled on Harriet and Bill Winlet's house over there on Beecham. You know that gorgeous turn of the century Spanish colonial with partial water views of which my living room interior was featured several years ago in one of our national monthlies? Anyway, she got them to list it for way less than it was really worth and promptly sold it to one of her own buyer clients in less than an hour after listing the place. And those new folks she put in that house, just complete trash. Relocated here from some god awful town in the Midwest, completely ruined all the gorgeous design work I had done for the Winlets. They just painted right over the custom entry lacquered peach that took forty coats to achieve its depth, with common yellow, flat paint from K-mart. Really! And that was just the start of it. Evidently Miss Share "advised" them on some other fine interior design touches. Ugh, just too awful! Now enough of all this, here let me show you my party pad," he said while getting up and walking over to the stone steps. I followed Percy up the stairs about twelve or so feet, at the top was another terrace with what appeared to be a small endless motion swimming pool inset. There were beautiful flowers in granite flower containers all around the terrace which also acted as a railing of sorts. The sloping suspended walkway on the right did in fact lead up to a balcony outside of the master bedroom. From up here you could see directly down into Serenity's back yard and the rear of her house, complete bird's eye view. From the other side of the terrace was a view of the other neighbor's back yard and way off in the distance was a small slice of Warner Sound sparkling in the afternoon sun.

"Well, here's my private oasis Alex. I am sure you notice that the back of Serenity's house needs some repair work. I have been after her for some time now to hire my dear friend and helper Arnie to get those gutters repaired and in working order and you can see that

Juliette balcony needs some shoring up. Oh well, now that she is listing I am sure you are going to make sure she takes care of those bothersome tasks. It really does sort of mar my view from up here, don't you think? Well at least it is not like that on the street side, you know what that does to neighborhood values now don't you? Oh and don't you just adore my endless motion pool? It is great for exercise, swimming just keeps one so tone and buff don't you agree? And I do have the jet and sauna features installed and of course it is heated so I use it all year long. It is so relaxing and the bedroom is just a hop away! I have electronic privacy screens that I can put up—they come out of the patio flooring over there, you know for intimate pool times or for when I sunbath *au natural*. I think it is so important to expose your whole epidermis to the sun, don't you agree Alex? In fact, we could do that right now, just soak up some good old vitamin D and you could tell me more about yourself. Here let me hit the button for the privacy screens. You know I custom designed this whole feature myself and it is just divine, if I do say so myself, isn't that right Hadley?"

"Ahh, thanks for the sunbathing offer Percy. However, nude sunbathing is really not my thing and in fact I really have to be going, lots of appointments to keep. I do appreciate the tea and your ah aunt's cookies and wow, your house is really unreal Percy." I said this while heading down the stone steps. Percy's house really was cool but damn if he didn't have to try and get all pervy. The thought of Percy *au natural*, gag.

"Oh my, you shy little guy! Hadley what are we going to do with this one? Well, I suppose we'll just have to take a rain check, maybe some moonlight *au natural* bathing is more to your liking, eh? Anyway, don't you worry about a thing Alex, not a thing. I'll just pop over and have a word with Serenity and I'm sure she'll be calling you again. "I will go over there in a minute. I mean there is just no way in hell she is going to list with that smelly woman. I for one will not live next to that whore's sign in the neighboring yard, I simply won't. Don't forget your shoes there Alex," Percy said as I stepped out the front door, "and we'll talk real soon."

I got to my car, noting that Share's SUV was no longer parked on the street. I thought about where to head next, truth be told I had zero appointments to attend to. I decided a nice long walk with Clyde would be the answer, I felt so alert and perky. Damned if Percy didn't serve a mean iced tea, I should make iced tea a regular break in the afternoon.

Seven

The next couple of weeks were the usual real estate whirl of start and stop. Turns out Share did not get the listing with Serenity. While scouting Capitol Heights for a buyer of mine, I noted that Serenity's patch of grass sported a sign from "U-Deal Realty." It appears Serenity had opted for a brokerage that basically provides the seller with a listing in the multiple listing service and does nothing else. Serenity was essentially going to list and sell the house on her own. If that wasn't a comical notion I don't what is. Serenity is a complete type A ego freak, running a company and with no time (or manners) to deal with prospective buyers and their agents. How did she begin to imagine she was going to handle the public? And like most owners who list their own property or who list with a company like U-Deal, Serenity would probably discover she was in over her head when an offer came in. She would then learn how complex the offer forms are, not to mention the many legal pitfalls she would not be aware of. Oh well, after my meeting with her it couldn't happen to a better person.

I was pondering all of this as I pulled up to the curb in front of an aging duplex in the Lee District. I had an appointment to pick up a new client of mine, Norman Kluntz. Norman is a middle age chemist who after decades of renting finally decided it was time to buy. I had met with Norman and we had reviewed the buyer intake packet and signed a buyer agency agreement which committed us to working together in his search for a home. The buyer agency agreement is a win for both sides. It commits the buyer to working with the agent and the agent has a contractual duty to actually get out there and look every day to find a property for the client. It is usually revocable by either party at any time. It protects an agent from showing a client sixty houses and then have the client turn around and have Aunt Mabel, who just got her real estate license, sell them the sixtieth house their previous agent showed them. In that nasty situation, if the agent has a buyer agency agreement with the buyer, then the agent is the procuring cause of that sale, even if Aunt Mabel does the actual transaction work. Believe me this kind of crap happens quite frequently and I have heard many an agent at Winterfrost whining about just such a situation. Of course, they are whining because they did not bother to have their buyer sign a buyer agency agreement when they started. So the agent has wasted numerous hours showing sixty houses to the *putz* of a buyer and now the buyer's aunt will get the commission.

I decided early on that I would not work this way. Most agents do not even do an initial intake appointment with their buyers. They just throw them in the car and go unlock doors. In my humble opinion, that is stupid on many fronts. There are specific legal notices and forms a buyer needs to be made aware of and acknowledge and the time to do that is at the start of the search not when they buyer is writing up an offer. The buyer agency agreement also protects the buyer because an agent is then legally obligated to search for them every day. The agent cannot be boating in the Bahamas and telling their client they are previewing houses for them. If they do go to the Bahamas they have a legal obligation to have another licensed agent cover for them while they are away.

So, Norman had signed a buyer agency agreement with me and reviewed/acknowledged the intake forms. He had gotten pre-approved for a loan with Wanda and I had his pre-approval letter on file. I then set up his search in the multiple listing service and sent him viable listings based on his price cap and criteria. And now, we were going to go on our first house tour this afternoon. There is a method to my madness and clients either get the way I do business or they don't. I think my method keeps things organized, keeps the client informed about what he or she is doing, and it takes a lot of drama out of the whole home buying process. At least that is what I would like to believe.

Norman had lived in the same duplex apartment in the Lee District going on twenty-two years. It was his first apartment after he got out of grad school. He works as a chemist for one of Clinton's industrial firms and judging from his pale pallor, I do not think Norman leaves the lab very often. In fact, when I met Norman he was wearing his white lab coat and had his scientific calculator and two pens neatly arranged in the coat's front chest pocket. To be honest, Norman is the quintessential nerd, and not in the intentional, pseudo hip, ironic way. Complete with thick rectangular glasses, pants that are a bit too short and a tendency to spray spittle when he gets excited while talking, Norman walks the nerd talk, so to speak. However, he is a nerd with a lot of spending ability and I had to agree with his mother, it was time to buy. Norman's mother lives in Philadelphia and it appears she calls him several times every day. One of her relentless beefs with Norman is that he should buy. He was finally relenting but only because the duplex he is renting is going to be converted into a condominium. He is not going to buy his apartment because the whole duplex is going to be gutted and the owner is going to subdivide the two apartments into four separate studio condo units. I guess the owner and developer both aspire to the whole "less is more" philosophy; why not live in three hundred square feet, who needs space?

Norman was anxiously waiting for me on the duplex's front porch and he quickly made his way down to my car. Today he was not wearing his white lab coat but he still had his scientific calculator and two pens tucked in his white shirt's chest pocket. He was sporting a dark brown and mustard plaid windbreaker jacket which seemed a tad unnecessary for summertime weather. I am sure Norman's mother had instructed he take his jacket, less he catch a cold.

"Hi Alex. I was worried that you were not coming or that I got the day and time wrong." Norman said while getting in my passenger seat. As if I would ever be late. "I am so relieved you are here. Oh WAIT! Alex, do not engage the gear until you hear the click. Auto safety is very important and all seat belts need to be completely fastened before engaging the gear. Mother always insisted we do this before she even started the car up. I am a bit lax with Mother's rule, I mean you have the car running and I can allow for that as the car is in park but really highway safety begins with you and me, as we always used to say in high school, right?" Oh, yes Norman that was my number one tag line when I was in high school.

"Oh, well are you all clicked in now Norman and ready to go see some houses?" I said all perky. I waited for him to nod and then I put the car in drive. We were off to see three houses he had picked from the queue of listings I had sent to him. I thought he would tend towards smaller houses, something maybe in Lee District where he currently lived. But no, Norman was leaning towards more suburban Brady Bunch style houses. The three houses we were to see are in Rosedale which is a neighborhood right next to the Lee and it consists of homes built between the 1930s and late 1960s. The first house was a bust as Norman did not think his mother would approve of neighbor's house color (it was a dull blue) and he was not fond of the open stair case, *a la* Brandy Bunch house style. "Those types of stairs are just inviting an accident." he said. So we moved on to door number two. This house was a mid sixties A-frame style on a quarter acre lot. It had a rear deck that overlooked a wooded ravine and had four bedrooms. More than enough space for Norman but he was not in favor, said the space wasn't right. I was now trying to figure out what exactly Norman meant about the space, with one person and seemingly no real requirements, what space issue could there be? By house number three we were getting warm but still no winner. This house was a split level and it had a medium sized rec. room but the ceilings were low on the rec. room's level. Norman was being a bit evasive so I decided to employ my new found assertive tactics from the Don't Step On My #ick book.

"Okay, Norman I hear you telling me what is not working with these three houses. But I am not hearing what is driving this vague criteria of yours. From your intake sheet, you did not indicate any specific rec. room requirements or other spaces needed for work or hobbies. So I need you to elaborate more or else I will not be able to help you find the right house."

Norman's eyes bugged out behind his thick rectangular glasses and he let out a gasp. "Ahh, well Alex, ahh, okay. You can't tell my mother but my girlfriend Amy is a dancer and she is going to live with me. Mother does not know about Amy, so do not tell her! Amy and I have been a couple for almost a year now and well ahh, Amy is going to live with me and she would like a space to you know, practice her dance routines."

"Oh a dance studio space, I see. And so you will need a large rec. room and the ceilings need to be high in order to accommodate Amy's practice?"

"Ahh, yes that is it Alex. But please, you really cannot tell mother. Mother does not know about Amy and it will just…"

"Not to worry Norman. I do not know your mother and you are a grown man. You are buying your own house without any help from your mother. So you are allowed to do as you please. Your secret is completely safe with me Norman. I have a legal obligation to keep all information you share with me confidential. Now would you like Amy to tour with us next time so she can see the spaces and give us feedback?" This seemed to completely catch Norman off guard; he looked simultaneously relieved and inspired. This must be like what a Catholic priest sees when people come to confession.

"Oh yes, we could bring Amy along because you don't know mother and well Amy is going to live with me and ah, yes I like that idea a lot Alex." Norman looked as if he had grown an inch taller as he replied. Amazing what light bulbs you can turn on in people's heads sometimes.

"Great, let's bring Amy with next time. And Norman, no worries. Your mother doesn't live in Clinton, not even close." I replied to reassure him. It always amazes me how when purchasing a first home, suddenly your buyer can realize that he or she is now in fact an adult. In Norman's case a middle aged adult but none the less light bulbs were going off and he was starting to figure things out. It is kind of fun when I can help out my clients in this way. I was locking up the front door when Norman's cell phone rang. He immediately looked panicked and picked up, "Oh, yes hello mother. No we just finished our tour. Yes, mother we saw three houses. Yes, I made sure to check for a large guest room mother. Yes, I made sure the kitchen layouts formed the right appliance triangle ratios we discussed mother. Ah, what? Oh yes Alex is right here, just a minute mother." Norman held up his cell phone to me, looking short again and panicked, "Ah, Alex, mother would like to speak with you and review what we saw today." Norman sheepishly said as he handed me the phone. God, some days.

Eight

Some days indeed. It was early evening and I was attempting to clip Clyde's nails out on my patio when my cell phone began to ring. I let it go to voice mail. I still had one paw to go and getting Clyde to cooperate with this annoying procedure is almost a miracle in itself. The phone started ringing again and once more went to voice mail. I was now on the final paw when it began ringing yet again. I had to answer. When it repeatedly rings like that it is most likely an emergency. I put Clyde's paw down, he gave me a triumphant look and took off to the back of my lot to see if the squirrels were still inhabiting his oak tree. I managed to grab my phone on the last ring before voice mail and before I could even say hello,

"Well, finally you pick up your phone. I have an offer here and it expires at 9:00p.m. this evening and I need your input right away Andy."

This barking missive was Serenity. I was completely taken aback. "Yes, hello Serenity, this is ALEX. I don't know what you mean about my input? I am not your real estate agent."

"Yes I know. But I have an offer from an agent and some of this does not seem so straightforward, so I need your input on this as to how best to proceed. It's important you know, that I sell my house. I think they are offering WAY too little and there…."

"Hey wait a minute Serenity! I am not your real estate agent, I do not represent you. You will need to speak with your listing agent and review the offer with them." I responded quite annoyed.

"I know that Alex but my listing company does not review offers. They are a limited service brokerage. I need you, a real professional, to review this and advise me as what is best to do. Of course I do not know the forms or the way to go about this. I think as a professional, it is your obligation to help me review this. After all, I let you see my house and I am sure it is not every day you get to see a house like mine or share a protein drink with the number one Lifestyle Diet and Wellness Coach and an up and coming national celebrity. You know I just heard from my agent in L.A. today, and he says I am top contender for a bacterial vaginitis info commercial. So it would be in your best interest to keep me happy! Who knows what doors I can open for you down the road Andy. Now, I need you to come over and…."

I was fuming, "You know Serenity you have a lot of nerve to call me and expect that I will help you out." I was thinking about addressing her comment about seeing her house, etc…when my restraint won out. "You have chosen to work with U-Deal Realty I believe. They represent you for better or worse Serenity. You made the choice to work with a limited service brokerage. Legally I am not allowed to help you review the offer or provide you with any advice. I can give you the name of a good real estate attorney. Perhaps she can help you review the offer and your options. Her name is Doris Havlon and her number is…."

"I don't want an attorney's number. I am not paying an attorney to review this. I need you over here now to help me out. Percy said you are the best and that is what I expect and need."

NO SERENITY

My knuckles were turning white as I gripped Clyde's nail cutter, "Serenity I am very good at what I do and that is why I have specific methods I employ when I take a listing. I tried to inform you of that when we met but you did not want to listen. And by the way, my name is ALEX not Andy! Now it is too late for my input or help. If you have a pen, I am happy to give you Doris' phone number."

There was a pause, "Unreal how unprofessional you are!" And with that she slammed her phone down.

I was seeing stars I was so angry. My phone started ringing again and just as I was about to throw it out in the yard, I noticed the number calling was Wanda's. I picked up.

"Hey baby, what's shakin' at your place tonight? I'm thinking maybe you and Clyde could come on over here and help me eat this batch of barbecued chicken I am fixing to fry up? Lexi is already on her way, she bringing us some of her nasty potato salad. I tell you, that woman needs to leave off the kitchen Alex. How are we gonna pretend again to like her fool potato salad? I never heard tell of no one puttin' no anchovies and apples in potato salad, humph, no sir. Oh and honey bring that blender I gave you for your last birthday. For some damn reason my blender is not working and you know how I feel about my blended frozen drinks. Okay then baby, see you two soon."

Before I could respond, Wanda hung up. So much for me ever getting the last word in.

I packed up the blender, rounded up Clyde and loaded us in my two-door Volvo and down the road we went to Wanda's house. Wanda lives in the Highmont neighborhood which sits atop a very high hill overlooking downtown Clinton and Warner Sound beyond it. Highmont is mostly black with a lot of left over hippies and artists thrown in. In my opinion, it has some of the best views and houses in Clinton but most people are too afraid of color literally and in the artistic sense. So the house values in Highmont have not climbed as fast as the rest of Clinton. The houses in Highmont were mostly constructed between 1880 and 1930 and some are of the highest quality Clinton has to offer. It was Clinton's premiere neighborhood back in the early 1900s but then the Bluffs was built and people began to own cars and drive farther out, so the Highmont went into a decline. I took Tenth Street up which is the steepest street in Clinton and goes right through the heart of Highmont from downtown. As I was turning off onto Wanda's street, Clyde's tail began its usually rapid drumbeat thump against the car seat. He knows when we are going to Wanda's and she is his favorite person to visit.

I pulled in behind Wanda's late 1980s, emerald green, Lincoln Town Car parked in front of her house. Clyde was practically jumping through the partially open window, something he is clearly capable of (see Volume One). Wanda's house is a three bedroom, late 1920s stucco bungalow complete with eyelet windows. It is painted a bright turquoise and currently her front door is a vivid hot pink. Wanda likes to repaint her front door several times a year to suit her mood I suppose. I opened the passenger door and unhooked Clyde's doggy seat belt and he immediately bolted up the steps to Wanda's front door. I was trying to hold onto the blender and butt shut the car door when Lexi pulled up to the curb in her aging yellow Bronco. "Hey there partner, I see you brought the blender and I'm bringing the potato salad to House Wanda tonight." Lexi said while getting out of her car. Lexi is somewhere in her sixties and a renowned installation artist of sorts in Clinton. She was wearing her usual green floppy hat and paint spattered overalls and sure enough she was lugging a plastic container filled no doubt with her nasty potato salad. How *do* you tell a friend their specialty dish sucks? Maybe my pop shrink book has a chapter on this?

"Hey Lexi, good to see you. It's been a while." I could hear music blasting from inside Wanda's house. "Clyde's already ringing the door bell." I said while walking up the front walk. Wanda popped the hot pink front door open. Clyde immediately put his front paws up on her chest and they began their usual (sickening in my opinion) greeting dance to the Martha Reeves and the Vandellas' hit, "You've Been in Love Too Long." Which to me indicated Wanda was on the outs with the upper end appliance salesman/boyfriend. Tonight Wanda was sporting a lime green and fuchsia swirl Mumu dress thing and a matching head thing to hide her curlers. "Come on in here baby and let mama fix you some of the best chicken parts. I know that Alex is starvin' you baby." With that Wanda left the door ajar and she and Clyde retreated inside to her kitchen.

Lexi and I let ourselves in. Wanda's living room has original leaded glass windows and an open arch way leads into her box beamed ceilinged dining room complete with original brass and milk glass chandelier. The dining room sports a bay window which overlooks the tall Camellia bushes and has views of downtown Clinton and the sparkling water beyond. This bay window with its large gem stone colored pillows is where Wanda spends most of her time. At some point, someone opened the house up and the kitchen opens up now into the dining room. Wanda's kitchen has gleaming new stainless appliances, with a neurotic glass fronted refrigerator which displays all of her not-so-tidy food inside. Wanda was already busy at work frying up chicken parts for Clyde on her enormous (and expensive) Viking stove top. Wanda has dated, on and off, an upper end kitchen appliance salesman and got most of her spendy kitchen toys at a major discount; the neurotic display refrigerator being her latest conquest/purchase. I set my blender down on her island countertop and almost immediately Wanda tossed a frozen bag of fruit at me. I began my concocting, Wanda stepping over to pour a large amount of rum into the blender. Wanda has a real thing for slushy, tropical drinks and the more rum the better in her world. Lexi will tolerate the slushy drinks but her drink of choice is a glass full of whiskey topped off with a scoop of Lipton's finest powdered iced tea. Yummy. Tonight Lexi was drinking slushies and dishing out her not-so-delicious potato salad. Once Wanda had fried up all the barbeque chicken (Wanda first barbeques and then fries) we sat down at her table. "Oh Alex look, Lexi brought us some more of her potato salad! And humpf, it has bananas in it?"

Lexi smiled proudly, "Yes, I thought I'd experiment a bit this time. I know how much you two adore my usual potato salad but I thought adding some bananas to the mix this time might help enhance the anchovy's undertone. Well, you know I guess my artistic sensibilities carry right on over into the kitchen. Plus, the bananas had turned brown so I figured this was the best way to use them up. Here, Wanda, let me scoop you out some more. It looks like you didn't get enough." Wanda gave me a sideways look, as if expecting what? For me to suddenly tell Lexi, gee your potato salad sucks and we hate it. But wait a minute; didn't my pop shrink assertiveness book proclaim this is exactly the type of situation where I need to speak up? I pondered this as Lexi scooped a large dollop of potato salad onto Wanda's plate. Nah, I think I'll let Wanda enjoy Lexi's culinary skills. "Now Alex I would offer you more potato salad but I know you hardly eat a thing so that little dollop you already have on your plate will probably hold you, right?"

"Oh, yes Lexi it will. Thank you for offering me more but you know I don't eat very much. This is so delicious Lexi, don't you think so Wanda?"

Wanda gave me sideways glare and then beamed a full teeth smile at Lexi, "Humm, sure is. Why I bet Clyde might like some of this here salad." She called Clyde over. He looked up, saw what Wanda was offering and went back to his bowl of chicken pieces. From there dinner proceeded and Wanda's chicken was as good as ever. Lexi told us about her new installation project that was via a grant from the Clinton Arts Council. This project was a new sculpture to go in front of the municipal building. Lexi was a bit peeved with the stipulations they had put on the commission. Lexi's installation sculpture pieces are usually beyond my comprehension. Her last award was for rusted out front ends of Cadillacs with barbed wire and cow horns or something attached to them. Went over my head. Who knows what she would be putting in front of the downtown municipal building. Wanda shared annoying client stories and how predatory lenders were getting away with murder putting buyers in negative amortization loans, she predicted a crash was imminent. I noted I was seeing the market slow down. I shared my recent Serenity story and told them about Norman and Amy.

Lexi cut in, "You know I wonder if your client Norman is dating Amy Foster? She is a renowned interpretive dancer here in Clinton. I always thought she was a lesbian but hell what do I know! It will be interesting for you to meet this Amy, Alex. If it is Amy Foster, she really is quite a classical artist and on the verge of being world renowned for her compositions and pieces." I told Lexi I would let her know if Norman's Amy was indeed the renowned Amy Foster. Lexi swore she wouldn't tell a soul. I did need to keep Norman's girlfriend under the wraps, lest his mother in Philly finds out. The rest of the night consisted of Wanda dancing with Clyde and way too many slushy drinks being made. I left my blender at Wanda's until she could get her high tech, rocket manual blender repaired. Clyde and I rolled into my little ranch a bit after 2:00 a.m. and we were fast asleep not much later.

Nine

The next morning I was setting up a tour for Norman and Amy for houses with high ceilinged rec. rooms and I hoped to take them out to tour over the weekend. I had just finished scheduling the last showing appointment for them when my cell began to ring and I picked up without thinking or looking to see who it was. It was Percy.

"Now Alex, it is Percy Emerson calling and I know you and Serenity didn't exactly hit it off. But you simply have to get over here this afternoon, and I won't take no for an answer. Serenity is beside herself! The deal she had fell through and she has no clue what she is doing."

"Hi Percy. Well, Serenity slammed the phone down on me last night and she is beyond rude, demanding my help on an offer when I am not even her agent. I offered to give her a good real estate attorney's contact information and as far as I am concerned that is above and beyond. Your neighbor is quite the entitled bitch. I am sure you will be relieved when she moves."

"Now, I know what you are saying Alex and yes, oh that interior is just dreadful and I know Serenity can be quite a handful. But you and I are both in the client relations business, so I am sure you are used to client tantrums. Well now it is time to kiss and make up because I simply cannot stand for her to list that house with the Winterfrost whore, Share, and that is what she is threatening to Alex."

That got my attention, Serenity listing her house with Stinky. I don't know if my ego could stand for Share to snag that listing, could I tolerate her endless jabs at how she ended up with the listing? "Ah, well Percy you know with clients I only choose to work with well behaved children who don't pitch fits and have tantrums. I do not think Serenity will listen to me or accept the way I work, so I still do not think this is a good match. I think Share might be the medicine she deserves, if she in fact dumps U-Deal Realty."

"Oh Alex, Serenity has already fired U-Deal, they are removing the sign as we speak. She has seen the light and knows that was a major mistake, believe you me. Why I know she said things that must be upsetting to you and for that she is truly sorry. Just come over to her house around 1:00 p.m. with your listing paperwork and I will be there with her to help smooth things over. I mean, really, you don't want that Share creature listing that house now do you? I promise I will act as the go-between with you and Serenity. Alex, she will behave."

There was that Share hook again. Oh god, did I dare? "Well Percy against my better judgment, I will come over there at 1:00p.m. But you better make sure Serenity is on her best behavior and ready to listen to reason. I will not list her place at some inflated price to assuage her ego and I am not playing any bullshit ego games with her either. She can find someone else to blow smoke up her ass but it will not be me. Is that clear? And you have to help me de-clutter that interior Percy, I'm not going to list it unless she agrees to clear out what I say. You are correct, short of completely redecorating that space, it is a nightmare. Her house looks like a knock-off Pottery Barn had a love child with a crafts and hobby chain store. Is she open to moving out and having the place painted a neutral white from top to bottom and removing all that wall-to-wall burgundy carpeting? She would get top dollar if she did."

"Oh, Alex I know, I know! But I don't think she would be willing to move out and do that, even for top dollar. She is so proud of that hideous décor, she fancies herself an accomplished interior designer Alex. But I could get her to agree to de-clutter the place as you call it and we can at least improve it a bit? Oh this is good news Alex. We will see you at 1:00 p.m. and I promise she will behave this time."

With that Percy clicked off and so it was decided. I quickly began to pull up active and sold comps and fill out the listing paperwork. I had the title company I use send me over a listing packet. I noted that the house was still legally listed in both her and her former husband's name. I also noted that they had her legal name listed as Brandeen Ramona Silvano. Quite different from her public "Serenity" name. That would have to be taken care of prior to listing or else the ex would have to sign the listing paperwork as well. My gut was telling me this was a bad idea but my ego was winning out and insisting I could not let Share end up with this listing.

Back to Serenity's I went and as I pulled up I noted the doggy day care van was out front. The dog guy was struggling to get Kali into the van. Percy and Serenity were watching from the front door. She was naturally gabbing away on her bright pink cell phone while occasionally calling out and admonishing Kali, telling her to cooperate. Percy immediately lit up, "Oh Alex, right on time! Come on in here and we'll get started. Serenity is on an important call."

Aren't they all? I walked in the house, Serenity led the way in her Lycra shorts, with a pink thong peeking over the top. She had on what appeared to be a low cut sports bra thing in a pale yellow which said "Power Up Serenity" on the midriff area and had her drink logo planted right between her inflated tits. Subtle. She was yakking away to some lifestyle client of hers, "Ohh, it is so important to honor your feelings and acknowledge your oneness. I think it is time for you to seek the divorce you are entitled to, to honor your wealth well being-ness and make your husband honor it via your divorce. You need to grow your boundaries and only allow your attorney to interact with him, feed your soul and…." On this crap went as she led Percy and me back to the living room area. I was already annoyed. We sat down on the ocean liner sized velvet burgundy sofa and waited as Serenity continued her phone dribble. I gave Percy a stare down look and pointed to my watch. He looked back pleadingly, and got up and went over to where Serenity was standing by the kitchen bar. He began to whisper and motion to her to get off the phone. She looked a bit peeved but Percy's motions became more dramatic and lo and behold she cut the call short and hung up. Percy immediately went into high placating mode and thanked her and asked she leave the phone for now. He re-introduced us, "Oh and isn't it just great to have Alex back here Serenity to help you out and what a professional he is right on time. Now Alex what is the first order of business to help get Serenity's house listed properly this time?"

I didn't even blink, "Well Serenity we can start by letting me have a copy of your cancelled listing with U-Deal Realty."

She gave a weak smile and said, "Ah, sure here it is; they removed the sign this morning. I had no idea they would be so unhelpful."

I took a look at the paperwork she handed me and it did appear she had in fact legally cancelled the listing. I noted however that they had listed her as "Serenity" in their paperwork which was a legal mistake on their part.

"This is all good Serenity. However, technically they never really had a legal listing with you because the contract does not have your full legal name on it. According to my preliminary title search you and your ex husband are still on title as the legal owners of this house and your full legal name is Brandeen Ramona Silvano. Serenity is your public name I take it and as such cannot be used on legal documents. You are going to either have to list this house with your ex-husband or else you will need to visit a real estate attorney to get the title transferred properly into just your name. I recommend you talk to the attorney I tried to give you information for last night, Doris Havlon."

At the mention of her legal name, Serenity blanched, "What, I mean how? How do you have my legal name? No one is to have that information. This is unheard of and…." I glared back at her and Percy and she actually shut up.

"Like it or not your full legal name is part of public records. Did you get this house as part of your divorce settlement?" She nodded. "Good, then you just need to have Doris or another real estate attorney properly transfer the title into your full legal name. I am assuming you have not legally changed your name to Serenity?" She nodded no. "Good, so all the paperwork will be written up using your full legal name. Once you have those title items taken care of then you can sign the listing paperwork and you will be legally listed with my company." She looked annoyed and was opening her mouth to speak. "No, this must be taken care of, your house was not even legally listed with U-Deal Realty and I am not surprised given their track record of failed deals and law suits." Normally I do not comment on other companies or agents publicly but in this case their bad reputation was so well known I didn't care.

Serenity looked a bit flustered, "Well I am a very busy businesswoman and I don't have time to go visit an attorney. You just make all this happen, that's why you are the agent."

I was instantly pissed, such an arrogant idiot. I collected my papers and began to get up to leave. Percy looked completely alarmed and cut in, "Oh no Serenity, Alex is completely right. You have to take care of this personally; no one can do this for you. Why I'll take you to this Doris Havlon's office, it'll be fun we can have lunch. Alex, she'll do this. Now what is the next step?"

I paused and then sat down again and Percy let out an audible sigh. "Assuming Serenity gets this taken care of ASAP she can then sign the listing paperwork and we are live. I need her to agree to a viable list price and here are my comps with a reasonable suggested range for the list price. I am assuming Serenity is too busy to go on tour of comparable properties with me to see firsthand how I arrived at this viable listing price range?" Serenity let out an exasperated sigh. "She needs to fill out the seller disclosure form, and the septic system form as well and I will post those forms with her listing. I will need to arrange for my photographer to come and take interior and exterior photos to post when the listing goes live. So we need to review the property together now and discuss what stays and goes and what needs to be repaired prior to listing."

Serenity took the forms and tossed them on the counter. "This is ridiculous what are these seller disclosure forms and a septic form? U-Deal Realty didn't have me fill out all this junk."

That got my ire up again, "That's because you were working with imbeciles, is that not clear to you at this point? Look, you either get what I do and want to list your house legally and get the most money for it or you don't. I am quite fine leaving right now and not listing you house. So what's it gonna be? Are you going to lose the attitude and work with me or should I stop wasting my time and leave now?" How's that for putting it on the line?

Serenity's eyes bugged out, "No one talks to me like that. Percy this is just, it's just, just unacceptable!"

"Okay, so be it. Enjoy your afternoon." I got up and proceeded to walk toward the front door. Halfway across the living room, Percy dove in between me and the hallway. "No, no! Serenity didn't mean a word of it Alex! She's just stressed that's all, aren't you Serenity? Serenity I know you are busy, so I'll arrange an appointment for us to see that lawyer tomorrow around lunch and Alex and I can go through the house today and he can make his list of what needs to happen before he lists and he can leave the listing paperwork and you and I will go through it." Percy said in a high pitched pleading tone.

I was still trying to walk around Percy when Serenity replied, "Oh god this is just so incredibly stupid! I need to go to the gym, I have a staff meeting. Just go ahead and take care of this Percy. List with Alex, whatever. I just have too much to do. Just make it happen. Oh, I can't wait to finally be out of this mud puddle of a city and in L.A. with *real* professionals!" With that her cell rang and she picked up and began talking. She grabbed her bag off the counter and shot off out the front door.

Percy immediately put his arms down from blocking me, "See all is good now Alex. You can just work with me and I'll make sure she does what you need. Let's go through this hideous place and see what we can do. I mean remember, we don't want that Share Shelton getting this listing and I'm sure you can sell this place and be done with Serenity in no time Alex."

Ugh, the Stinky hook again. "Okay, let's look through the house and I'll give you notes. She does everything I say and you get the forms signed properly and I'll take the listing. But I'll cancel it in a heartbeat with any more of her crap, you saw how she acts. Complete idiot, she won't even listen to much less recognize things that are in her best interest."

"Deal." Percy said. With that we toured the house and room by room I wrote down what needed to go prior to listing. Percy and I were in complete agreement with the "to go" list. In the back yard, I noted the gutters needed repair work and the Juliette balcony could use a new and more stable railing installed. It is important to take care of these kind of items prior to listing so a prospective buyer does not focus on them and offer less and then still demand the items be repaired via their inspection. I noted that Percy needed to have Serenity identify where the septic cover was, as that would have to be inspected and a condition report provided to any buyer, per the law. Percy assured me all would be done. I left and called Wanda up and we went for a late lunch.

Ten

Percy did deliver. The next day I had a call from Doris Havlon. She told me that from what she could tell via the divorce decree, Serenity did not get the house as part of the settlement and in fact her ex-husband was still the co-owner with her. For the house to list, both needed to sign the listing agreement and when it sold both would be splitting the proceeds, per the divorce decree. What an interesting fact for Serenity to over look. Was she really so stupid as to think she could sell the house solo and take all the money? Percy called to let me know that per our list, the items I thought needed to be removed were being removed that day. He wanted to know if I could stop by tomorrow and meet up with his repair person Arnie. He said I could bring my camera person to take the photos and drop off the official listing paperwork so he could get Serenity to sign. Serenity would not be there but he would. Sounded good to me. No Serenity is a good thing.

I went to meet with my new clients, Sam Olson and Robert Fraige. They are a couple who were referred to me by a former client. They have been together for twelve years and are finally getting around to moving in together. Sam is a general practice doctor and Robert is a CFO at one of Clinton's industrial companies. They certainly seemed as if they had money to spare. I put them in touch with Wanda to get pre-approved and entered their search in the multiple listing service. This would be a high end purchase which is good for my bank account. Also, Sam had a condo to list and yours truly would be taking care of that too. I called Lexi to make sure she could come with me and take the photos for Serenity's listing and with all that taken care of Clyde and I went for a long walk along the rotting piers.

The next day I arrived at Serenity's house at 10:00 a.m. and Percy was there to let me in. As he was unlocking her front door, Lexi pulled up to the curb. Percy said he'd meet us inside and I went to help Lexi lug her camera gear and deflectors into the house. I introduced Percy and Lexi.

"Ohh, you must be Alex's top notch artist friend I have heard so much about? I just know you are going to take awesome photos, even if the décor in this place leaves much to be desired. I am Percival Emerson. Percy to all my friends and I just know we are going to be best friends." He said holding out his meaty, pinkie ringed paw to Lexi. "My last name is Emerson but alas I am not related to *the* Emerson. But I do descend from Woodrow Wilson on my mother's side. I am familiar with some of your public works and I am sure you have seen an interior or two of mine peeking from the magazine covers."

Lexi shot me a quick look, "Well, darling I am just delighted to make your acquaintance Percy. Such a cute name and descending from Woodrow Wilson to boot. My, you must have such a rich life with magazine interior covers and all." I could note the sarcasm in every word she said but to the untrained ear, Lexi's words were just pure ego boosting compliments. True to form, Percy was beaming with joy.

"Oh, Alex your friends are just so artistic and wonderful. See I knew we would all be best friends. Now let us take a quick tour so Lexi can see what she is up against in photographing this interior from

75

hell. My friend Arnie should be here shortly to start the repair work out back Alex." And with that Percy led the way. "Now you will note Alex, I did get Serenity to remove the fabric from that original wrought iron stair railing. I have opened these poor excuses for draperies in the dining room so there is bit more light. Unfortunately Lexi, you will note that Serenity's color palette tends towards the darker range." Darker range was putting it politely, how about cave like? "I got her to remove her used wine corks from the dining table Alex and trust me that was no easy feat." We moved upstairs, Lexi tsk-tsking as we went.

"This place is so dark and all this nasty wall-to-wall carpeting in the bathrooms too?" Lexi commented.

"Oh, just unreal isn't it? You would not believe how beautiful this house looked when I did it for Adele. Why if Adele could see it today she would be absolutely mortified." Percy responded.

We had arrived outside the "closet" bedroom and there were still racks of clothes. "Ah, Percy you promised she would remove these racks of clothes prior to listing so one could envision it as a bedroom not some glorified narcissist's closet."

Percy quickly scampered up to the doorway, "Oh Alex yes I know. But I simply could not get Serenity to part with her clothes racks. You know her image is important and she has to have the wardrobe to fulfill her public appearances. I did get her to remove two of the racks."

I was pissed, "Appearances? The only thing I have ever seen her in is Lycra shorts and a midriff top to show off her enhanced friends. Lexi is there any way to shoot this room or should we just forget it? I can always state in the verbiage that once the crap is cleared out a nice sized bedroom awaits. Fine, we won't sweat this. If Serenity is this stupid and vain and wants to hurt her own listing and offer odds, so be it."

The other bedroom/office had some of the boxes removed and the work-out bedroom had the curtains pulled back and a few exercise machines had been taken out. It still looked like shit. The master bedroom was okay, once I opened the curtains. "Percy, she has to promise to keep all of the curtains open for all showings. This place is like a vampire's lair."

Lexi was looking at things through her camera and adjusting her light meter. "I think I can do something to lighten up these rooms but boys we all know it is just so tacky that no matter how nice I can shoot things, crap is crap." Percy nodded in agreement.

I suddenly had a thought, "Percy, when you did this house for Adele didn't you have photographs taken?" He looked confused but nodded yes. "Awesome, can you get a hold of those photographs? We could put them in a binder and leave that out for prospective buyers to flip through so they can see the potential of the house. You know most buyers cannot visualize unless you show them? We could make it sort of tribute to your interior design services and hopefully a potential buyer would realize we are trying to show them this house does not have to be so hideous. Perhaps they'd even hire you to redo the house once purchased."

Percy leaped over and bear hugged me, gag. "That is just sooo clever Alex! I just knew you were a little dynamo and such a marketeer to boot! Oh, I could restore Adele's house to its glory! We'll just make Serenity think it is an advertisement for me and it is but still this is genius Alex."

"Ah, yes, now could you stop hugging me Percy, I can't breathe." Eewe, Percy cooties. "I don't think I would call this genius Percy but you gather up the interior photos from Adele's time and we'll see what we can do." At that moment the door bell rang and Percy was off to answer it. Lexi and I gave the master bedroom one last look and she said she'd start her shots up here and work her way down.

I went downstairs. Percy had let a gruff looking man, no wait it was a woman, in. Percy introduced us, "Alex this is Arnie my number one fix it man. Arnie this is Alex, he's the listing agent for this house."

Arnie flashed me a gold toothed grin and stuck out her hand. She cleared her throat and said in a powerful baritone, "Yup, Percy sure has that one right. I'm more man than he'll ever dream of being. Arnie of Arnie's Repair, please ta meet cha Alex." Her grip just about broke my hand. "Ah, nice to meet you Arnie. There are some items out back that need attention." I said taking my aching hand back. Damn, what is it with butch lesbians and power handshakes?

Percy led the way out back and I followed along behind noting Arnie's enormous tool belt, her beat up steel toe boots, backwards John Deere tractor baseball cap, and of course the *de rigueur* Carhartt cargo pants and flannel shirt top. Nothing like a rad dyke when it comes to repair work. I swear by it. Put Arnie to work and I bet she'll do the job of ten men and a better one to boot. I'll take Arnie any day over some hetero, butt crack showing, Cletus. Percy's contacts were already paying off for me. If Arnie's work proved up to par, as I was ninety-nine percent sure it would, I'd have a great new resource for my clients and listings.

Serenity's back yard is fully enclosed by a fence and a tall laurel hedge on Percy's side of her yard. The lawn was pretty torn up from Kali and it could use some serious tidying up before listing. Arnie assessed the sagging gutters and noted the railing that needed replacing up above. "Oh, this is a piece of cake, I'll get her done this afternoon, no problem." She said while spitting in the grass. "Want me to fix up the lawn and those bushes as well? Gonna need to re-sod her, take out those dead plants. Take me about a day to get her all show ready fer ya. Owner is gonna have to keep the dog out of back here if you want it to stay nice." I nodded yes while Arnie hocked a loogie into the brownish grass. And then I added, "Oh and Arnie, Serenity is going to need to check the septic tank and probably have that pumped and inspected prior to listing if possible but definitely once she has an offer. Could you by any chance locate the septic cover lid? I am sure it is a very old system, maybe original to the house because the county records have no as-built drawings on file for this property's septic system."

Arnie grinned, her gold tooth shining in the sun, "Ahh, septic needs a pump huh? Sure, I can locate the lid fer ya." Arnie placed her thumbs in her tool belt and bounced up on her steel toe boots. I had no doubts Arnie was going to be my new go-to fix it man.

Eleven

Arnie was going to fix the gutters and railing that afternoon and Percy said he was going to be at the house to baby-sit things. Lexi was happily clicking away and doing her photography magic. I let Percy know what Doris Havlon had reported back and that Serenity would need to contact her ex-husband so he could review and sign the listing agreement. I mentioned that I found it odd Serenity said she got the house as part of the divorce settlement when in fact that is not the case. Percy shrugged it off as Serenity being such a celebrity and so busy. I thanked Percy for babysitting things and left to take my new clients Sam and Richard on their first house tour. I had four upper end houses to show them and based on their pre-approval from Wanda, they could just about purchase any property within reason that caught their collective eyes. Must be nice. We had agreed to meet at the first property and caravan to the others, which I vastly prefer. I hate having to make small polite chit-chat while navigating to the next showing. And most of my clients appreciate traveling in separate cars so they can talk freely amongst themselves about what they've seen. I think the caravan tour is win-win for all concerned. Although I know a number of agents who try to "close the deal" with the clients in their car and insist upon always driving the clients on tour. I guess that is the difference between me and the hard sell agents; I have zero interest in pushing or selling in the classic sense for that matter.

The first house we were scheduled to tour is in the Beaumont. The Beaumont is a gated community on the outskirts of Clinton. It is where all the new money in Clinton strives to live. It comes with the rent-a-cop at the gate, a members club house, required Beaumont stickers for your cars (I am sure that is just a status item they cooked up when developing the place) and it has all the zero lot line eclectic (most tacky) mcmansions you can imagine. Most of the Beaumont has been constructed since the late 1990s and one of its features is enormous multi car garages usually stuck on to the front of the house. And this was the case with the first house we were set to tour. I had previously notified the gate of my clients' names, so the guard had let them in and they were parked in the drive of the first house when I arrived. This five bedroom, Beaumont special came with huge white columns (fiber glass) and was a mixture of *Gone With the Wind's* Tara meets English Tudor. One ugly bastard of a child. It boasts a four car garage and a double Jacuzzi/hot tub out back, set in the wooden deck which takes up the entire back lot, so zero yard/grass.

Sam and Richard were impeccably dressed, Sam in a sports coat and a brightly colored "doctor's" tie and Richard in a three piece dark business suit with a sedate tie. I had tried to look presentable and had on khakis that the dry cleaners had pressed and a bright blue plaid shirt which wasn't too terribly wrinkled. My belt matched my brown slip on shoes and my hair wasn't completely sticking up like Dennis the Menace in the back. I never do the tie routine. I think they look nice and when they are in bright colors and patterns even more so. However, I made a decision long ago that I wasn't going to wear them. First off, they are a literal noose around your neck—gee what sinister entity created that symbolic gesture for the corporate man? Second, when I do wear a tie it inevitably ends up with food all over it, getting stuck in keyboards, doors, etc.… Just too much of an aggravation. So I was hoping my two corporate model men here weren't going to judge my less than perfect attire. Turns out there was nothing to worry about, they were already busy gabbing away about the house's exterior and from the sound of it, they too thought the child was an ugly bastard. However, in we went and toured it bottom to top. Many of the interior features were cheap developer crap but the price tag did not reflect that. When we were through, I gave them my blunt assessment of the Beaumont and suggested they might want to skip the second scheduled house on our tour as it was also in the Beaumont and even more hideous in my opinion. They quickly agreed and so off we caravanned to the Buffs.

The Bluffs is one of Clinton's oldest, most prestigious neighborhoods. It literally sits on bluffs to the north of Clinton's downtown and has stunning views of Warner Sound. It is not a gated community and it is home to most of Clinton's old money elite. The lots are large and most of the homes have old wrought iron entry gates that are usually left open. The Bluffs was designed by a famous architect and developed between 1905 and 1930. The house we were scheduled to see is a 1921 four bedroom Mediterranean Revival. It is a very stately, two story, house with a half moon brick paved drive and established flower gardens and beds out front. It does not have direct views of Warner Sound but does have a beautiful in ground, mid-size swimming pool that is surrounded by a slate terrace, old and very fragrant rose bushes and a fountain at the north end of the terrace. The interior boasts original hardwood flooring, a formal dining room and living room. The kitchen is a good size and had been updated somewhere in the early 2000s in keeping with the historic character of the house. Most buyers these days would prefer an open kitchen, living room layout and no formal dining room. I could not get a good read as to how this house's layout was striking Sam or Richard. They liked the large bedrooms and told me they were considering adopting a child once they were settled, so they liked the fact this house had good sized bedrooms and would be child friendly. They definitely had interest in this property, I could tell by the way they were pacing and the little mini conference they were having with each other. I locked the house back up and we were off to our final house.

This one was in the Lee District which is situated to the south of the Bluffs and borders Capitol Heights to its north, Rosedale to the east and downtown directly to the south. The Lee is a mixture of really nice sound view properties that up and coming lawyers and doctors seem to gravitate towards and its eastern end has lots of duplexes, small neighborhood green grocers, cafes. It is more urban without being directly urban I suppose. Our final house in the Lee is one of its premier properties with direct sound views and a midsized city lot. It is a classic arts and crafts style two story, four bedroom, house built in 1915 but fully restored and updated. The entire back of the house overlooks the sound and the backyard is fairly large and a good play area for children. I could tell this house was of interest. They liked the smaller formal dining room which is paneled and has an original brass and milk glass chandelier. The radiators for heat did not seem to faze them; in fact Sam said he preferred radiator heat. The upstairs had a screened in porch which ran the entire length of the house and the sound views were unbelievable. If I had to bet, this would be the house they chose but I am not a betting man, so who knows. I told them I would send them detailed active and sold comps for the house in the Lee and their other choice in the Bluffs. They could ponder the statistics side of things and then get back to me.

As I was pulling away from the curb, my cell began to ring and I did not recognize the number. Probably one of the listing agents for one of the houses I just showed eagerly calling to find out what my clients thought. If they bothered to listen to my voice mail message, they would note that I do not take calls about showings, they can email me and I will be happy to provide feedback. If they are smart, they will email a photo of their listing as well. Some weeks I can see as many as fifty houses and they all tend to blur in my mind. Also, calling for feedback right away is annoying. I could still be showing clients other houses and I am not going to provide feedback in the middle of a tour. The other obnoxious thing is when they insist on specific feedback; i.e. what did my clients think of the price? Like I would ever provide that information right away. If my clients have an interest in a property, I am not about to tell the listing agent what their thoughts are on the list price. Basic poker game principles do apply. They can find out what my clients think about the list price when and if they see an offer. If I know for absolute certain my clients will not be making an offer on the property (i.e. the Beaumont bastard) then I might provide price point feedback. Otherwise, get a life and find someone else to bother.

I drove back to Serenity's house to check on things. Lexi was just leaving.

"Got all the pictures I could stomach. I'll get them formatted for you tonight Alex and I'll try and lighten them as much as I can. That Arnie is the real deal Alex. I'm going to have her out to my little farm and get things looking right around my yard and studio. She says she can make my studio roof more secure." That would be a good thing considering Lexi's studio is this ad hoc addition to the front of her house which consists of a metal carport like roof with heavy plastic hanging down for walls and bare bulbs hanging from above for light. She had cement poured where the front lawn used to be and built this make shift studio over it. All very ugly and wacky. But hey, she's the installation artist after all.

"Sounds good Lexi. Thanks again for snapping the pics and I'll call you."

I went inside and found Arnie and Percy talking at the kitchen bar. Looking through the french doors, I noted that Kali was home and was digging up a storm in the far back part of the yard. Trying to escape?

"Oh, here's our premier listing agent now Arnie. Alex, Arnie got those gutters all repaired and replaced the railing on the little balcony. The doggy day care brought that beast back and we had to put her in the yard, she was starting to tear up the house. Arnie is going to come back later this week to redo the back yard but I am going to have to get Serenity to do something about that bad dog. She'll just wreck that back yard again in no time."

Arnie replied, "Yup, that dog is a wild one. But she just needs love and exercise. I'm guessing the Missus around here ain't much on those things?" Arnie said while handing Percy a bill for the repair work. "Shame, nice pretty dog she is. No one has taught her to behave. Well, Alex it was nice to meet you and I'm outta here fellows, gotta get Pearl over to the Beaumont and fix some fencing on one of those mansions. Catch ya later…oh, I found the septic tank lid Alex. I uncovered the top for you and it is one them old iron bastards. That's an old septic system out there, best to get her checked out. Later gents."

As Arnie left I asked Percy who Pearl was. He informed me Pearl is what she calls her truck. Humm, maybe my car should have a name? Nah, I don't think so, not something I would do with an inanimate object. I pulled out the listing paperwork which had Serenity's legal name as well as her husband's. I gave it to Percy and let him know both signatures and initials would be needed on all forms before I could list. He promised me he would take care of it. He then suggested I should come over for a dip in the pool. I politely declined and said I had tours to set up, which wasn't too far from the truth. I got in my car and was about to drive off, when Serenity arrived back home. I watched as she simultaneously yakked on her cell phone and proceeded to unload what appeared to be bags of new clothes. Great, just what her overfilled bedroom/closet needed, more freakin' clothes. Percy appeared and she literally thrust all her shopping bags at him, while continuing to gab on her phone. Percy almost fell over from the force of the bags hitting him. He quickly picked them up and followed Serenity's Lycra covered, thong showing, ass into the house.

Twelve

The next day Percy called to let me know that he had gotten Serenity's signature on all the listing paperwork and her legal name not her public one. He had the ex-husband's name and address and I would need to contact him and take the listing paper work to him, as Serenity did not speak to him since the divorce. Well, at least she was catching on to the pertinent legalities involved in selling her house and since Percy handled her signing the paperwork, I could hunt down the ex I suppose. I called the number he gave me for the ex and got a voice mail that identified the number as Hayes Brighton, CEO of Wealth Creation Advisors and Imports; whatever that might be. I left him a detailed message and asked that he call me back. I took Clyde for a quick morning walk and then was off previewing houses.

I was looking at some houses in the Highmont when I got a call from Wanda. She was down at Salon Wanda, checking out the receipts no doubt, and wanted me to come down, pick her up and go out to lunch. I decided that was a great idea, and quickly sped down Tenth Street. At the bottom of the hill on Fulton Street where the Highmont ends and downtown begins is Salon Wanda. This is the hair salon Wanda started when she was barely twenty years old. It is a 1930s clapboard house, which she had repainted a vivid lime green. The front yard was long ago turned into a gravel parking lot. The house had been through many incarnations before Wanda purchased and transformed it. When she bought it, the back yard was full of rotting tires, which Wanda removed. She put in a very nice bricked terrace with potted plants, a trellis and the famous (or infamous) statue that Salon Wanda is known for: a life size copy of Michelangelo's *David*. This *David* however, was altered per Wanda's instructions, by Lexi, and he sports a porn star size organ which spews a fire hose stream of water night and day. I went up to the somewhat tilting front porch and opened the bright yellow entry door. Inside was the usual buzz of hair stylists busy at work, the odor of hair chemicals wasn't too strong today. Miz Liz was at her station busy on a head of hair, but she stopped to say hello to me.

"Oooh, honeys look what the sunny weather done brought to us this afternoon! The fine real estate man, with his thick head of hair. Alex when you gonna let my clippers loose on that mop of yo's?" I immediately blushed. "Humph, okay then not today. Well Miss Thang has her ass parked out back, guess she's waitin' for you." I smiled at Miz Liz and headed for the back door and the brick terrace. Miz Liz is one of Clinton's well know drag queens and most weekends you can catch her Diana Ross act. She and Wanda are always in some kind of tangle. Wanda turned the salon over to him when she decided to get into the mortgage business and Wanda is supposed to be a silent partner. As if, Wanda has ever kept her mouth shut. Miz Liz is no better and they are always mouthing off at each other. When they really get into it, the patrons will flee to the front porch or back terrace, literally, with glop in their hair and vinyl capes on to wait out the fracas. This usually happens at least once a week. They still can't agree, over ten years on into their business arrangement, what kind of neon sign they want to put out front, so there is no sign.

Wanda was indeed out back, her feet propped up on the edge of the pool of water that surrounds the *David* statue and waterfall. Today's outfit was no disappointment. Wanda had on a lemon colored dress with some kind of green leaf pattern, her hair was at least a foot high all piled up top and she wore bright green ear rings which almost touched her shoulders. A couple of ladies with glop in their hair and vinyl capes were sitting in chairs on the terrace reading magazines, I guess waiting for the next step in their hair do-ing process.

"Bout time you got your bony butt down here Alex. Not too hot out here this afternoon, good summer breeze today. Damn, I'm starving. Where we gonna eat at? I'm thinking some Mama Honey's might hit the spot just right. Course she don't have no slushies so that might be something against that decision. What do you think?" Wanda said as way of greeting me.

"Yes, delightful to see you too this fine afternoon Ms. Billings. No slushies is a good thing in my book. As you know, I do not drink in the middle of a work day. So are you ready, let's go."

Off we went to Mama Honey's. When were just about finished eating my cell rang and it was Hayes Brighton calling back. I explained what I needed from him and he gave me an address where I could meet him and get his signature. I asked if I could stop by in the next half hour or so as it was nearby and he said he'd be there. Wanda and I finished up and she decided to tag along while I got Hayes' signature. Wealth Creation Advisors and Imports is a lone storefront in a mostly abandoned strip mall, located on the south end of downtown.

"What does this man do Alex? Ain't no wealth creation happening down here in this skanky strip mall. Seems pretty off to me." Wanda chimed in as I pulled in a parking place in the deserted parking lot.

"You got me Wanda, I'm just here to get his signature, list Serenity's place, and hopefully sell it in record time. This man must thank his lucky stars he is divorced now. I can only imagine what it must be like to be married to a vain viper like Serenity. I wonder if he knows she tried to list and sell without his knowledge or signature."

The Wealth Creation Advisors and Imports store front had one large plate glass window with the shades drawn and a single glass door also with the shade pulled down. I pushed the door but it was locked. So I knocked. A minute or so later, a tall blonde man pulled the white vinyl shade back looked out at us and unlocked the door.

"Hi, I am Hayes Brighton and you must be Alex Campbell, the unfortunate one who has to work with Serenity. Please come in." He said while motioning us into a fluorescent lit office with dark grey industrial carpeting. There was one large wooden desk with a dark green landline on top, two white plastic chairs in front and a brown leather chair behind. A few black metal filing cabinets lined a wall, a plastic tree sat in the corner and that was it. Behind the desk was a closed door, which I suppose led to where all the wealth creation happens. Hayes motioned for us to have a seat and I introduced him to Wanda. Percy was correct, Hayes was not hard on the eyes but he seemed a bit off to me. Nothing I could exactly pinpoint though.

I explained the listing forms to him and he dutifully signed where needed. I also let him know how Serenity had previously listed the house without his signature. He did not act surprised, "Oh, Serenity and all her wheeling and dealing. What did she think she could sell it herself and I would not figure it out? Go figure. Okay, well looks like that is my final signature and you should be good to go. Best of luck working with that bitch, don't put up with all her crap. Best day of my life was when the divorce was final. Please let me know when there is an offer and I will be ready to review and sign off. The sooner that house sells the sooner Serenity will be completely out of my life. Nice to meet you Alex and Wanda." He said while showing us to the door.

That was easy. I dropped Wanda back at the salon and headed off to input the listing and upload Lexi's photos with it. The broker's open was scheduled for the day after tomorrow and Wanda had agreed to sit it with me. I left a voice mail with Serenity confirming things, letting her know Wanda and I would be there to both sit the broker's open and we would serve snacks. I then went back out to do an evening showing for a chronic client of mine. Chronic meaning this man has been looking at houses going on one year now. Who knows when or if he will ever buy. I have politely suggested professional psychological help but that fell on deaf ears. It is really bad when you get this far in with a client like this. You know they most likely will never buy but on the other hand you have so many hours in that you don't want to just give it up. Ugh.

Thirteen

Thursday arrived soon enough and it was the day for Serenity's broker's open. Brokers' opens are open houses for brokers/agents only. In theory, it is a great way to get the word out about your new listing. In the old days brokers would caravan around for the broker open tour. I say the old days because this practice was especially important prior to the real estate industry going online. Now, most agents simply preview (if they do that) online and call it good. There is still a hard core group of us that prefer to preview in-person and still do the brokers' open circuit. But in the past few years, this core group has dramatically fallen off in attendance. Quite a few listing agents do not even bother having brokers' opens anymore.

Therefore, I had let Serenity know that the broker's open might not be well attended but that Wanda and I were doing our best to announce it to our email spheres and we would be serving snacks. Nothing like food, to entice the agents to waddle through your listing. And that is what most brokers' opens have deteriorated to in the last few years, free food for greedy agents. It has reached the point where the agents attending will come in, make a bee line for the food platter, stuff their fat cheeks, take a quick glance at the living room and leave. If it is a two story house, forget about most of them even bothering to go upstairs, too much exercise I suppose. I am on the fence about brokers' opens as I don't really think they lead to sales. I still schedule and do them because in my mind any exposure can't hurt. But I do understand why many agents are no longer hosting them and perhaps I will join them, who knows.

I arrived at 10:45 and parked down the street. This way there would be ample curb parking for the horde (hopefully) of agents who would be stopping by. I placed my "open house" A-board over the yard sign, to let them know they had the right place and rang Serenity's doorbell.

I could hear Kali barking and what sounded like Serenity yelling at her. Serenity opened the door and stuck her head out while screaming, "Kali get back! Stay, damn it! Bad dog! No!" I could tell Kali was jumping up on Serenity from behind. Serenity looked at me with a scowl on her face, "Oh, you are here already. Where is the damn doggy day care van? They were supposed to be here twenty minutes ago. Down Kali! Wait there, the van should be here shortly to pick her up." With that she slammed the door and the barking grew louder. I was just about to sit down on the stoop when the doggy day care van appeared. The young twenty-something guy got out. "I'm here to pick up the dog named Kali that lives here." I motioned toward the front door, the barking and yelling were growing louder. "Oh, this again. What's up with the owner? She can't control her dog. The dog is so cool once we get away from here but man when she's with the owner it's always like this." I stepped down to the walk, so the doggy day care guy could get to the door and collect Kali. While he knocked and went through the head out the door drill with Serenity I noticed Wanda parking down the street. I wandered down the sidewalk to greet her.

Wanda got out of her emerald green Lincoln Town Car, "Looks like they got a dog commotion going on over there Alex. Here help me with these pastries I brought. I'll bring in the coffee urn and cups." Wanda had brought a few boxes of pastries from the French bakery. The dog care guy had Kali on a leash and was pulling her into the van, Serenity stood at the front door scowling and yakking on her bright pink cell phone. She stood aside as we approached the front door and back to the kitchen we went to set up shop. I returned to the cars to get Wanda's brochures and mine as well. When I came back in, Wanda had set up the pastries on a plate and the coffee and cups were all nicely arranged on the kitchen bar top. I was setting up the listing flyer copies and her mortgage brochures when Serenity entered, still talking on her phone. She walked out to the back yard.

Suddenly behind me a deep voice said, "Ohhh, hello, you must be the listing agent Serenity told me about." I quickly turned around and was a bit stunned. There stood a six foot tall, football player build woman (I think) dressed head to toe in a white, three piece man's suit. She had yellow hair, from a bottle, which was cut in a man's crew cut (literally). At the top of her no collar white shirt was a quarter sized gold pin covering the top button. I guess this replaced the tie? She wore very large dangly earrings to let you know she was a woman I suppose. Her feet were in white, flat sandals and her toe nails were painted a noxious acid green. The toenail color and sandals actually made her large feet appear hoof like.

"I am RG Boysun with Cooper's Hawk Mortgage. You must be Al?" She said in her deep voice while setting on the counter what appeared to be a mortgage brochure display.

"Ahh, yes I am Alex Campbell. Are you here to tour the house? We really haven't started yet."

RG pursed her thin, faintly red lip-sticked, lips and her pug nose nostrils flared out a bit, "Oh, tour. Sure I'd like to see the house before we get started. Serenity said this will last until 1:30."

I was confused, "Serenity told you about the broker's open? Yes, we will be here today until 1:30 but you are welcome to tour it right now."

RG's face grew a bit red, "I don't think you get it Al, I am here for the broker's open. I am the mortgage rep and I will be sitting this open with you."

This was news, "Well Serenity knew that I would be here today with Wanda from Safety Mortgage, so I don't know why she told you to come and sit this open."

RG's face grew redder and her nostrils were beginning to flare pig style big time, "Well, Serenity who is the owner of this house I believe, told me I could come here today and sit this broker's open and that is certainly what I intend to do. I am one of Serenity's VIP clients. She is my official Lifestyle Diet and Wellness Coach. She is so impressed with my weight loss progress and my top-notch mortgage abilities that she asked me personally to exclusively represent mortgage options available for this property."

What a load of crap. No one issues or gets rights to exclusively represent mortgage financing on a property except for new construction. Even then, only an imbecile of a developer would not permit a buyer to use his/her own financing person. "I don't know where the miscommunication is RG but Serenity knew I was coming here today with Wanda from Safety Mortgage. If you would like to sit an open house with me sometime, perhaps you can send me information about how you do business, your company's current rates, etc.... There is no exclusive or preferred mortgage rep for this property. It is a resale, not a new construction project. As you know, even new construction projects that have on-site lenders are not exclusive, per the law."

RG's face turned beet red, accented even more so by her all white men's suit. Her beady eyes narrowed, thin lips pursed, as her nostrils flared out completely pig style. All she needed was steam coming out from her piggy nostrils. "How DARE you insult me! You clearly do not know what you are doing or who you are working for. I AM Serenity's exclusive mortgage representative, personally and for her property. Why you are so rude, I might just have to call your company's designated broker and report you!" She directed her beady eyed glare towards Wanda who stood frozen next to the kitchen island and said, "You are clearly in the wrong place and need to leave right now. I have been doing mortgages for years and I am the exclusive rep for this property."

Wanda looked perplexed and then smiled, "Honey, I don't know how long you have been doing mortgages but you need to go read up on your law books baby. It is against the law to have an exclusive mortgage rep on a resale and it's a grey area on new construction. I don't know any new construction projects that require buyers actually use their preferred on-site lenders. They might require a buyer to get approved by their on-site lender but the buyer is still free to choose whatever mortgage company and financing he wants. So you are misinformed. I was contacted by the listing agent here to sit this broker's open and he informed the seller I would be here. I will be here until 1:30. You can make all the huffing and puffing you want but it won't change anything. There is no law against two mortgage brokers or more sitting on opens. So if you want to stay here with us, just put your pile of flyers up there on the counter and here, have yourself an éclair. You look like you could use some sugar to even out your blood."

RG grew so red I thought she was going to explode and beads of sweat were popping out on her brow. She looked exactly like a bull that was getting ready to charge after a red cape, all she lacked was a brass ring through her pig nose. She slammed her meaty hands down on the counter top and bellowed out in a deep baritone, "No one talks to RG like that, RG is NOT happy! You WILL leave. I AM the only mortgage broker that is going to be here! Serenity only wants me here and she is the owner. And take that sugar shit with you. Serenity does NOT allow sugar in her wellness program. We are serving her Power Up Serenity drinks here today. I will be setting that table of drinks up. Now clear up that sugar crap and get out or I will be forced to call Serenity."

Wanda was speechless for once. So I interjected, "Excuse me RG but Wanda will be staying. If Serenity led you to believe something else I am sorry. As Wanda said, you are welcome to stay if Serenity has in fact asked you to be here. There is no need to call Serenity. She is out back and when she comes in you can speak with her directly. Wanda is not removing the pastries, they are for the brokers and Serenity was informed we were bringing snacks with us. If you want to set up and serve her powder drinks be my guest."

RG got a smug little smile on her pig like face, "Ohhh, we'll just see about all this when Serenity comes in. You'll be doing good to keep this listing. You should be honored I am even here today. I am a very well known mortgage broker in Clinton but you obviously are too new or do not do enough player transactions to know how fortunate you are to have me here today." With that she pulled out her cell phone and hit a speed dial button, "E-E-E-E! Where are you at? Well hurry up! I need the table and cups in this house pronto!" She looked back at Wanda and me, did a smug little chuckle and said in a sing song stage whisper, "Yes, we will just see."

There was a commotion at the front door and then a short and very skinny (as in barely ninety-eight pounds) aging man appeared in the kitchen area lugging a card table and other items. He was completely bald and had a grey beard which looked very much like ZZ Top's. "Here they are dear. Where would you like for me to set them up?"

"Set it up in the corner over there near the refrigerator so we can have ample ice, there's an outlet over there for the blender."

He proceeded to do as told and then he put out his hand towards Wanda and me, "Oh hello, I am Eddie Boysun, RG's husband. Are you the real estate agents?"

"EDDIE! Shut your mouth. I said to get that table set up, now do it! These two here are in trouble with Serenity."

"Oh, my! Oh dear. Well, okay then dear, I'll just set the…"

"Shut up EDDIE and do what I told you."

Just then Serenity walked back in from the back yard and for once her ear was not glued to her cell phone. RG immediately began to tell Serenity what had happened and how Wanda needed to leave. Serenity looked at me and I calmly began to explain to her that she knew Wanda and I both were coming today and would be bringing snacks. I told her she should have let me know she had arranged for RG to attend but as Wanda and I had told RG, it would be fine if she stayed and served the Power Up Serenity drinks if she wished. RG kept trying to interrupt and was huffing and puffing. Serenity looked completely bored, "Oh okay then RG, you just sit with these two today and serve the drinks. No biggie. RG is my personal mortgage person and she is in my Power Up Serenity Winner's Circle this month! She has lost twenty-one pounds on my lifestyle wellness plan. She is off all her prescription meds and aligning her inner body's wisdom while synergizing the outer and inner for a complete whole and wellness lifestyle. You are going to be in the VIP Winner's Circle next month aren't you RG?"

With that RG leapt over to Serenity and put her meaty paw up for a high five with Serenity and barked out, "Ohh totally, RG is going to be there! Gonna be a VIP next month for sure. Eddie, it's time to POWER UP SERENITY!" She looked like a rugby player trying to start a scrimmage. Serenity just gave her a condescending smile and replied, "That's great RG, I like your enthusiasm and I know you will make it. Oh, RG don't forget to call the office with your credit card today. We need to run it now, if you are going to do next month's Winner Circle meetings."

"Oh, totally for sure Serenity. I'll have Eddie call my card number in this afternoon. Eddie! Make a note!" RG started adoringly at Serenity, who was now busy texting.

"Oh, yoo-hoo! I am here to purchase this house. Ha, ha, ha. Mercy me it is shaping up to be a hot one today! How's it going Alex and oh---you have Miss Wanda here and you are?" He said stopping at the drink card table where RG was perched in front and Eddie was hovering behind. Before Percy could introduce himself to RG, a six foot tall man appeared behind him in the living room entry. He was a South American man in his late twenties. He had shoulder length black hair, wore no shirt and had on black Lycra shorts and running shoes. He was clearly a body builder and tattooed on his perfectly waxed pecs was a hang loose sign. Serenity glanced up, tossed her phone in mid-text on the counter and rushed over to the man, "Ohhh, its Javier!" She said while literally leaping up into his arms. Instantly she started speaking in baby talk, "Ohh, me missed my widdle Javey! Did you miss your kitty?" She said while he held her up like a baby.

"Ahh, my little kitten has been lonely. It's been four hours sweetness, too long to be without you." Javier replied. I couldn't believe it. First, he looks like a model from one of those drugstore romance novel covers and second he speaks like some Don Juan from a 1970s coffee commercial. And Serenity's baby talk was enough to

101

make me hurl. I glanced over at Percy and he was almost literally drooling and about to wet himself. RG appeared to be getting ready to tackle Javier, while Eddie fidgeted nervously behind the table with the blender. Wanda was in the corner taking it all in with a very odd smile on her face. Javier put Serenity down, and smoothed her hair back, "Has my little kitty had her late morning protein shake?" She then kicked her foot like a pouty child and tilted her head all coy and replied in baby talk, "Maybe, maybe not. Me not hungee this morning." Hungee? You can't be serious and this from a woman who I know for a fact just turned the corner past forty-five.

"You need to Power Up Serenity baby."

"Okee- dokey daddy. Maybe RG can make me a shaky?" She replied with her back to RG.

RG instantly jumped into gear and stood up an inch taller and snapped her fingers, "You heard the lady Eddie, hit it! And not too much ice Eddie, you know Serenity doesn't like a lot of ice. Well? What are you waiting for EDDIE, move it!"

"Ohh, ahh, yes dear, I'm still setting up the--(RG gave him a dead cold look)—oh yes, right away dear." Eddie nervously mumbled as he scrambled to put powder and ice into the blender.

Serenity and Javier kept up their goo-goo talk while we all stood there. Eddie quickly whipped up a shake for Serenity and RG snatched it out of Eddie's hand, wiped off the glass and handed it to Serenity like she was making an offering to some goddess deity. Serenity took the glass, with her back to RG and proceeded to gulp it down. When she finished she looked up at Javier smiling and said, "All gone-y now. Am I a good kitty? Uh-oh, I tinks I has a shaky mustache now."

"Oh, yes you are a good girl. But oh, it does look like my little kitty has a shake mustache. And you know what daddy does to shake mustaches don't you?" With this Serenity got all five year old girl squeal-y and Javier proceeded to lick the shake mustache off of her upper lip. Now I seriously needed a barf bag. Percy had popped out his monogrammed handkerchief and was mopping his brow, I swear too much more and the poor man was going to just keel over. With each passing second, RG looked more like pit bull pulling on its chain leash in a junk yard. Wanda now had her eyes bugged out and mouth hanging open.

"Okay baby now we need to go to TOTAL for the staff meeting. Are you ready for that kitty?"

"Me all ready but him has to carry me."
With that Javier hoisted Serenity over his shoulder and proceeded towards the front door. Serenity called back, "Okay team, you all sell my house before I get back so Javier and I can get to L.A!" And we watched as he carried her out, her Lycra-ed ass hanging over his shoulder with yet again, a pink thong rising out of her tiny butt crack.

Fourteen

Sell her house indeed. Eddie finished setting up RG's table and they set out Serenity's protein powder drink canisters, fired up the blender and made a batch of her mango, jalapeño flavor. RG promptly drank an entire batch herself while barking at Eddie to make another one, this time the chocolate mocha, raisin flavor. Wanda and I stood on the other end of the kitchen giving each other amazed looks, trying not to laugh. So there I was standing between Wanda who was wearing a billowing orange dress with hot pink accents and shoes, her towering hair in a hot pink headband and flipped out. On the other side was RG the man/woman in her men's three piece white suit and acid green toenails along with her lap dog Eddie, his cue ball all shiny and his ZZ Top beard hanging down to his naval. Near the hall stood Percy decked out in one of his large, un-tucked, tropical Mumu shirts, busy mopping his brow with a lavender, monogrammed handkerchief. I stood in the middle in my plain-Joe khaki pants, a short sleeve green plaid button down, black belt and matching slip on shoes. What a picture this must be. Right on cue, a gaggle of real estate agents did actually stop by.

They looked around the house, ate Wanda's pastries, checked out the back yard, and passed on Serenity's Power Up Serenity drink. Well, one agent did take a sip but promptly grimaced and asked for a glass of water. RG extolled the virtues of Serenity and her program while the agents gave her odd looks. One asked me about the condition of the septic tank, and I said that was being checked on very soon. Another agent commented on how dark the house was and bad the color choices were. RG abruptly cut in and told her, "You obviously are not good enough to sell this house. Do you know who Serenity is? Do you have any idea how fortunate you are to be allowed to walk through her personal house?" The agent gave me a quizzical look and I replied, "This is RG Boysun of Cooper's Hawk Mortgage. She is the owner's personal mortgage rep and lifestyle and wellness client." To which the agent looked more perplexed and moved on.

After this group of agents left, there was a long awkward silence in the kitchen. Eddie stood behind the blender nervously puttering with the ice cubes while RG pulled out her Blackberry and used a little stylus to type.

"Stop fidgeting Eddie and stand still!" She barked while tapping with her stylus. "Al you two obviously need to recognize a pro at work when you see one. This is my new Blackberry which I use for work to always stay in touch with my clients. I am always on the cutting edge, in with the players and that's how I have become a VIP. I also take time to care for myself by aligning myself with the upmost of professionals and celebrities like Serenity. You should study and learn while I am presenting you with this opportunity."

Wanda and I gave each other open mouthed looks. This woman was just plain bat shit crazy. Neither of us chose to respond and there was an awful silence only slightly interrupted by the feint tapping of RG's stylus. Percy walked over to RG's table, "Well, where were we before that gorgeous man interrupted us?"

"I am RG Boysun. This is my husband Eddie. Eddie, make the man a drink, now! I am Serenity's personal mortgage representative and I am here to assist you with all of your mortgage needs. I only associate and work with VIP's and I can just tell you are a player."

Percy looked a little confused, "Well, it is nice to make your acquaintance. I am Percival Emerson, not related to *the* Emerson but my mother's side does descend from Woodrow Wilson. Ohh, it is a bit of a hot one today. One of those Serenity drinks with ice would hit the spot. I am Serenity's neighbor and good friend."

I suppose Percy telling RG he was Serenity's neighbor and good friend hit her jealously button. She began to turn a red color again. "EDDIE, I said to mix the man a drink, now do it!"

"Oh yes dear, I am so sorry let me just get this ice and aagghhhhhh...."

With that, the blender started up on high, the lid flew off in the air and the mocha protein drink sprayed all over RG's white suit, hitting Percy just a bit as well. "God DAMN YOU EDDIE!" RG shrieked in her deep baritone. She kicked the card table over in anger and everything fell to the floor, the blender still running. Eddie let out whimper and ran for the front door. "You get your RUNT ass back here EDDIE and clean this mess up! You SHIT, look at my suit. Come back here NOW!" And RG took off for the front door after Eddie.

Percy stood there, sputtering and wiping the drink's spray from his face with a fresh, pale yellow, monogrammed handkerchief. "Well hells bells Alex, who is that woman and what is she doing here? Did she say that tiny man was her husband? Husband; her? How in god's name could she possibly know Serenity?"

I unplugged the blender that was now on its side sputtering on the floor. I located a mop and bucket and Percy took the paper towels and all three of us set to work cleaning up the drink mess while Wanda and I filled Percy in on the morning's events.

We had most of it all cleaned up and Percy was attempting to refold the broken card table when RG and Eddie reappeared. "Help that man out Eddie, get the stuff." RG said as she picked up her Blackberry and flyers. "I think Eddie and I are going to call it a day. I will let you take over the mortgage part of this open house Wanda. Al, I do look forward to meeting you again and reviewing what I and Cooper's Hawk Mortgage can offer you and your clients. Only the best for the best is what I always say. Percival it was nice to meet you and I apologize for my husband's complete incompetence. I hope the drink spray did not do too much damage. I am sure I will see you again, as I am part of Serenity's inner circle. I know you said you are her neighbor and friend. Well I know for a fact, that Serenity's *real* friends are exclusive members of her Winner's Circle program. Perhaps someday you too will achieve the status of that circle as I have. Okay, bring the gear Eddie and get a move on it! It's time for my noon Power Up Serenity shake and I am getting hungry!"

Eddie was scampering to gather all the items; I picked up the broken card table for him and carried it to the front door. I was about to carry it to their four door white Cadillac Escalade Ext pickup truck, complete with gold wire hub caps, parked out in front of the house but

Eddie motioned for me to stay, "Oh, ah, thank you Alex. Please just leave that right there by the door and I'll dash back and get it. I ah, don't want to upset RG any more than she already is. Her blood sugar is awfully bad today, you'll have to please excuse her…" he was cut short by the Cadillac pickup's honking horn, which sounded exactly like an eighteen wheeler's horn, some kind of custom add-on I suppose. Then equally loud, RG's baritone bellowed, "E-E-E-E, bring the damn table and let's go! RG does NOT like to wait!"

I went back inside and found Percy and Wanda eating éclairs. Wanda stopped in mid bite, "Damn Alex if that ain't one fucked up honky man/woman I don't know what is! Percy you should've heard what that woman said. Humpf, I'm gonna have to find out some more about that there RG Boysun and her bird's nest mortgage company. What the hell? You know Alex, she reminds me of a lezzy version of that TV show Boss Hog character. Just plain crazy. You think she on drugs?"

I shrugged and Percy cut in, "Well I can tell you Miss Wanda, that woman is quite the confused one in the gender department. She was wearing a man's suit for god's sakes and her hair is shorter than a ROTC trainer. As an openly gay man, I pride myself in my gaydar and I can tell you both, that woman is a lesbian, husband or no husband. I mean who really cares? It works for those two I suppose, but lord that Eddie must fear for his life. Did you hear her yell at him and see how he ran out the door? My lord, I bet that woman abuses him. Of course maybe that's what he's into, who knows! But winner circle or not, I can tell you that creature is no close friend of Serenity."

108

This conversation continued and 1:30 rolled around soon enough without another group of agents coming through. We packed everything up and left. I mentioned to Percy that I needed to get Serenity to have the septic tank's condition checked and most likely pumped. I told him Arnie had already identified where the septic tank's lid is so it should be pretty straight forward. He said, "I will work on it Alex."

Fifteen

Later that afternoon Norman Kluntz called and asked if I could possibly move up his tour to today instead of Saturday. Seems Amy had the day off and was going to have to work double shifts on Saturday. Nothing like a last minute scheduling change to know you are working in real estate. I had to scramble to call the houses that required appointments to tour. Fortunately, I caught two of the owners live and they said it would be okay to show today and the other I left a voice mail. The fourth was vacant so it wouldn't matter. All of the houses were in Rosedale so that made it a bit easier. I managed to take Clyde out for a quick walk. He proceeded to mark every light post and mail box he could lift his hind leg to. I got him settled in the back yard and sped off to meet Norman and Amy at the first house.

When I pulled up to the mid-sixties split level house I spied Norman in the driveway. He had on his brown and mustard plaid windbreaker again and his green slacks were about an inch too short. Towering over him stood a woman who I guessed was Amy. This certainly couldn't be *the* Amy Foster, creative artist/dancer that Lexi spoke of. This Amy was in seriously tall, porno stilettos, which were shimmering white and glittery. She wore fish net stockings and a barely there micro mini which was also white and glittery. Let's just say her friends up top made Pamela Lee Anderson look flat and they were literally spilling out of her hot pink, low cut stretch top. Her black, permed hair spilled down to her shoulders. She kind of looked like Cher circa the late 1980s. She was leaning down on Norman's shoulder and appeared to be stroking his cheek with her stick on hot pink talons. Amy looked up at me as I got out of the car and gave me a huge smile, her inflated lips slathered in a lilac colored lipstick. Oh my god, Norman's mother in Philly was going to have a coronary. Amy was not the kind of dancer you would take home to show mommy. Norman you horn dog!

"Hello there Alex, sure is the right weather this afternoon for touring. Ahh, this is ahh Amy. She's you know, going to be living with me and all and well honey Alex here is my real estate agent. He's going to make sure we find you the perfect rehearsal space in our new home."

Amy practically purred with glee, "Ohhhhh Normie you are just my little baby!" She oozed while her talons squeezed his cheeks. Norman turned a bright shade of red and appeared a bit flustered.

I stuck out my hand, "Hi Amy. A pleasure to meet you. I am Alex Campbell with Winterfrost Real Estate and Norman has told me that you need a rec. room that can work as your dance rehearsal space. Hopefully the four houses we'll see today have rec. rooms that will work for you."

"Ohhhhh, Alex I so appreciate all of your *hard* work." Was this woman making sexual innuendos with me? "Normie knows how much I like to rehearse and he just loves to watch me, don't you Normie? He's my number one fan Alex. Maybe you've seen me perform? My stage name is Fantasia. I'm pretty well known at Scandals if I do say so myself! I have been there going on two years now and Normie and I are just so excited because Ron the floor manager says I'm gonna be getting top billing starting this weekend!

He wants me to headline their retro 1960s a-go-go night this Saturday! Can you believe that? I mean most girls don't achieve that kind of star billing status in three years, let alone just under two like me. My Normie here says he's very proud of me. I'm gonna make you even more proud with my first top billing performance this Saturday Normie." She let out a little titter and began caressing Norman's arm.

"Well, Amy I don't think I've caught your act but I am sure it is good. So folks, why don't we get this place unlocked and let you all have a look." With that I unlocked the house and we went in to take a gander. Unfortunately, this house had the open kind of Brady Bunch stairs that scare Norman. We caravanned to the other three houses, Amy oohhing and ahhing at each one. The second house was a complete no, as the rec. room's ceilings were too low. The third one was okay but did not have a lot of privacy. It looked like house number four was the best bet. It was built in 1957 and its basement was a day light basement and had eleven foot ceilings, a rare find. Amy said she definitely could fit her practice pole in the space and Norman said maybe they could install a mini practice stage with lights. That made Amy just about orgasm on the spot. This house would need new windows installed, no cheap item. The windows were the original late 1950s single paned aluminums which were molding in places and are notorious heat loss offenders. I suggested Norman might want to price out the cost for new double paned vinyl windows and reminded him the large plate glass windows upstairs would be spendy. He seemed to take it in stride and appeared to be more focused on the pleasure den he could build for Amy in the basement. We did a complete walk around the house outside and the backyard was right next to the Rosedale ravine so no chance of someone building behind this house, always good for long term value. I pointed out to Norman that the gutters might need to be replaced soon and noted a crack in the front drive that should be sealed. I left them in the driveway to ponder things and told him I would email him the active and sold comps for house number four so he could see firsthand how it stacked up price wise. Amy was so busy caressing and oohhing and ahhing with Norman that I'm not quite certain he heard me. However, as I was getting into my car Norman's cell phone began to ring and he immediately bolted upright into a soldier stance and looked completely panic stricken, "It is mother calling! Ohh, I have to answer this Amy. Now you'll be good won't you? Remember, you have to be silent when I am speaking with mother." To which she smiled big and wide and put her index finger up to her inflated lilac lips.

I had to drop some paperwork off at an escrow company located near the airport so once that was done, I decided to take the interstate down and drop in on Lexi. Lexi lives on the outskirts of Clinton off the interstate on a "little farm" as we all call it. I pulled onto her dirt/gravel drive noting the new installation sculptures that lined the long and winding drive. Lexi has been in an "organic" sculpture phase for a while now. This means her metal creations have honey, food or something to attract wildlife to interact with them. Something about the live critters interacting with the inorganic, who knows. I think they all just look like rusted metal poles with crap welded onto them. I passed what appeared to be a family of possums licking one blob of a sculpture. When I rounded the corner, I noticed Arnie's truck, Pearl, parked out front alongside Lexi's aging yellow Bronco. They were standing in front of Lexi's makeshift studio and having a discussion.

"Well hello there stranger." Lexi said, "Arnie is here letting me know how she is going to fix up my work space. She's going to get this metal roof all secure and put in real lights for me. We are still debating whether or not I should keep the hanging plastic for walls or put in real walls. What do you think Alex?"

What do I think? Hell no. Lexi already burned down one of her ex husband's 1800s family's homestead with her sculpting torch, though she claims pot was to blame, I highly doubt it. Anyone who has seen Lexi with her blow torch knows to duck and cover. "Ah, hello. Well Lexi, you know I think the plastic walls are working for you now so why change? Also, it allows you to get fresh air and it makes it easier for you to wheel your metal installation pieces in and out, right?" Lexi adjusted her green floppy hat and pondered my two cents worth.

Arnie was finishing up some notes she had been taking, "Good to see you Alex. So I got that septic lid at Serenity's all i.d.'d for you. She gonna get the pumper out there or should I pop the lid when I'm over there tomorrow laying the sod and fixing up that back yard?"

"Go ahead and pop the lid please. I can then show Serenity firsthand that the tank is full and needs to be pumped. She is going to have to get it pumped and inspected, per the law, so might as well get it out of the way before there is an offer."

114

"Gotcha chief, sounds like a plan to me. You know it's one of them old-school iron bastards she's got out back there. She's probably gonna have to have the whole damn thing replaced. D-box is probably one them concrete bitches, just all wasted away by now. But I'm hearin' ya, git her done before someone makes an offer. Probably save her some money in the long run without that hassle in the negotiation mix."

"Couldn't have said it better, now if I could just get Serenity to listen and serve her own best interest and not her ego."

Arnie gave me a sly grin, "Yeah, well good luck with that one. Okay Lexi, I got my notes, we'll talk more." She banged her hand on the rear panel of Pearl, her mint green 1973 Ford F-100 pickup, and said, "I'm outta here, gotta take Pearl down to my friend PK's garage and give her a lube and tire swap tonight. Later."

Lexi and I chit-chatted and I thanked her again for the listing photos she took and put on a disk for me and I gave her a check. She showed me her latest piece of work in progress, part of the installation that was going to go in front of the municipal building. I have to say I don't think I grasped the overall vision and what I saw just looked like rusted car parts to me but what do I know. I told her I had to get going but we'd all need to meet up for dinner soon, hopefully not at her pigsty house. I was pulling up to where her driveway meets the rural road connector to the interstate when my cell began to ring. I stopped and picked up. It was Serenity.

"Alex I need you to be at the News Four studios tomorrow morning at 5:00 a.m. Make sure you wear a blue, non-patterned shirt and bring flyers for the house with you." Naturally, no hello or any of the usual telephone etiquette pleasantries.

"Yes, hello Serenity. What is the occasion, why meet up at News Four tomorrow?"

She let out an annoyed sigh, "Because they are featuring me on their *Clinton AM* program tomorrow and I am going to be promoting my Power Up Serenity drinks as well as trying to help you sell my house. Not that you have done a single thing thus far to sell my house. I suppose I'll need to coach you on how to act on live TV and..."

I cut her off, "No Serenity, actually you don't need to coach me. I was on a number of live TV shows a while back when Wanda and I caught a local killer. My dog Clyde made national headlines for knocking the killer over and keeping the killer from harming anyone else. I am quite well versed in the local and national TV studio protocols. No need to worry, I'll see you at News Four tomorrow at 5:00 a.m. If I remember correctly, the producer there is Teri Roberts and she can clue me in as to how she wants me to plug your listing." With that I hung up. I had more than enough of Serenity for one day. I guess her cute baby talk routine wears off the second Javier goes away and then it is back to rude bitch mode.

Sixteen

I had to wake up at 3:00 a.m. if I was going to be remotely perky and awake for the 5:00 a.m. studio call and early morning live TV. Clyde gave me a groggy eyed, what the hell are you doing up look and promptly burrowed deeper under the covers. I stumbled into the shower, and then was busy making coffee. I dragged Clyde out back for a quick squirt but he wasn't having any of it and let me know in no uncertain terms by grunting as I dragged him on his leash out back. He did a little business and then dragged me back inside and promptly jumped up on the bed, walked around in a circle a few times, plopped down, glared up at me, and went directly back to sleep. I threw on a t-shirt and jeans, packed dry cleaner pressed chinos, three blah solid color shirts, and my navy blue blazer in a travel garment bag and was off to the News Four studio.

I arrived at the studio a little before 5:00 a.m. and checked in with the security guard at the front desk. He had my name on the list, so he gave me an entry badge and directed me down the hall way. The studio was buzzing with activity, all the workers obviously used to working early morning hours. The bright studio lights are always a bit jarring, not to mention the heat factor which is always high regardless of how much A/C they run. I spied Teri Roberts the producer of *Clinton AM* and walked over and let her know I was there. She remembered me from when Clyde and I had been on the show. Teri told me the segment was about Serenity's Power Up Serenity drink and her testimonial client. Then towards the end they were going to mention that Serenity's house was for sale and show a couple of pictures. The camera would focus on me and I would provide basic listing answers to questions the host would ask me. Simple enough. Teri then directed me back to make-up and said Serenity was already there.

I made my way to make-up and Serenity was in one salon chair, yakking on her cell phone while a make-up person was setting her hair. Another attendant was about to brush some make-up on her checks but she slapped the make-up brush out of his hand and snarled, "What do you think you are doing? I didn't say you could put that crap on me! I am already pretty enough, I don't need any blusher. Don't you know who I am? I am completely healthy and my skin tone reflects it without your artificial blusher." The make-up guy picked his brush up off the floor and shook his head as he walked away. Serenity went right back to her cell phone. I sat down in an open chair and they put a vinyl cape around me and started glop-ping on make-up. Unlike Miss Perfect two chairs down, I knew my pallor was pale and I also understand how the bright set lights can alter your skin tone's color, thus the necessity of some make-up. My make-up lady asked me how I was doing and we chit-chatted a bit. She then asked me in a whisper, if Serenity was always this bitchy. I rolled my eyes upward and replied, "You don't even want to know." She shook her head and tsked. She was starting to un-Dennis the Menace my hair when into the room in a blaze of white came RG, Eddie running in tow.

"E-e-e-e, you put my bag down over there." She sat down in the next salon chair and they were wrapping her in a vinyl cape when one of the show's associate producers approached her. Apparently they were not thrilled RG would be wearing white from head to toe, as white is not the easiest of colors to work with on live television.

"Excuse me," RG bellowed to the associate producer, "But you obviously do not know who I am! I am one of Serenity's VIP, Winner Circle clients and her personal mortgage representative. This white suit is my signature look and I have no intention of altering any of it for the likes of your small, little morning show. No, RG does NOT adjust her signature look! You should count your lucky stars that Serenity has even agreed to show up here and introduce her extraordinary Power Up Serenity shakes on your piddly TV show. I came only as favor to Serenity. Oh and watch it with that make-up! I prefer my look to be natural." The associate producer attempted to cajole RG to at least wear a shirt that was not white with her suit. RG was not having it and she started to stand up. "Okay, Eddie that's it we are out of here!" She called down to Serenity, "Serenity we have to leave. I am afraid the producer does not care for my signature look and wants me to not wear all white. They are also attempting to put make-up on me that I do not like or wear. I have on a bit of red lipstick on and that should do it."

Serenity put her cell phone aside, "You are right RG. This is just too unnatural. If you feel you need to leave then go, I understand. These people don't seem to grasp the favor we are doing for them or how powerful my drinks are. I will stay only because I reluctantly agreed to be here. But they will just have to rewrite the segment without a live testimonial from one of the winner circle VIPs." The associate producer appeared panicked and began to placate RG into staying. RG huffed and puffed but agreed to stay and do the show. She ordered Eddie to mix her up a shake and then glanced over at me. "Oh, you are here too today I see. EDDIE! Mix a shake for the real estate agent too, he could use one. I see you are allowing them to put their make-up on you, very unnatural." I made a mild attempt to explain to RG that the make-up was necessary given the lighting and it would appear natural on the set. She just scoffed. "I do hope you intend to actually promote and sell Serenity's house this morning. After your awful attempt at selling the other day, I am really not certain why Serenity still has you on the job." She said admiring her piggy nose in the brightly lit mirror, while the make-up person attempted to do something to her yellow dyed crew cut.

Before I could respond, Eddie was passing out shakes. I set mine on the counter and made no attempt to even feign sipping it. RG guzzled hers and held the empty glass up for Eddie to scurry over and take away. Next the producer wanted us on the set so out we went. We would be on the segment stage which was right next to the faux living room set for *Clinton AM*. We watched in the wings as the hosts Katie Katori and Skip Kenny finished a live bit and then went to commercial. They quickly lined Serenity and RG up on the segment stage where a Power Up Serenity shake display table was set up and shakes were ready made to be sampled while on the air. The producer quickly reviewed with Serenity and RG the drill and then she showed me where to stand. Everyone was on their marks and it was live again. Skip did a lead in and then cut to Katie who was standing with Serenity and RG ready to hawk the drink.

NO SERENITY

"So, we're back here at *Clinton AM*, I'm Skip Kenny and of course the lovely Katie Katori is here with another one of her special features!" Skip oozed with such excited glee that I could swear the man had a personal vibrator buzzing in his ass as he sat on the taupe sofa. He was all perky and buffed, waxed, shellacked, wearing a perfectly pressed blue suit and green tie, with his manicured and clear glossed fingernails, his teeth whiter than floodlights, his blonde hair sprayed, coiffed, and windblown all looking perfect under the hot lights. The camera cut to Katie standing with us. She is a pencil thin Asian woman and was dressed in a tight Chanel pink and black suit with pounds of make-up on her face,

"Oh, you are too kind Skip! But yes I do have a special friend here with us today to share. Now folks in full disclosure, I want everyone to know that I am this woman's number one fan!" Skip gave a loud hee-haw off camera. "No really! My guest Serenity is the best Lifestyle Diet and Wellness Coach in Clinton, well anywhere in my humble opinion! Important for our viewers to note Skip, that I too am guilty of belonging to Serenity's gym TOTAL and I've been a personal client in her wellness coaching program. And as anyone around the station knows, thank god for Serenity, she's made me a new woman. Ha, ha, ha! Just ask anyone here and they'll tell you I have so much more energy and zest now since I've been on Serenity's trademarked program and have participated in her wellness training. So here for everyone to meet is Serenity and she is going to share with us her line of protein drinks called Power Up Serenity. Which I just have to add certainly get me through my hectic day here at News Four!"

The minute the camera was on her, Serenity lit up like a Christmas tree. She was decked out in her usual Lycra shorts, flip flops and her barely there, letting it all spill out Power Up Serenity midriff sports bra top. Again, why the entire room full of clothes if this was all she ever wore? She smiled all big and warm and giggled with Katie like they were long lost sorority sisters. Katie was very interested in the drink's diet angle and quizzed Serenity about her Lifestyle Diet and Wellness Coaching business. Serenity gave her standard new age dribble combined with corporate double talk nonsensical answers. "It's soo important Katie, as you know firsthand," she purred while reaching out and touching Katie's arm, "that we strive towards living authentically and my Power Up Serenity shakes are designed to help facilitate that transition. They are not only balanced nutritionally with all the protein you need for energy, I have also ensured they are balanced on a chakra level. They help to synergistically align all of your seven chakras so your inner and outer well being can become one. They help us achieve as the famous *Rinpoche* once said, *alive awareness of being.*"

Oh that *is* deep, Serenity. I guess she wasn't aware *Rinpoche* is the generic word for teacher, so which famous Tibetan teacher exactly is she quoting here? I guess the Tibetan For Dummies book didn't specify. Katie cut in to ask her how her rising notoriety on a national level was affecting her. Serenity gave a closed mouthed constipated smile, "Oh Katie, you've known me for years and I'm just the same old Clinton Serenity I've always been. You know I'm still down with all my peeps." Oh sure, another Jenny from the Block or rather that is the status you are jones-ing for. "It's so important to me that I remain faithful to my core, not just all the loyal clients whose lives I have facilitated in transforming but my own inner essential core as well. Again, grounding in authentic living. It's just sooo important." She concluded that spew by placing her palms together right in front of her inflated friends and doing a little Namaste bow directly into the camera.

Katie ooohhed back at her and then had them sample some shakes. She acted like she was having a live TV orgasm after she sampled the new mango-jalapeño flavor and gushed over how tasty all the flavors were, while holding her glass up to the camera. She then put her microphone in front of RG, "Now I understand you are one of Serenity's VIP Winner Circle clients and you have lost over twenty-one pounds, is that true?" RG appeared somewhat like a deer in headlights as the camera moved in on her face for a close up. Her beady eyes appeared to be looking directly at the monitor rather than looking at Katie as the producer had instructed.

"Oh, ah, me? Yes, yes, I am RG Boysun and I am part of Serenity's Winner's Circle. Her coaching and Power Up Serenity drinks have given me a new life. My husband Eddie is just amazed at the results. Everyone out there in Clinton should go to Serenity's gym TOTAL and sign up for her coaching and wellness program. It will totally change their lives." Katie smiled and was about to cut away but RG actually reached out and held onto the microphone Katie was holding. Then RG spoke directly into the camera, "And if anyone out there needs a good mortgage, they should know I am Serenity's personal and exclusive mortgage rep for her house. I am with

Cooper's Hawk Mortgage and a very big VIP player in the Clinton
mortgage market." Katie abruptly pulled her microphone back and
RG's face got its smug, superior piggy look, I guess she was proud of
herself for getting her company plug in. Katie immediately took
control and stood in front of RG. "Well Serenity's drinks sure are
delicious and good for you! Our viewers can check out her gym
TOTAL, the address should appear at the bottom of the screen. Now
before we go, we did promise Serenity that we'd show a few pictures of
her home that she is selling. Of course we at *Clinton AM* are always
happy to let the public know about a local celebrity's listing. So
exciting! Now what you are seeing is an exterior photo of her house,
tres chic, in the Capitol Heights neighborhood. I know our viewers like
that. And this is the living room, ohh so cozy and such an earthy color,
and an open kitchen it looks like with stainless appliances. Can't show
anymore I'm afraid we are running short on time.

Now we have here today Alex Campbell with Winters Front
Realty and he is the listing agent for this property. Alex can you
quickly give us the rundown as to the number of bedrooms and baths
and our list price?"

The camera panned over to me. I corrected the Winterfrost
name and let her know it is Real Estate not Realty. Winterfrost really
gets their panties in a knot if anyone refers to them as "realty," they see
that as too down market. Then I went over the house's basics. Katie
smiled and purred in response and asked me to let the viewers know
when the next public open house would be so they could all stop by.
So I let the idiots out there who were awake at such an ungodly hour

listening to this brain dead drivel know that I'd be there on Sunday with my mortgage sidekick Wanda Billings of Safety Mortgage from 1:00 to 3:00 p.m. and that we just couldn't wait to see everyone and show them Serenity's terrific house. How's that for on-air fake and perky? With that the camera cut to back to Katie and she just giggled with glee, "Oh, thank you Alex. Now that address for Serenity's house is on your screen folks, so take note and who knows maybe I'll even stop by in person to take a look on Sunday? It's not every day you get free access to a local celebrity's house!" And then her big smile faded and she went all somber and looked gravely concerned as she spoke directly into the camera, "Next Skip and I are going to chat with a woman who is recovering from a serious toenail fungus that she claims she got from a *major* Clinton nail salon! So stay tuned, you won't want to miss this startling and alarming exclusive News Four Investigates interview!" And then we were off the air.

They hustled us all off the set as a woman in a foot bandage and what appeared to be her ambulance chasing attorney were being seated in the faux living room with Skip. RG tried to get in my face as the make-up woman was removing my make-up. "Nice plug for your mortgage person there. But as you know I am the exclusive mortgage rep for Serenity. However, I will allow you to have your loan person there on Sunday as Eddie and I already have plans and will be at the Seadogs game with some big Clinton players and VIPs."

I sat up straight, the make-up removal halted, "RG, legally there is no such thing as an exclusive mortgage rep. Not for Serenity or anyone. The law clearly states that requiring someone, a buyer in this situation, to work with someone, such as you, is illegal. It's a tie-in and tie-ins are illegal in this state. But don't take my word for it; I'll have Doris Havlon contact you with the pertinent legal codes and laws so you can see for yourself. You really are putting yourself and your company in legal jeopardy when you continue to publicly state that you are the exclusive mortgage rep for Serenity and her property." I was done with the make-up removal and was taking off my vinyl cape when Serenity walked up and stood between RG and me. "Well Alex I certainly hope you appreciate all I have done for you this morning. Not everyone gets to be on TV with someone as famous as me. And you'll note that I have once again done ALL of the work to sell my house. You should learn a thing or two. I get your listing on live TV and what have you done for me besides have a dead open house and send out postcards and email your lame sphere. But I'll just have to accept the fact that when you are as famous and hard working as me, you just have to do everything yourself and that's just the way life is." With that she snapped on her cell, put it to her ear and was already beginning to gab before she was no more than three steps away from me. RG gave me a smug and condescending look and brushed past me, tailing Serenity. She snapped her man paw fingers impatiently and Eddie came up the rear dragging an enormous suitcase that probably weighed more than he did while holding a blender, his ZZ Top beard flung over his bony shoulder. He smiled weakly at me when he passed by, following in RG's dust. The more I see that man, the more I visualize the dog that pulled the sled in *How the Grinch Stole Christmas*.

Seventeen

Later that morning after I had given Clyde a good long walk amidst the rotting piers and we had stopped by Sasser's Bakery for strong coffee and pastries, I had Clyde parked out back and I was sitting in the sun enjoying the silence. Not to be, my cell began to ring and when I picked up it was Arnie.

"Hey there chief, how's it hanging? I'm over here at Serenity's gittin' that sod laid so you are good to go for your open on Sunday. I've popped the septic lid and she's full. Princess is gonna have to git her pumped. Wanna come and take a look and get the Princess to take a gander too?" Arnie then cleared her throat and it sounded like she was hocking another loogie.

"Thanks for letting me know. I'll come over right now and take a look. Sounds like Serenity is there?"

"Ohhh yeah, little Miss Lycra is here and in rare form. She's inside battling with her dog right now. See ya in a few."

So much for silence in the sun. I left Clyde to play or do whatever he does in the back yard and motored over to Serenity's lair. The white Ranger Rover was parked in the pad and Pearl was right out in front parked at the curb. I didn't see any sign of Percy lurking about as I dashed to the front door. I could hear Serenity screaming at Kali inside as I rang the bell. Serenity popped her head out the door, "Oh what the hell do *you* want? I thought you were the fucking doggy day care. Down Kali, stop it now!" I let the pleasant home owner know that Arnie had called and the septic tank's lid was open. I was there to take a look and she could as well. Serenity gave me nasty scowl, "Just

go around back through the gate for god's sake. Don't bother me!"
And she slammed the door while cursing at Kali. As I walked around
to the side gate that led to her back yard, I pondered just canceling the
listing there on the spot. Who needs this shit? Well actually I suppose
my bank account needed it. I found Arnie out back laying and rolling
the sod. It looked really nice. She led me over to the side area and
showed me the enormous cast iron lid she had removed. The lid
opening alone was easily accessible by an adult. I had no idea septic
tanks were so big and mentioned this to Arnie.

"Oh yeah, especially these old cast iron bastards they are
usually really big Alex. Plenty of room in her for you to stand up and
judging from this old one it's at least six foot tall or more. As you can
see she is sure enough full of shit and is gonna have to be pumped, no
doubt. I'll betcha the D-box is totally eroded and this whole tank and
system is gonna have to be replaced before the sale closes. Real shame
to lay out all this fresh sod when they are just gonna have to back hoe
her and lay out the new system. Speaking of which, they are gonna
need one of them mini Bob cats to get back here and remove and lay
out the new system. Not really sure a mini Bob is gonna fit but you'll
have to see what the septic company says. For sure, the county and
city ain't gonna sign off on this here."

For better or worse, Arnie was one hundred percent correct.
Per law, all sales with septic systems now require the owner have them
professionally pumped and inspected prior to the sale closing, via the
required septic inspection addendum to the purchase and sale
agreement. I still couldn't get over how big this tank was. It was big

enough to be a small, underground bomb shelter room. The water/sludge was totally filled almost to the lid's top. I told Arnie I was going to go get Serenity and have her take a look at this. Hopefully seeing it would convince the bitch that she did need to have it pumped and inspected pronto. Way better to have this taken care of prior to an offer, so the buyer would not have this as a negotiation tool when making their offer.

I went to the french doors, noting that Arnie had arranged the furniture on the rear patio and put some flowers in the pots. It looked really nice. I rapped on the glass paned door. Serenity was still yelling at Kali, who promptly appeared at the rear door and put her paws up on the door as if pleading for escape. Serenity appeared and screamed, "What the fuck do you want? I am busy!" I was ready to smack the living shit out of this lycra assed bitch. However, I managed to say in a loud voice, "Arnie is correct this needs pumping right away. Come out here and have a look for yourself." She snarled and pushed Kali down and opened the door. However, Kali outsmarted her and knocked her down on the floor and took off into the back yard, making a break for the far end of the narrow enclosed lot, back where Arnie was laying the sod. "God damn fucking dog! Now look what YOU made me do you idiot." Serenity said while standing up. "I already told you I am NOT having that tank pumped or repaired or whatever. It is NOT my concern. You deal with it and make it happen as is. That is how this works you dumb ass! I am a VERY important and busy woman in case you haven't noticed and you are here to SERVE me." With that she promptly took a call on her cell phone and instantly was in her soothing and caring tone of voice, "Yes, how are you dear? I agree! It is so important that you honor your inner wisdom and flow with the changes of life. Live the talk I always say! Now do you have your credit card handy? Because I DO want you in my inner wisdom outer body series next month, it is so crucial for your continued wellness and your journey toward your safe harbor...." She continued her pseudo psycho babble as she slammed the french door in my face.

That was it, I was done. I turned around and stood in awe. Kali the wild dog was sitting and acting completely well behaved for Arnie. Arnie was petting her and teaching her to sit and stay. I waved to Arnie and walked out the side gate. Just as I reached the side walk, who should appear?

"Yoo-hoo, Alex it's me, Percy! Wait just a minute." He shouted as he bustled up the side walk, mopping his brow with a royal blue monogrammed hankie while his monogrammed, leather fanny back swayed back and forth around his fat belly and Hadley led the way on a leash. "Ohh, you all were just to die for this morning on *Clinton AM*! Such stars, well except for that RG, she looked like a Klansman all decked out in her white. But Alex wasn't it just too exciting being live on the air? And that Skip Kenny, now isn't he just delicious? So handsome and personable he is. Was he as hot in person as he appears on air? Why I'd like to get him out of that studio and on my pool terrace and see..."

I gave Percy a cold look. "No Percy it wasn't fun, it was hell. Skippy is as vapid in person as he seems on air and he appears to have a vibrator shoved up his ass and running on high. And the Katie

130

whore is no Einstein either. As for Serenity, total bitch and I'm done with this listing. I am heading back to the office to get the cancellation paperwork right now." I then stormed off to my car and got in. Percy was on the curb all flustered and calling out to me saying to wait, he'd fix everything. Wailing about how I couldn't let the listing go and he wouldn't stand for Share's sign or any others in his neighbor's front yard. I didn't care; I just fired up my car and drove off.

I decided to cool off with Wanda first, so I drove over to Safety Mortgage to see if she was in and available. The whole way my cell kept ringing. I flung it in the back seat. I would have preferred to toss it out the car window but then I'm too cheap for dramatic acts like that. I'm not going to pay for a new phone even if tossing it out the window would be all made-for-TV dramatic and alas, very satisfying! Wanda was in and as I walked in her office she immediately started up. I half way listened as I took in today's Wanda work place ensemble. Her hair was all shellacked up in a helmet dome around her face, an electric blue headband thing making it go up towards the ceiling even more. She had on sparkling silver chandelier earrings that almost touched her shoulders. Her billowing dress was electric blue with white and hot pink swirls; nothing like a sedate, conservative banker dress approach to lending. Thank god she defied that boring routine in spades.

"Baby, what have you done over at Serenity's? That Percy has been speed dialing me and he's all in a fluster. Says you is dumping the listing and he's practically hysterical. He don't want that Stinky bitch to get the listing. Says he's gonna make everything right and for me to make sure you don't go canceling that listing. So what is going on Alex?"

I shrugged, "I'll fill you in but first we are going for a major SLUSHY lunch. And we are going down to that seafood restaurant on the waterfront, Barnacles is it? And you are driving."

"Damn sakes, if something ain't got your rattle but good today! Ewe, wee- and you telling ME it's gonna be a slushy lunch, don't that just beat all. Okay honey, here let me grab my bag and we'll roll on down to Barnacles in Miss Emerald." Miss Emerald being how Wanda sometimes refers to her late 1980s rebuilt, custom painted emerald green, Lincoln Town Car. She hoisted up her fifty pound fuchsia pocket book and off we went for lunch.

Barnacles is an ancient seafood restaurant that skirts the edge of downtown Clinton, right on the cusp of the redone, gentrified downtown Clinton and the rotting former industrial, wharf, factory part of Clinton's waterfront. Barnacles sits on pilings out in Warner Sound and was originally built in 1936. The name sure does nothing to stimulate the appetite. Yummy, nasty calcified crud on the bottom of dirty boats, gee I'm ready to order! Its interior is honeyed pine paneling with open rafter ceilings. Hundreds of historic, black and white Clinton seafaring photos line the walls with assorted stuffed and mounted fish and three hundred and sixty degrees of large windows overlooking the water. It is not five-star dining but not junky fast food either. I like Barnacles because they don't deep fry all their seafood and it is fresh. Wanda and I were seated at one of the honey colored wooden booths and had ordered a pitcher of Pina Coladas from our waitress. I filled Wanda in on the morning's events from 5:00 a.m. up to when I appeared in her office.

"I hear what you are saying Alex. No doubt that Serenity is a class B rude bitch. But you have already spent money and time on this listing and Percy says he's gonna smooth things over. Said he's gonna have Serenity look at the septic tank before our open house on Sunday. She should then see reason about completing that required septic addendum and getting it all repaired. Sounds like she is gonna have to replace the whole septic system, but one step at a time. She's a fool that's for sure, just let her be a fool in her own time." I suppose the frozen colada had gone to my head because I reluctantly agreed to Wanda's way of thinking. Ugh, what's the expression about suffering fools gladly?

Eighteen

After lunch I got a call from Norman and he wanted to write up an offer on the fourth house we saw in Rosedale. I quickly drove home, fired up my computer and began to fill out the offer paperwork. I called Norman back to find out what he wanted his offer price to be and then did a three-way call with Norman and Wanda so I could get the financing information directly from his lender for the financing contingency offer forms. Nothing is more stupid than agents who fill out the financing part of the offer for their clients and just guess at the loan terms, financing timelines and any pre-paid or closing costs to ask the seller to pay. Worse yet are the agents who don't bother checking with the loan officer to see if the closing date the buyer is asking for is going to work for the lender. Duh! Or so I thought. Recently Doris Havlon and other real estate attorneys have told me that most buyer agents do not bother checking with the loan officer, hence the deals become very dramatic and a good deal of them crash and burn. I thought it was just common sense and basic organizational skills to go to the loan officer for the loan information when writing up an offer. I guess common sense is not part of agent training?

I typed in what Wanda said for the loan terms and then told Norman I could swing by his office to get him to sign the offer paperwork. He agreed. He was not too daunted by the prospect of the offer paperwork because I require all of my clients (buyers and sellers) to review a sample purchase and sale agreement prior to starting to work together. They are included in all my client packets. Of course, some clients like Serenity do not do their homework and review them, no surprise. But it's to her own detriment not to. The purchase and sale agreement is not exactly a stimulating read but it does allow a client to get a general idea of what is coming down the pike and allows them to understand when they initial and date each page what exactly they are putting their name on the line and agreeing to do or not do. Naturally, some deals require a few forms more or less than what I have in my standard purchase and sale agreement sample packet. But at least my clients have a chance to review the basic nuts and bolts and are more relaxed and informed when they do put pen to paper.

I printed all the paperwork out, including a cover letter. Wanda emailed me a specific pre-approval letter for his offer and I printed that out as well. Off I went to Norman's office. Norman works at Clinton Chem Labs which is some kind of industrial outfit for something or another. Its headquarters and labs sit on the outskirts of Clinton north of the airport just off the interstate. Living in Rosedale will provide Norman with easy access to the interstate and he'll be to work in no time. Clinton Chem Labs is a locked up fortress. First there is the gate and I had to wait while the guard called in to get clearance for my car. He handed me a laminated placard to place on my dash board and directed me to the visitor's parking area. The front of the building is a mid 1970s austere design. It features spindly white metal columns and then a sheet of gold reflective glass panels. To the left of this entry/office building is an enormous white rectangular concrete blob which seemingly stretches out for miles with very small rectangular windows, also in gold reflective glass, popping out at certain intervals.

The unhappy bushes that line the white blob part are trimmed in rigid rectangular square shapes. Ugly. Inside is a dark Richard Nixon era lobby, complete with gold metal sputnik chandeliers, gold shag carpeting in the seating area with black vinyl low slung sofas and simulated wood paneling. A large aging oil portrait with what I suppose is the original Clinton Chem Lab CEO was dimly lit in the seating area. The CEO's scowling face peering out from the black frame, complete with thick rectangular black glasses, his grey hair all Brylcreem-ed back, wearing a dark blue suit and tie. So unlike today's psychopath/megalomaniac CEOs who are made over to look like rock stars. Flying around on their corporate jets, dressed in $2,500 pre-distressed designer jeans, with a $1,000 pre-ripped t-shirt, their hair coiffed and dyed by $400 an hour stylists, running to and fro with their personal publicists, photographers and assorted lackeys in tow. I suppose their official portraits would be painted in a pseudo Warhol style in bright acrylics. Yes, this grumpy CEO of the past would probably turn over in his grave if he could see his piglet cohorts today.

Another guard sat by the front door and he searched my briefcase, checked my driver's license, called upstairs and finally gave me a visitor's lanyard to wear. He instructed me to go up to the third floor and someone would meet me at the elevator. Once the bell dinged and doors opened, there was a pasty faced woman with dishwater hair dressed in a hunter green polyester suit. She asked if I was there to see Norman and I nodded. Down the white and black speckled linoleum hallway we went, the fluorescent lights buzzing louder with each step. And there it was, "Room 322 Kluntz." Inside was what appeared to be a somewhat more sophisticated college lab room. Brunson burners and paint shaking like machines, other assorted chemical geek crap. And there was Norman in his white lab coat complete with clear acrylic goggles over his eyes. He put the test tube he had been working with down and we sat down at a metal desk in the corner. Norman whizzed through the forms, signing everywhere he should and making no mistakes. Another reason to let your clients review the purchase and sale agreement in advance, saves time when they sign. We were done in no time. I told Norman I would get his offer in and email him a complete copy of what he just signed for his records, per the law. He was all excited and wanted to know when we'd hear back. I let him know the sellers would have until Saturday night to accept or counter and I would be in touch with him as soon as I heard anything. I asked he keep his cell phone with him at all times until he heard from me and he agreed.

I exited the gorgeous work environs known as Clinton Chem Labs and sped off to get Norman's offer in the listing agent's paws. That night I got a call from Percy who let me know that he was going to make sure Serenity looked at the open septic tank before Sunday's open house. He said he had already spoken with her and she had promised to go out back and look on Saturday. I was to the point where I almost didn't care anymore. Percy also understood that this was all in Serenity's best interest to take care of this now. But he wrote it off as Serenity being a busy woman, etc…. I told him no, it's because she's a rude bitch who can't even look out for her own best interest. "Oh my, you *are* the feisty one Alex! Who knew? You must be full of surprises in the buff, why…"

"Goodnight Percy." That said, Clyde and I went for a quick night time walk and we were in bed asleep by 11:00 p.m.

Nineteen

Saturday started out slow with a long walk with Clyde and coffee at Sasser's Bakery but soon gained momentum. Sam and Richard called and wanted to see the two houses they had narrowed things down to again. So I quickly called both sellers and arranged appointments for that afternoon. It was between the house with water views in the Lee District or the non-view house in the heart of the Bluffs. Both had hefty price tags so my bank account would be more than pleased with either choice. After our quick two house re-tour they decided they wanted to make an offer on the house in Bluffs, but the one in the Lee was a very close second and good Plan B. We went to the Winterfrost office and I printed out the offer paperwork. The Winterfrost office is always a ghost town on weekends, which I never have figured out because most offers I do seem to happen on weekends. I suppose the usual coffee klatch of agents who spend their weekdays walking the halls of Winterfrost bemoaning their lack of business and ripping other agents to shreds with their gossip, while drinking gallons of "free" second rate Winterfrost coffee, I suppose those agents have to rest sometimes and that's what weekends are for. Just a tip no one has bothered to tell them, if you plan to be successful in real estate the entire concept of a weekend and weekday needs to be firmly erased from your consciousness, every day is a work day. Anyway, I was thrilled the office was free of vipers and I could write up Sam and Richard's offer in peace. The first page of their purchase and sale agreement listed their legal names and I indicated by their names "joint tenants in common with right of survivorship." This is what legally needs to happen to protect their rights of ownership in the property, since legally they cannot marry and take title as "a married couple." The way I wrote in for them to take title protects any claims from their prospective families to the property if, god forbid, one of them should die. This also applies for straight couples who live together but do not choose to get married. It is also what I use when there are just two people, not a couple, who are buying together and want the ownership rights to be exclusive to them. I told them I would get their offer to the listing agent right away and to keep their cell phone on hand and I would call with any news as soon as I heard, yada, yada. The seller would have until Sunday at 9:00 p.m. to accept or counter, let the games begin!

I was not thrilled that the listing agent for the house Sam and Richard were making an offer on was Larry Wilcox from KMA and Associates Realty. Otherwise known in real estate circles as Kiss My Ass Realty. And for good reason, talk about attitude and lack of service! Larry especially is a complete ass. He is a thirty-something, ex frat boy wanna-be (doubtful he made it to community college classes much less graduated high school). He thinks he is god's special gift to the real estate world. He is all surface slick and zero substance. Larry always has his spray on tan just so, his teeth are so whitened they blind and he wears the latest in upscale male gigolo business world fashions. This usually means he has on trendy loafers which have the too long toe part that curls up like Elf shoes and in my opinion look absurd. His suits are all shiny and shark suit like and he usually wears a black shirt or some neo-psychedelic, retro disco shirt which looks like someone barfed Technicolor prescription pills onto fabric. Larry is always fake happy, and says, "You da Man" in his white boy wants to be ghetto wigga voice. He talks down to everyone as if he is some complete Einstein and the world has not yet caught on to his unique brilliance. Larry is also completely passive aggressive, my pet peeve. His trademark and annoying unconscious habit is he constantly grabs his crotch while talking. Is he worried his dick has fallen off or does he want to make sure he's still a male or does he have serious castration anxiety? I don't get it but he's known for it.

A possible deal with Larry as the listing agent, such a thrill. I called him up, "Heeyy, this is Larry, it's always an awesome time to buy or sell, so what can I do for *you?*" I clued Larry in that I was an agent calling. Contrary to his phone shtick, I don't think it is always an awesome time to buy or sell. I let Larry know I was dropping off the offer at his office and would also email it to him. I also reminded him the offer expired Sunday at 9:00 p.m. "Awesome! You da Man, Alex! Yeah, I got me some major party plans tonight dude but I'll make sure my peeps get a gander at your offer tomorrow, if I'm not too hung over. Ha, ha, ha." Yeah right stupid jackass. Legally you are supposed to notify the seller right away when an offer comes in but god forbid your party time be interrupted so you can do your job for your clients and hey, also maybe *earn* your commission.

Why people fall for and use the Larrys of the real estate world never ceases to amaze me but they seem to eat up Larry's bullshit with a snow shovel. Never mind that the Larrys are almost always incompetent. I suppose they are awesome manipulators and great ass kissers and that is what the public appears to want. Water seeks its own level and all that.

Twenty

My Saturday seemed to be slowing down a bit. Now it was the "wait and see" holding pattern for my clients' offers. Somewhat akin to circling the airport and waiting to land. This meant I kept my cell phone glued to me so I could pick up right away if one of the listing agents was trying to reach me with questions. I knew it was doubtful Larry would get back to me tonight but Norman's offer expired at 9:00 p.m. tonight, so I should hear something. I fussed around the back yard for a bit and was in the process of trying to add a fountain to the small stream which goes through my back yard. I had already successfully diverted the stream to make it run by my patio. Now I had to figure out the fountain part. The sound of running water is my valium and I can't wait to get this all figured out so I can fall asleep to the sound of running water outside my bedroom. Clyde had given up trying to assist, thankfully, and was out at the very edge of the yard under the big oak tree waiting for his nemesis, the squirrels, to appear. My cell phone rang, and I jumped up to grab it off the patio table. It was Wanda.

"Hey baby, I'm thinkin' you and Clyde should come over and we should figure out something to cook up and something to do! I tried Lexi but she ain't in. I know we got that open house tomorrow but I just can't be sittin' home alone on no Saturday night. Why don't you two just come on over now?"

My psychoanalysis of her music choice the other day was correct. Wanda and the upper end appliance boyfriend must be on the fritz for her to be calling and wanting to do something on a Saturday night. I really didn't feel like going out but I did feel bad for Wanda being all alone. Wanda doesn't do solo or quiet time very well. "Oh, sure Wanda. I can pack up Clyde and we'll pop over. You have my blender so you should be good on the slushy front. Want me to bring anything with?"

"Just brang that Clyde with you and get on over, we gotta cook us up some kind of food and entertainment honey!"

I changed clothes, closed up the ranch and loaded up Clyde in my two door beater and off we went to Wanda's. I pulled onto Wanda's street and was parking when I spied Miss Lyla walking up the sidewalk with what appeared to be an electric mixer in her hands. Miss Lyla is somewhere in her late eighties if not older and has lived in the same house in the Highmont her whole life. She has literally never left the Highmont neighborhood once. She says it is the highest hill in Clinton and she can see everything just fine from there so why leave the neighborhood. "Hey Alex, how you doing chile? I ain't seen you round here in no time, you still sellin' them houses?"

"Yes, hi Miss Lyla, you are looking well. I am still selling houses, got some crazy ones right now but seems like that is always the way." I replied.

"Ohh, baby ain't that the truth, I hear that! I hear tell you got yo'self one fussy devil of customer right now. Wanda say she some kind of celebrity and you be on that channel four on the TV the other day. I am sorry I missed that Alex, I surely am. Baby you should be lettin' Miss Lyla know when you gonna be on the TV. Not every day somebody I know be up on the TV and you know I likes to keep up with all my children and family. Anyway baby I am so proud of you being on that TV, ahhum, sure is. Well let me get on up the street. Wanda lettin' me use her mixer here and I gotta go bake some cookies for the church Sunday school children for tomorrow. I tell you what, I don't know how I get myself into these thangs, baking one hundred fool cookies for them brats. You be good now and cheer that Wanda up baby, she all up in a knot cause that boyfriend of hers done moved on. Course she did get herself a nice new kitchen out of him so I don't know what all the complaining is about!" She let out a long loud cackle and then walked on up the street.

There it was, the official confirmation of her boyfriend problem. Wanda on the rebound can be tough. Last time around with this, she had the famous, or infamous, statue of *David* made for Salon Wanda. I managed to get Clyde out of his doggy seat belt before he knocked me over and took off for Wanda's front door. I noted a can of bright orange paint next to the front door. Was this going to be the new door color for Chateau Wanda? Before I could ring the bell the door flew up and in went Clyde and their usual greeting dance commenced. "Go get yourself a slushy Alex." Wanda shouted as she went over to her stereo to turn down the volume. Blasting from the surround sound speakers was Grace Jones' *Bullshit,* just another confirmation that appliance man was no more.

I walked into her open kitchen, all the stainless appliances were shiny and streak free. However her glass front refrigerator was different. It appeared someone had installed-- what?--curtains on the inside of the refrigerator's door panel! So the whole purpose of the neurotic show-off expensive glass fronted refrigerator had been defeated. I looked more closely and opened the door. Yep, tightly pleated orange patterned curtains had been mounted on a custom installed rod inside the door's panel. And no wonder, judging by the compete wreck the refrigerator's interior was. Spilled goo, molding containers of leftovers, a bag of veggies shoved on an open shelf, open canned tomatoes, etc.... I warned Wanda about just this problem when she proudly showed off her new refrigerator. She said the see through glass front was good, it would make her eat better and keep things neat inside since everyone could see in.

Wanda walked into the kitchen with Clyde in tow. She was wearing hot pink Capri pants, with a large citrus yellow top and her hair was up in a knot on top and she wore enormous turquoise beaded earrings. "Aupt! Not a single damn word Alex! Not a word! Don't wanna hear no nothing about my refrigerator there, except that you like the fabric I chose for the curtains."

Well what to say? I did like the brightly patterned fabric, but curtains inside a refrigerator that might be one for the books. "Sure Wanda, I like the fabric's pattern and color and it looks like you had the curtains all professionally hung up?"

"Yes, I had that Arnie come on out here and she welded on a custom made curtain rod for me, also got my fence out back repaired and she took a good foot off the top of that Camellia hedge that runs around my entire lot, that weren't no easy trimming job let me tell you. But honey, that Arnie works better than three men put together. I am telling you no lie here baby, she can work her tools like a real pro!

146

Now let's look around in my refrigerator and see what we got in here to eat."

We discovered more molding food, a long lost bottle of unopened champagne, and Wanda found one of her expensive stick-on eyelashes that had been missing. We didn't find anything edible, so we called out and had Dim Lung's deliver Chinese, with extra fortune cookies of course because Wanda needs several cookies until she can find the fortune that suits her best. The food arrived soon enough. She and Clyde enjoyed her order of pan fried duck (which makes me want to gag) and I had garlic prawns. The slushies were not too bad either, too much rum but what else is new when Wanda makes a drink? The night was progressing and we had moved into the dining room where we had set up her Rummikub game and were busy contemplating number combinations when my cell began to ring. It was just past 10:00 p.m., an hour after Norman's offer technically expired. However, the listing agent had called me at 8:00 p.m. to let me know she was on her way to meet with the sellers to review the offer and she would call me as soon as they were done. Imagine that, common courtesy letting me know she was going to do her job! Wonders never cease. This listing agent, Lisa Stanton, I have never worked with but thus far this lady appeared to have her shit together, what a welcome and rare thing! I picked up the phone and Lisa let me know her sellers had accepted everything in Norman's offer except they wanted an extra week to close, thus they created a counter offer asking for closing to be a week later. She told me she was faxing it to my office, per the law, and she would also email me a PDF of the seller's counter offer. I thanked her and told her we would respond no later than tomorrow at 9:00 p.m. per the terms of the purchase and sale agreement.

However, I'd be responding tonight. I never let these things hang. I take the "time is of the essence" clause very seriously. I do this because: A) It is the law and all agents should, B) If you wait, another offer could come in and the sellers are more than free to accept another offer at any time until you have reached mutual agreement with them (and this does happen), C) I like to complete things and would be on the hamster wheel myself until I know this deal is done and mutual agreement is reached. So this meant I needed to track Norman down and get his signature and date next to the closing date/ counter offer change the sellers made.

First I needed to use Wanda's computer and printer to access the counter offer and print it out. That was easy enough and once again Lisa surprised me. She actually had gotten all of the necessary seller signatures, initials, dates, and had scanned all of the contract's pages in numerical order! I needed to pinch myself. It's pretty sad how cheerful this made me. I couldn't remember the last time I had worked with a listing agent that could remotely do their side of the job without constant barking from me or worse, me just stepping in and doing the job for the incompetent and/or lazy ass. I called Norman on his cell phone and it went to voice mail. I told him about the seller's counter and that I needed to meet up with him tonight to get his response. Wanda and I started in on a new Rummikub game and were bickering over whether or not a particular tile could be moved or not to create the necessary three series, when Norman called me back.

"Alex, it is Norman Kluntz here calling you back." The background noise was pretty loud. Was Norman actually out at some bar on a Saturday night? Shouldn't he be in his lab doing something geeky? "Listen, it is hard to hear Alex but I'm over at Scandals, tonight is Amy's big debut performance. Could you bring the papers down here so I can sign? I don't want to miss Amy's debut." I shouted back that would be fine and I'd be there in a bit. I think he heard me. I looked up at Wanda, "Well, Wanda looks like you and me have a Saturday night entertainment engagement after all. Ever been to Scandals, the strip club before?" Her eyes bugged out, "Me neither. Here let's look up the address on your computer and take in Amy's debut performance at one of Clinton's finest titty clubs. I'm guessing that technically this will be a legitimate, tax write-off, business expense."

Twenty-one

S candals is evidently Clinton's premier strip club and is located near
the airport, actually down the street from the Tiki Bar, where
Wanda and I have been a few times. It sits just off the airport access
road that runs parallel to the interstate. A large neon sign is out front
with lit yellow bulbs that flash all around the sign's perimeter. There is
a nude black silhouette of a very buxom woman in platform stilettos on
the sign, highlighted in red neon and the name of the club in a huge
cursive font in violet neon. The paved parking lot was completely full
and we had to park my Volvo in the gravel overflow lot. I put the
counter offer in a small leather document holder and up to the front
door we went. A very burly bouncer was on hand and he seriously
checked both our i.d.'s and then charged us both twenty bucks to
enter, cash only. Once we paid him, he put Day-Glo yellow vinyl
bracelets on our wrists. I asked for a receipt and he gave me a hard
look. I held up my document holder and said this was a business call,
my client Norman was inside and his girlfriend Amy was tonight's star
attraction. That changed his attitude, "Oh sure, let me get you one of
our receipts and I'll put today's date on it. So you two know Fantasia,
huh? What a fox. Ron's got her doing star lead tonight, she's heading
up the whole 60's go-go theme. I'm gonna try to slip inside myself and
catch part of her act. It should be starting real soon. Okay, here you
go that should keep the government happy. You two enjoy your
evening and welcome to Scandals."

Wanda smiled and said to me as we walked in, "Now see there
Alex, see what dropping the right name can do for you, us! Ahum,

that's what I've been talking about, us getting the right names out there with us and…"

"And what, we can be Clinton VIPs like RG? Oh, I so aspire to be more like her. Can you help me with my *signature* style Wanda? Taking a note off her page, perhaps I'll only wear white dresses everywhere and grow my hair down to my shoulders, you know the whole flip gender side of her confused style." With that Wanda swatted my shoulder and pushed me into the main room of Scandals.

The place was packed and a stage act had just ended. The topless waitresses were busy buzzing all around filling drink orders. The blue neon bar was jammed, off to the left side of the main floor of tables was a dark booth section and I saw a business man and an extremely busty dancer get up and leave for the private lap dance room. I bolted through the people and snagged the little booth for us. When our topless waitress, Candy, appeared Wanda just started laughing. I ordered us Pina Coladas, mine a virgin. Candy smiled, her cherry red glossy lips looking like some kind of fish and said, "Oh a virgin! That sure is a first around here! Want me to start a tab? Are you two interested in some private entertainment this evening?"

"No Candy. Actually we are here to meet my client Norman. He is Amy, I mean Fantasia's, boyfriend. You wouldn't happen to know where Norman is would you?" Candy said no but Amy's act was scheduled to start next and she bet Norman was in back with her and would soon be in front of the stage taking in her act. "Norman is always down front cheering her on for all her dance routine debuts." My god they all seemed to know him here by first name, boy would

151

mommy in Philadelphia have a complete shit fit over this news. So much for my theory of Norman's Saturday nights being spent in the lab, little do I know. Candy brought our drinks, her jugs rubbing against my bare arm as she placed the drinks with green umbrellas in them on our small table. Oh the feeling of flesh and silicone just sends shivers up my spine, not really. Wanda paid for the drinks and then grabbed my arm. "Alex, look over there near that hallway next to the bathrooms! Honey that is Tony over there, I ain't lying and look who he is with, it's that bitch's boyfriend Javier!"

Wanda was correct. Tony is a mob boss we recently met via Lexi. It's a long story (see Volume One) but Tony knows us and yes that is his real name, he's pre-*Sopranos*. Tony was dressed in pressed black chinos, had on a black and gold golf shirt, a thick gold necklace and a large ruby ring on his pinkie finger. Javier was actually coming out of the private lap dance room and had two very well endowed topless women hanging on him. Naturally Javier was shirtless too and was wearing what else but black Lycra shorts and work out shoes. They were walking toward the dark area where we were seated. The lights began to flash to indicate the next show would be starting soon. A low wall separated our seating area from the aisle Tony and Javier were walking down. As they got closer we could overhear their conversation. Tony was annoyed, "Look youze come here to do sum bidness wid me or what? Save the lap dancin' for later and put on a shirt! I ain't doing no bidness with some fruit wearin' no shirt, I wanna see HER titties not yours! Follow me around the bar to the office and we'll talk shop. But I'm serious, youze gotta put on a shirt before

152

youze meet wid me. I'm Tony for god sakes!" Neither of them saw us and we watched as Tony headed off toward the back of the bar and Javier sucked face with and felt up the two topless dancers. I suppose Percy would have fainted on the spot. Then Javier pulled a skimpy white Power Up Serenity tank top out of the rear of his Lycra shorts and slipped it on, hardly a difference.

Wanda and I looked at each other, our mouths busy sucking Pina Colada through tropical colored straws. Before we could speak, the lights completely dimmed and the stage lit up. An announcer welcomed us to Scandals a-go-go, Scandals' tribute to the 1960s. And with great dramatic flourish he announced tonight's premier, the new star headliner for Scandals, *Miz Fannnn—taaayy---sia*! There was lots of yelling and cheering and then Mitch Ryder's 1967 song, "I'd Rather Go to Jail" began blaring at top volume from all of the speakers and the stage lit up like a retro *Shindig* a go-go special. All the topless dancers were made up in retro 1960's dos and go-go dancer outfits complete with the ubiquitous white go-go boots. Which still looked ridiculous forty some odd years later. Then Amy, a.k.a. Fantasia, appeared and the dancing became as wild and frenetic as the fast paced song. The lights were flashing rapidly and before long Amy was completely nude and her background dancers had flung off their sequined tops. The high tempo music had them doing lots of pony and jerk dancing moves and Wanda yelled in my ear, "Honey they keep that type of dancing up and them girls is gonna have some SERIOUS black eyes and I ain't kidding!" I spit out my drink while laughing. It was true, their inflated friends were going to cause bodily harm if they didn't slow down. I must say though, Amy is one tireless dancer and performer. She did moves all over the stage and up and down her pole, sideways, upside down, all around and she never tired, despite the song being extremely fast paced. She was shimmy-ing her heart out and taking no prisoners. Sure enough down front, right in the center was Norman. His rectangular framed eyes were staring straight up at her on stage and never left her. The last beat of the song, Fantasia fell to her knees and skidded right to the edge of the stage directly in front of Norman. The crowd went wild with applause and yelling and Amy stood up and smiled and blew kisses to her fans, while some roses pelted her and fell on the stage. Stage lights went dark and she exited as the curtains came down. That was our cue, Wanda and I made our way through the excited crowd and managed to push and shove our way down to Norman.

Along the way who should crash right into me? None other than Larry Wilcox. He had his hair all spiked up, was wearing a Technicolor retro disco shirt, expensive pre-faded jeans and of course his elf loafers. He was way into his cups and sweaty and threw his arms around my shoulders, ewe sleazy real estate agent cooties! "DUDE, I'm out partying hardy tonight! You da' Man Alex, out here part-ey-ing too I see! Awesome titties all around, huh? You gotta check out the private lap dance booth Alex? It's awesome dude, totally rocks! Catch ya' later, party on!" He screamed out the last bit and putting his hands over his head and his fingers up in a hang lose pose. No one paid attention, thankfully.

I moved away from Larry quickly and once I had Norman's attention, he led us to a side door that took us back stage. It was relatively calm backstage; the next act was setting up. We went in a small dressing room that was currently empty. Norman said he would take us to Amy but she didn't like to be interrupted between acts when she was working and she had two more sets to do tonight. I showed him where to sign to accept the seller's later closing date. Wanda assured him he was good to go money wise and I told Norman I would check in with him tomorrow night. We both sincerely praised Amy's dancing abilities and he promised to tell her. He thanked us for coming down to Scandals and meeting up with him and for taking care of his deal tonight. So rare, common courtesy and manners! Mommy had done something right back in Philly.

Wanda and I headed back to her place, where I was going to scan and fax Norman's offer back to the listing agent, and I explained to her who Larry was but she was more interested in Tony. "Alex, what was Tony doing at Scandals? I bet you he runs that place too. We know the Wharf Rat and the Ridge (see Volume One) ain't the only games in town he gots going on. I tell you them mob people is in it all Alex. I don't know how Lexi got you and me all mixed up with them folks. You know he owes us a favor from last time."

"Sure, right Wanda, Tony owes us! That's rich. Anyway, I'm sure he runs Scandals and they must pay off the cops because I'm fairly certain full-on nudity isn't allowed under Clinton law, topless yes but no thongs or bottoms on, I doubt it. And what was Javier doing there sucking face with two bimbos? Looks like his *widdle kitty* isn't the only one he licks and carries around! But who could blame him, she's such a bitch. Still, can you imagine if Serenity found out Javier was at Scandals?"

"She'd cut his balls off and tell him it was spiritual. But what gets me Alex is what kind of business was he doing with Tony? They running numbers, guns, selling drugs?"

"Oh, god slow down Nancy Drew. Just leave it, none of our business. I am not doing any more investigative gigs with you. We sell houses and do loans, period."

"Ahh-um, that's what you always saying anyway."

We got back to her house and Clyde was busy sleeping on her leather sofa. I used her fax and email and we now had mutual agreement for Norman's deal. One deal down, one left to go. We played a few more rounds of Rummikub then I took Clyde home and was in bed snoring away by 2:00 a.m.

Twenty-two

Sunday morning was off to a somewhat fast start. I woke up around 9:00 a.m. and took Clyde for a long walk. I needed to have him settled in before I took off for the open house. Naturally, we stopped off at Sasser's so I could get some strong coffee and wake up. They had a copy of the *Clinton Observer* handy so I checked out my open house ad. Very old school of me as most agents no longer place open house ads in the newspapers and I have to say it really does not lead to any "traffic" through the house anymore. I polled all attendees of my open houses, asking where they heard about the open. In my first years in the business it was almost exclusively through the local newspaper. In the past year or two that is almost non-existent anymore. It is now rare if anyone says they learned of the open house through the paper. Things have changed so quickly.

Now they hear online or through friends or they drive around and see the open house sign. Along with this change has been less "traffic" in general through public open houses. The public has wised up I suppose and now gets a buyer's agent to exclusively represent them and have them set up tours and show them applicable properties. The secret in the industry for years was the public open house was used as a tool to show your sellers what a good job you were doing when in reality you were sitting the open to drum up new business for yourself. Most open houses do not in fact sell the house but that said occasionally they do. I also like open houses, because they keep me up on the public, what questions people are asking, etc.... However, for better or worse open houses appear to be dying out. There is way less "traffic" through them and many sellers now prefer not to have them at all. They are a pain for the seller. The seller has to prepare the house and leave for a few hours on Sunday and many do not want the general public tramping through their house without an agent accompanying them. There is the safety factor, the many stories of burglars scouting a property first via the open house, of items being stolen at the open, etc.... I always provide my sellers with a long list of items I suggest they remove from their house prior to an open house. Some listen, some don't. There is also the safety factor of the agent who sits the open house. Far too many agents have been injured or killed while holding an open house, especially when it is in a remote or secluded location. Even in the city, like Serenity's house, safety is still a concern. I always have a mortgage rep agree to sit with me the whole time while I do the open house. Two people are better for monitoring the property, and safety in numbers.

I was downing my strong coffee and Daynia was giving Clyde some treats when I found my open house missive. I had placed it in the Winterfrost Real Estate ad section. We do get somewhat of a discount for placing our open house ads there and naturally it makes Winterfrost look good so they are always after us to place these ads. *"Come live in a local celebrity's wonderful Spanish style house in Capitol Heights. This 4 bedroom, 3.5 bath house boasts original old world charm and plenty of high end upgrades. Lots of potential to express your own style! Open 1-3. Alex Campbell, xxx-xxxx."* Normally I would not have mentioned the celebrity part but since Serenity had made sure it was all out there on live TV, I figured what the heck, push it. And many people are just dumb enough--or bored enough?--to actually come see the house just because someone "famous" sleeps, showers, and shits there. Wow. I thanked and paid Daynia for the coffee and paper and got Clyde back home.

I showered, put on my open house drag which today meant I was wearing stone colored chinos that had been pressed at the dry cleaners not by my inept ironing hands, black slip on shoes, a belt that matched and a blue and red short sleeve button down shirt which the cleaners had also pressed. Recently, I have discovered the advantage of paying the cleaners to press everything. My rational being: A) They do a much better job than me, B) The cost isn't that much higher than me taking the time to do it myself, C) People actually notice if you are pressed or rumpled. I guess this means I am going all slick and business world now. With my perfectly pressed and oh-so-wholesome look, I just need Ward and June Cleaver to show up and be impressed with me and buy the house.

I loaded up my A-boards in the car's trunk, put my pile of flyers and promo crap in a box and tossed that in the car. I also have a metal bowl with little candy bars in it. God only know how old they are, which Halloween they are left over from. But I usually toss this bowl on the counter with the flyers. I figure the lure of chocolate might entice some viable tour-ees to stick around. There is an agent in my office who has been selling houses since before I was born, Ida Simmons. She has been lugging the same frozen apple pie around with her to her open houses for years. She swears the smell of a baking pie in the house makes people linger and buy. She throws the rock-in-the-box in the oven and turns it on the lowest setting. That way the pie never really cooks but the odor permeates the house. Once she's done, she takes the pie-in-the-box home and throws it back in her freezer for the next open house.

I arrived at 12:30, so I would have time to place the A-boards and get everything opened up and ready. I put my A-board over the yard sign, the other directional A-boards I had strategically placed on prime sidewalk corners. Serenity's white Range Rover was parked in the mini-drive space. I hoped she would clear out soon, as we would want that parking space open. Plus I did not want to be around Serenity any longer than necessary. I rang the bell several times but no answer. I walked around back through the side gate, peered in through the french doors, no sign of anyone. I knocked on those doors but still no answer. I noticed Arnie had made the yard look picture perfect. The flowers in the pots looked terrific and the freshly laid sod also looked nice. At the rear of the fenced yard I thought I spied Kali. I walked back there calling her name and sure enough it was Kali. She ran up to me and actually sat, her tail wagging. I began to pet her and asked her where her bitch owner was. Kali just smiled and wagged back. I noticed the iron lid was back in place covering the septic tank. Hopefully Serenity had taken a look yesterday and realized it needs to be inspected and pumped ASAP. It appeared Kali had dug some near the rear fence and bushes but at least she had left the new sod alone. She followed me to the patio area. I banged on the french doors again, still no response. "Where is your human, Kali?" I asked and again Kali wagged her tail and tilted her head grinning back at me. I left her in the back yard and went around front again. I dialed Serenity's cell phone. It went to her voice mail. I left a message and rang the front door bell a few more times.

Okay, I was pretty sure no one was home, despite her car being there and her dog out back in the yard. I accessed the agent key box and took out the entry key. I opened up the door and called out for Serenity. No answer. I immediately began turning on all the lights, it was such a dark cave. It appears Serenity had not listened and shut the burgundy velvet drapes in the dining room which I promptly threw open. Anything for light in this dank burgundy nightmare; it really is akin to swimming in a bottle of deep red merlot. She had however, removed the used wine cork display from the austere concrete dining table. I kept calling out for Serenity as I made my way through the house. No one downstairs, so up I went. Upstairs I followed the same drill turning on every single light, opening all curtains, blinds and still no Serenity. I opened the doors in the master bedroom that lead out to the little Juliette balcony. I waved to Kali below. She was so happy and calm. The doggy day care guy must be right; Kali is only a wild, misbehaving dog when Serenity is around. Along with that thought, where is the stupid pain in the ass? The bed was all made up and the bathroom looked dry and clean. We were ready for the open. Maybe she met up with Javier after Wanda and I spied him at Scandals last night? Perhaps he swung by and picked her up? I'd love to see her face if she saw him at Scandals, she'd rip his entrails out. Or knowing her, she'd first eviscerate the young twenty-something dancers in true cougar fashion and then kill her man.

161

I went back downstairs, set up the flyers, and expired candy bars on the kitchen counter top. Thankfully, no display of Power Up Serenity drinks had been set out, although several cases of the powder drinks had been left stacked up next to the kitchen. Not the best thing when your house is on the market, boxes piled up but some like Serenity never listen. It was ten minutes to show time, I needed Serenity to move her car and take the dog away. I dialed her cell again and nothing. I realized the best thing would be to call Percy, ugh. Which I did, and he immediately picked up. I asked if he know where Serenity was and explained my dilemma.

"Well Alex, I haven't heard from Serenity since yesterday. I did get her to take a look at that septic tank yesterday. I called her and she promised me she was going to go right out back and take a look before Arnie got there to put the lid back on it and do the final yard tidy for today's open house. I don't know where Serenity is Alex. She usually has her car with her. She puts Kali out back a lot but Serenity has to know Kali will dig up all that sod and destroy the nice things Arnie has done, so it is a bit odd Kali is out back now. I have never known Serenity not to pick up the phone. Let me try calling her and I'll call over to the gym to see if she is over there or if Javier knows where she is. If I can't reach her I'll come on over and take Kali to my house while you have your open."

I thanked Percy and continued to get things set up for the open house. I think I had every single light turned on in the entire house, it was still fairly dark but better than the dark cave look it usually has. Wanda arrived as I was propping the front door open. "Oh honey it was hotter than hell at the church this morning. They still trying to fix that air conditioning system. And Reverend Stiles just would not shut up! I had to leave early out the side door or I was gonna run late to your open." She walked back to the kitchen and set up her flyers while she tossed her large egg yolk yellow church hat which matched her billowing dress on the back counter. She noticed Kali out back and I clued her in to recent events. Right on cue, Percy appeared.

"Yoo-hoo, I want to buy this house!" Ha, ha, ha. "Well, Miss Wanda is sure looking all sunshiny today. I tried calling around for Serenity, Alex but no answer on her cell and no one at the gym has seen her or Javier. Well, here let me get Kali and she can come over and visit with Hadley and me this afternoon. Did you see what a great job Arnie did out back?" He and Wanda talked about the great work Arnie had done over at Chateau Wanda. Kali was calm and obeyed Percy as he clipped her leash on her collar and took her out the side gate to his house. I thanked Percy again for helping out and then Wanda and I opened up shop.

Twenty-three

The first hour of the open house was a bit slow. The usual gaggle of curious neighbors walked through. They murmured good and bad comments about Serenity and most found the house's décor lacking. Some actually recalled how nice the house had been back when Adele Cory owned it. These curious (nosy) neighbors always attend the first open house. They have no intention of buying and I have never seen them refer a friend or relative to buy the house they toured. Mostly they just want to make sure they are keeping up with the proverbial Joneses or better yet, are superior to them. They also want to see why the house is listed at the price it is and make sure their own castle is better and would list for more money.

These visiting neighbors always want reassurance from the listing agent that their house is worth more. As if I can psychically tune into their abode and reassure them? It's always, *Well our house has a bigger master bedroom, or a pool, or we have an extra bath, etc…, so that means our house would list today for how much more than this one?* I then calmly explain to them how I only list viable properties based on the active and sold comps and any unique features a property has to offer. To arrive at a realistic list price requires research and work, thus I cannot offer an off-the-cuff opinion of what their prize pony home would list for. This really annoys the egomaniacs in the bunch. They will persist in asking me what their house would be worth if they listed today, *Yes of course I know you do research and that is just great, but in your opinion knowing that we have a custom pool, what would our home probably go for?* One more time for Jerry's kids, I don't know jackass! I will then try and smile and politely tell them again how I do business. I suggest if they are serious about listing their property in the next thirty days, I will be more than happy to come take a look at their house, meet with them, and explain how I work. Then I will do the necessary work to come up with a viable list price. I always end by placing one of my business cards in their hands and sending them on their way. They usually leave in a huff, like the pouty little brats they are. The big bad agent wouldn't reassure them that their gorgeous home is better than everyone else's and thus worth more. They have no intention of listing and selling. They just want to know they are superior and wiser than their neighbor whose house is for sale. Such fun on a Sunday!

After the neighbors, came the few lost souls who had seriously watched the *Clinton AM* show and had to come see where Serenity lives. These folks filtered in and out during the next hour, mentioning the TV show, or how they attend one of Serenity's groups or belong to TOTAL. Quite a few had their bright green portable Power Up Serenity sippy cups with them. I learned you were given one of these special plastic to-go cups (complete with matching plastic straw) when you reached the second level of Serenity's wellness program. Evidently at that level your inner and outer body has attained enough alignment to fully benefit from her protein powder drinks. I wonder how much alignment their credit cards had to reach to arrive at that special level? A couple of the Serenity groupies actually had Wanda take their picture in Serenity's house, such a treasured keep-sake! I whispered to Wanda that we should keep a sharp eye on these folks as they were likely to try and swipe some *chotska* for a personal memento and a direct link to

Serenity. Too bad the hundreds of dirty wine corks weren't still on display on the Soviet style dining room table, we could give each lucky groupie one of those to take home with them.

Around 2:30 p.m., Wanda and I were starting to count down the remaining thirty minutes. All the traffic was gone and the house was dead. Wanda was working on some numbers for a client and I was trying to organize my upcoming week, when the stench hit us. A sickening fog of freesia, rose, musk, and some other noxious spice, attacked both of our nostrils simultaneously. We looked up at each other.

"Oh howdy, you still here playing open house Alex?" I could hear her clacking shoes and other footsteps coming down the hallway towards the kitchen. Yes, there was Stinky and she had two clients with her in tow. She told them to go and take a look around and she'd wait down here. Share was in one of her Sunday bests. She had on tight (camel toe) white pants that flared at the bottom and had some kind of large lilac and gold flower appliqués around the leg flare. She wore her usual foot tall stiletto, pointy toed, bitch boots, today's were white to match her pants. She had on a shiny lilac satin blouse with gold buttons that were unbuttoned to her navel. This way you would be sure not to miss her freckled tit valley and her prized inflatable friends. Her gleaming gold cross was nestled in between her girls, along with a few strands of purple colored beads. Her hair was more orange than usual and spiked up very high. She wore thick gold rimmed sunglasses, her lips painted three shades of lilac which naturally matched her stick-on, inch long talons. The bracelets on her arm jangled as she removed her sunglasses, and she flared out her nostrils as if smelling her own stench? Her lips turning down, "Oohhh, look we have both of our little friends here today playing open house on this sunny Sunday! Someone has to enjoy not working while the rest of us are out showing houses. Well, well, this sure is *the* listing for Capitol Heights! I see you were not successful in getting her to change anything prior to listing? Pity. It is so dark in here. Oh and look who you have here with you Alex, your *little* friend for the side show, Wendy isn't it? And Wendy is all dressed up to match our sunshine I see. Where is your usual plate of pastries or cookies or have you eaten them all Wendy? It's important to stay fortified when you work this hard Wendy. Oh, but I see Alex must have brought a bowl of candy bars to keep your strength up, how sweet. Well I suppose it is better you than me having this listing Alex. I mean I am just *so* busy with my buyers and Serenity really just isn't my kind of folks. Besides, I'll probably find the buyer and sell this place anyway, just won't be a dual agent on this deal I guess."

Before I could respond her cell phone went off with her custom ring tone, *Yellow Rose in Texas*, "Share Shelton, your personal real estate agent. How may I assist you with your purchase or sale?" Just as she was picking up, her clients made their way into the kitchen, looked around and then went out in the back yard. I noticed Wanda was clenching her fists, looking down at her spreadsheet. Stinky's clients came back in and thanked Wanda and me. Share proceeded to herd them down the hallway to the front door while still yammering away with some agent on her cell. She looked back over her shoulder, gave me an insincere upside down smile, winked and mouthed she'd be in touch.

Wanda went over to the stove and turned the exhaust fan on high, "That stinky, smelling bitch! I tell you Alex, me and that woman gonna come to blows one day. Acting all hincty with me! Lord and the stench she leaves! Even with all the doors open we gonna be smelling her vapor trail until we close up shop here. Damn, I hate me that woman something fierce, calling me Wendy when you know she knows my name."

"I know, I get it. I don't know who dislikes her more you or me and you know Wanda, Percy despises her too. That's the main reason he has been so pushy to keep me on here as the listing agent, he's terrified Serenity will list with her. He hates Share so much he's jumped in and is doing all this work to keep the listing with me."

Wanda smiled, "Well that may be partly true but we both know that Percy man got himself a serious case of the hots for you! Now you can be all fudge ripple or say you not seeing anyone, but it still don't mean that man ain't out for you. I'm not saying you should bite, but at least it's a sign honey."

I shuddered, "Wanda if that is a sign then it is a sign of impending Armageddon because there is no way there will ever be Percy and me as a couple, ever."

"Humph, I hear that but at least he's trying. You ain't even trying for nothing Alex."

I was real close to bringing up her ex appliance salesman boyfriend and asking her just how well that went, was it worth it but I decided that was too low and kept my big mouth shut. Finally it was after 3:00 p.m. and we closed up the house and locked up. Naturally Percy appeared on the sidewalk and insisted we stop over for "refreshments" before we left. So over to Percy's we went. On the way up the walk to Percy's front door I asked Percy if he had heard from Serenity and he said no. I mentioned I left her a message letting her know things were locked up, the open house went well and that Kali was over at Percy's house.

I have to say Percy's house really is magazine cover material and a much lighter and nicer (well nicer if you can get over the fear of spilling something) place to hang out than the burgundy wine colored nightmare next door. We took off our shoes outside Percy's entry and followed him into his sunlit living room. All the glass and metal surfaces were brightly shining, the white fabrics and colorful needlepoint throw pillows completely perfect, not a thing was out of place. Percy proceeded to show us his latest acquisition that was prominently displayed atop his Hepplewhite chest. "Now this is my latest find and quite rare! It's a Ming Dynasty vase and I had to outbid this nasty Japanese businessman to get this. It arrived last week and well you can see she is just at home here with my Hepplewhite chest. It is so important to have antiquities to blend with the custom modern furniture, don't you agree?" Wanda and I nodded, me feigning more interest than I really had. We all went out on Percy's terrace where Hadley and Kali were both sitting calmly in the shade next to the cool waterfall. Percy had made a pitcher of fresh lemonade and baked oatmeal cookies, these apparently not from some obscure 1700s family recipe but tasty nonetheless. Percy let us know the lemonade pitcher and matching crystal goblets were from his mother's family, mid 1840s something another. He set each glass down on perfectly pressed coral linen cocktail napkins. I complimented Percy on his freshly made and not too sweet lemonade and Wanda chimed in, "Yeah, Percy this is some nice tasting lemonade and perfect for the sunny summer weather we are having. And baby, yo mama's glasses is something special too. But you know Percy, what we need in this here lemonade is some gin or vodka. Now I personally like my drinks all slushy but whatcha got in there for this here lemonade Percy?"

Percy lit up, "Ohh, Miss Wanda you are an afternoon devil now aren't you! Why I too just love my drinks spiked. Of course I have some Bombay Sapphire gin inside. And you like your drinks slushy? Well, let's just break out the blender and remake this pitcher of lemonade. Come on back inside with me girls and we'll make it right." With that Percy picked up the crystal pitcher of lemonade and bustled inside. I gave Wanda a withering look but she just pretended not to notice and followed Percy. Once inside, Percy was setting up his blender, adding ice and gin and Wanda was quizzing him about his sound system. Percy showed her the cabinet it was tucked away in and then proceeded to tell us how it was piped in throughout his entire house, outside as well. "Well, damn skippy you got the show right here then baby! Now lem-me put this tuner on that satellite soul groove station. There we go, now that's what I'm talkin' bout honey!" With the satellite station set, Wanda cranked the volume up and blasted Sly and the Family Stone's "Dance to the Music."

Twenty-four

Sunday night I had not heard from Larry, so I left him a voice mail around 8:30 p.m. reminding him the offer expired that night and to please give me a call and update. I called Serenity's number but it went to voice mail again. By 9:30 I had not heard back from anyone. I left another voice mail with Larry, asking him to please let me know what was up, the offer had expired, it was a full price offer and all the seller's stated terms had been met so this should be a slam dunk sign around, please advise. I took Clyde out for a night walk and when I returned, still no messages. Sometimes things are just left hanging, drives me crazy. Around midnight, Clyde and I went to sleep.

The next morning I had a voicemail from Norman letting me know he had scheduled his home inspection for tomorrow at 10:00 a.m. I am required by law to be there and make sure he and his posse of people do not break or steal anything. I wrote that on the calendar while listening to the next message. This was from Larry Wilcox and he let me know that the sellers had decided to pass on Sam and Richard's offer. Pass? God this guy is clueless. They legally can't pass. My clients made a full price offer and adhered to all the terms of sale the sellers had indicated in their listing report. This is insane. I had a message from Percy letting me know he had not heard a word from Serenity, no one came home to her house last night and Kali was still staying with him. He thought this was very odd and asked me to call him back. It did seem odd, Serenity lives on her friggin' cell phone.

First I returned Larry's phone call. He was all breezy and perky as usual. "Larry, it's Alex Campbell with Winterfrost. I got your message but I am not clear what you mean the sellers are passing. My clients submitted a full price offer and agreed to all the sellers' terms stated in the listing report. Legally the sellers are obligated to take this offer, unless there has been another offer?"

"Heey, Alex, good to talk. Craaaazy weekend huh? I don't know about you but I didn't leave Scandals until 4:00 a.m. and not alone if you know what I mean dude? I didn't peg you for a Scandals kind of guy, but awesome place huh, I did shots off some major tits dude! So listen, yeah my sellers are passing on you guyses' offer they just want something else."

"Larry, they can't just want something else. Unless there is a competing offer that is better than my clients' or the sellers accepted an offer that was submitted prior to my clients' offer, your sellers have to legally accept the offer."

"Ahhh, yeah well, ahh, you see, and this is just between you and me Alex, my sellers ahh, were not good with selling to fags. They are elderly and want their house to go to a straight couple, preferably with young children. I am sure you understand. They just want to keep their home and the neighborhood you know, as it should be, maintain the character of the Bluffs. The whole two guys owning a Bluffs house just doesn't sit well with them. I am sure you get it. There are some great houses in the Highmont."

This guy had to be insane. "Larry I hope you have let your sellers know that what they are doing is illegal and it breaks all sorts of local Clinton municipal laws. It doesn't matter who or what my clients are, they met all of the sellers stated terms, they are therefore legally obligated to sell."

"Well, yeah Alex they just don't see things that way."

"Then let them know I am fairly certain my clients will file a lawsuit before week's end and it will of course name them, KMA and Associates and you as the listing agent. Please advise them of this and my next call after we hang up is to my clients who will then be calling a real estate attorney before lunch."

Larry hemmed and hawed and I hung up and did just what I had stated. I reached Richard at his office and explained, he said he would be calling Doris Havlon when we hung up and letting Sam know as well. I then called my designated broker Todd Blund and filled him in. He acted all indignant and said he would call the KMA designated broker. I am sure Todd would call the other agency but the indignant part was a complete act. The only thing Todd cares about is covering his own ass and keeping the Winterfrost name out of any kind of lawsuits or publicity that might be seen as negative. This was all very stupid. Regardless of who my buyers were, straight, gay, bi, friends/roommates, it did not legally matter. They offered full price, and met all the stated seller terms. The seller is then legally obligated to accept their offer and go through with the deal. There is no changing your mind as a seller once a full term offer comes in. You can't just randomly change your stated terms or tune as these people apparently were doing. A good listing agent would have advised the sellers of this prior to even listing the property so they were clear. I doubt Larry had done this or even knew to tell them this was a problem when he finally presented my buyers' offer to them. He also should have told them to not just assume Sam and Richard are "fags." They could just be two straight people investing in a house together, which is not so uncommon these days, especially with prices continuing to shoot up. This was like real estate world circa 1965 when certain areas were redlined, and whole neighborhood had legal covenants which restricted prospective buyers; i.e. no Jews, blacks, single moms, etc....

Well this was a nice Monday morning fire that did not appear to be on its way to being put out. Next, I rang Percy up and he let me know he had heard nothing from Serenity, no lights on in her place. He wanted me to stop by later and let us in the house so we could give it a look through. I agreed to stop by after lunch. In the meantime, I suggested he try contacting Javier and the gym and let them know Serenity was not anywhere to be found. I said I would give her ex husband, Hayes, a call, which I did. I got the voice mail for Wealth Creation Advisors and Imports and I summed up what was going on and asked Hayes to give me a call back. I got dressed, took Clyde out for a good walk and then went out to preview some new listings. I had lunch on the road and rolled up to Serenity's around 1:00 p.m. I called Percy and he came over as I was removing the key from the agent key box. I let us in and nothing was different from the condition Wanda and I left the house in yesterday afternoon. Percy spied Serenity's purse and her cell phone was in it on mute. Her laptop was still upstairs in the office and her suitcases stored in her room full of clothes. No toiletries appeared to be missing. Percy said she had missed her morning coaching group meeting which was highly unlike her and her mid day aerobics class had been missed as well. Javier had not heard from her since Saturday, said they didn't have plans for Saturday night or Sunday. He was miffed as to why she had not shown up today for her clients and classes and said she always arranged subs in advance and never missed things. It was not adding up. She apparently had not gone on a trip anywhere and her cell and pocket book were in her house, even odder. There was no sign of a struggle but still no Serenity anywhere. I decided we should contact the police. They would probably not let us file a missing person report but we could at least start the process, find out if there was anything to do. So I called my friend Detective Davies. "Oh you are that agent with the crazy loan lady who has the big dick statue outside of her hair salon right?" Nice, Wanda and I are known for her porno statue. "The whole Tilberts' family drama thing, right?" (see Volume One)

"Yes, that would be me." I then proceeded to explain the current situation to Detective Davies. He said we couldn't file a missing persons report for some time since Serenity was a legal adult and had no obligation to notify anyone of her whereabouts. He did say it sounded very strange that she was not around and her cell phone, wallet and purse were in the house and no sign of an overnight bag being packed, etc.... Still there was nothing the police could do to help out at this point; she'd only been missing since Saturday and we didn't even know the last person who saw or spoke with her. He suggested trying the ex-husband again and see what he might know, contact her family/relatives and call all of her friends, check her email and email all of her contacts to see if anyone might know where Serenity was. And that is exactly what Percy and I then proceeded to do. We called Javier to see if he wanted to come over and help but he said he had to cover Serenity's afternoon and evening groups and classes. He did give us the password to Serenity's email account. He didn't seem very concerned but then again Javier did not strike me as the sharpest tack on the board so perhaps none of this had really sunk in?

While Percy and I were making calls and emailing I had a call from Doris Havlon, the real estate attorney. She said we should try one more time to meet with the sellers in person and present the offer, then she would have a complete slam dunk case. "They certainly have a case right now but I want you to try and do this tonight and see if you can make any headway. Take their finance person along as well so there is no doubt these two are okay in terms of financing. If you two can do this, then it is completely iron clad, an open and shut case. I am going to make a call to the sellers' listing agent when we hang up, can you give me his number? Perhaps I can let him know the dark water they are swimming in. I am going to let this Larry Wilcox know, Alex, that you and Wanda will be attempting to meet with the sellers in person tonight and it is in his best interest to help facilitate such a meeting. I want you to reprint Sam and Richards' offer again with today's date, have them resign with the appropriate date and have this offer expire tonight at 9:00 p.m. Ideally you will meet with the sellers this evening at 7:30 or 8:00 p.m. When you all meet, make sure you just present the offer you originally submitted as is, no changes except for today's date and expiration. Let them know your clients have met all the stated terms and you are presenting it one more time for review and acceptance. Say nothing more, give no legal advice, etc.… Call me when you have done this and let me know if they accept or decline. I am going to call Wanda as well and encourage her to keep her mouth shut. I just want her to show up with an updated loan pre-approval letter and say nothing more except that Sam and Richard are fully pre-approved and there are no financial issues at this time to hinder the sellers from accepting their offer."

I told Percy that I had to leave to go and reprint Sam and Richards' offer out and get fresh signatures. He said he would continue making calls from his house. I thanked him, locked up, and motored off to my house to print out the paperwork. I then took the offer to Sam's office and had him resign and then drove over to Richard's office and went through the same fire drill. I spoke to Larry and said I would like to meet with his sellers in person along with my clients' loan officer tonight at 7:30 p.m. He seemed flustered; I said we would plan on going to the sellers' house at that time unless I heard back from him otherwise. He wanted to talk more, no doubt to try and cajole me in to making this all go away, as if, but I kept it short and said we'd be at the seller's house at 7:30 p.m. and would see him there. I then updated Todd who said he would be calling the KMA designated broker again to let her know what was going to take place and hopefully she could get the sellers to meet and agree and all would be good.

Wanda called me, "I just got off the phone with that Doris Havlon and old Dorothy Hamill told me what I should do." Wanda calls Doris "Dorothy" because Doris has a haircut that is exactly like the famous figure skater's bowl cut hairstyle circa the mid 1970s. It drives Wanda nuts, she's always trying to get Doris to visit Salon Wanda. "I spoke with Richard earlier today and baby this is some shit, huh? What these folks think it is 1967 again? And I talked to Percy and he tell me no Serenity no way no how, ain't that damn strange too? I will meet you at the sellers' house in the Bluffs tonight at 7:30. I got the address; it is in their pre-approval letter."

"That is right Wanda, 7:30 and please listen to what Doris said. Not a word, just their updated pre-approval and assurance all is good on the money end."

"What you think I'm thick like that Javier bimbo? I heard what Doris said, I hear you, and I got it. I ain't gonna say nothing, just show up, smile and show the approval letter. No need to go and get all worked up, I swear some days you treat me like I'm ten years old! Now I got business to do, I'll see you in a few hours." Huffy but some days are like that.

Twenty-five

I pulled up to the sellers' house in the Bluffs right on time. There was a shiny black BMW coup parked in the drive which I naturally assumed was Larry's and which I knew was his once I noted the vanity plate, "LARRY." How's that for original? I approached the french glass front door and rang the bell. Soon enough Larry appeared in a black button down shirt, shark suit looking blue pants and of course, black elf loafers with buckles on his feet. His hair was slicked back rather than spiked and his one hundred watt smile was all lit up. "Heeyy, Alex right on the money, huh? Good, good! So my peeps are back here in the study, I see you have an offer in hand for them? Just so you know, I've spoken with the sellers and my designated broker, Marla Watkins is here as well. I'm sure we can hopefully reach some nice common ground," he said while leading me back to the study. Common ground my ass, just have the fuckers sign the deal you *putz* and let's get on with it. I went in the cherry paneled study and was introduced to Marla and the aging sellers, the Hoffmans. I was being seated when the doorbell rang and Larry went to get it. Must be Wanda. Marla was de-icing the meeting as best she could and I mentioned how I had recently sold the Tilberts house in the Bluffs. Mrs. Hoffman sneered, "Yes the house where they found the dead body. Such disgraceful children that bunch of Tilberts children are." Okay, so much for common ground via neighbors or children. Marla was quickly interjecting happy talk, "Oh yes, that was quite the news story you had there Alex. It is not too often that we real estate professionals come across a body in our…"

Marla stopped speaking in mid sentence and the Hoffmans' eyes bugged out and they looked quite alarmed. I turned around in my chair and did a double take. Wanda had arrived.

However, Wanda had remade herself. Instead of her usual explosion of bright colors, Wanda was dressed in a black dress, what little there was of it. She had on an extremely short black mini dress, made of rayon? I'd never seen Wanda wear anything too far above her knees, I guess because she is larger sized. She wore vintage clunky black platform shoes. Her hair was a huge mushroom afro and she had on enormous, thin, gold hoop earrings. She looked like a cross between an overweight Ikette (from the Ike and Tina Turner days) and Angela Davis circa 1971. "I hope I didn't keep everyone waiting. I am Wanda Billings of Safety Mortgage and this is an updated loan pre-approval letter for Sam and Richard. It was updated this afternoon and everything on the financial end is all checked out and they are one hundred percent okay to go ahead with this purchase." She said while sitting down in an overstuffed chair, trying to keep her knees together so everyone didn't get a free peep show.

Larry looked like a deer in headlights and Marla quickly cut in, "Why thank you Wanda, I'll take the new pre-approval letter you have brought and Alex you have a revised offer for the Hoffmans to review?"

"Yes, here you are Marla. The only thing that has changed since Saturday is the date has been changed to today's date, and this offer expires at 9:00 p.m. tonight and of course I have had both of my buyers resign all of the pages of the offer. Otherwise it is exactly the same as what we submitted on Saturday."

"Why thank you so much for bringing us this and…"
Mr. Hoffman appeared agitated and fiddled with his hearing aid, "You bring us the same damn offer as Saturday's? I already told this good for nothing Larry we are not selling this house to a couple of queers, period. It is a disgrace and you two should be ashamed to be representing such deviants!" This he said while pointing his finger at Wanda and me while Mrs. Hoffman reached out to pull his arm in. Marla was sputtering when Wanda replied.

"Honey, let me tell you something and I KNOW you is old enough to recall what I'm about to tell you. My mother, god rest her soul, Bessie Mae Billings she worked up here in the Bluffs all her life cleaning one house or another and helping out with your parties and holidays. She had to walk most days just to get here 'cause no bus ran up here in the Bluffs back in the day. Now she worked hard to raise us children to be the best we could be. As you know, back in her day no blacks were allowed to live up here in the Bluffs, couldn't even live in the maid's quarters. No sir, had to be a white maid to live in the maid's quarters up here. That's not that long ago. Times have changed, you now got one or two black couples who own houses up here and your maids are now almost all Hispanic but you lets them live on-site if need be. I am quite sure you got some fairies and lezzies living up here already that you don't know about Pops. Hell, could be your neighbor for all you know! My point is times have changed and laws have too. It ain't the same as when you first bought this here house and there is nothing you can do about that. That is just the nature of the world, change. Some of it is good, some is bad and a whole bunch I gotta say myself I ain't so sure of. But I do know you can't stop change and you are certainly old enough and educated enough to see that for yo'self. I'm sure your mama didn't raise no fool! You need to save yo'self a world of legal trouble and sell this damn house and move on baby. Your life is too short as it is to go on acting like this over two grown men that want to buy your house. Ain't ya'll got some grandbabies to go and concern yourselves with? This just stupid, plain and simple and there ain't no way in hell ya'll gonna win. You don't have to agree with it, not one bit, no sir. But ya'll do have to move on and get out the way. Now that's all I got to say about this here."

You could have heard a pin drop. Marla looked like she was about to shit a brick and Larry looked more deer in headlights and stupider than ever. I was taking it all in when Mrs. Hoffman spoke up, "Thank you for your opinion Wanda. I am not sure Clarence here gets it but I do. I agree with my husband and I too think it is awful that two men are buying our lovely home. However, you are right we do not have much time and change is inevitable. I think we are going to discuss this some more with Marla and Larry and I believe we will just sign and move on. You are correct, I remember when they had those live-in maid restrictions up here and I thought they were ludicrous at the time, even when they were legal. You know Wanda, I think I knew your mother, Bessie Mae was it? I think she used to polish the silver for all the holiday parties way back. In fact I am quite sure of it. Yes, I knew your mother."

Marla gave a manic smile and quickly interjected, "Oh such a small world we all live in! And thank you Wanda for your insight. Larry, why don't you show Alex and Wanda to the door and we can review this offer with the Hoffmans. Thank you both again for stopping by tonight and I will be in touch Alex." She smiled big and wide and Larry woke up from his deer in headlights trance and turned on his smile and led us to the front door. "Thanks dudes and ah like ah Marla says you know, we'll give you a jingle hopefully in a few."

Wanda walked over towards her car, pulling the too short rayon dress down in back as she walked. She said over her shoulder, "Why don't we meet up at Mama Honey's, all this work has made me something powerful hungry." She got in Miss Emerald, her mushroom fro flattening against the car's ceiling. I agreed and got in my two door Volvo and followed her down out of the Bluffs to Mama Honey's.

Twenty-six

We parked and went in Mama Honey's, the big plate glass windows were steamed over and sweating and the air conditioner units in the transoms were whirling away as fast as they could. Inside was warm but not insufferable and there were a few tables filled with diners. Mama led us to a table by one of the steamed over windows. "Oh I do see that Miz Wanda has herself a new and purtty look, now don'cha? You be wearin' the black Miz Wanda, not like you, I hope there ain't no funeral troubles or nothing?"

"No baby, just borrowed me a new look for this evening is all." Mama went off to get our usual beers and orders of seafood jambalaya. I gave Wanda a long what gives look. "What you all so Curious George about? I decided I needed to show those bigots a thang or two. So I decided to go all retro Black Panthers and scare their honky asses. They definitely old enough to remember that time and be afraid. So what do you think, did my look capture the time and the Panthers?"

"Wanda, you were supposed to just show up and say nothing, Doris told you what to do. Your Black Panther look? What are you trying out for acting roles? This is the real world Wanda, you might have really botched this up and now Sam and Richard may have to file a law…" My cell began to ring. I picked up and listened as Marla spoke in her manic chipmunk tone. I said I'd look for it and thanked her for helping out.

Mama placed two cold bottled beers on the table and Wanda had a bird that ate the canary smile on her face. "So, that was Marla wasn't it? And them old fools signed the offer as is, now didn't they?"

I sighed and managed a weak nod. "Okay then, so I would say my costume and my speech got the deal done. I don't care what old Dorothy Hamill lawyer woman say, looks like I done got Sam and Richard in their house." To that she held up her bottle to toast me.

I began to laugh, it was too surreal. "Wanda, what the fuck? And where did that fro wig and that dress and shoes come from?"

"Oh I had Miz Liz whip up the fro for me. This dress and shoes, and the earrings is all from my older sister Syreeta. You know Syreeta just holds on to everything. Come to think of it Alex, I betcha I could get her on that TV show, you know the one that's all about them crazy people that keep all this crap up in they house and won't throw nothing out? Anyway, this here outfit is one she really wore back in the day when she was in high school. I could barely fit in it but you know Syreeta always been a big girl so she was big even way back. And damn, let me tell you I ain't never walked around in public in nothing this short. It's creepy, you gotta always be making sure your coochie ain't hanging out and keep your legs all together when you sittin'. Not to mention, Syreeta and them girls must have froze they asses off back then. Now it's summertime, so it is nice but I still feel like I am walking around naked or something. Yeah, I figured a little Black Panther flashback might be some good visual intimidation for those crackers. Sure 'nuff worked too now didn't it?"

Oh my god, but she's right, it worked. "Yeah, between your outfit and that story you told. I didn't know your mother had worked as a domestic?"

Wanda let out a loud cackle, "Oh, wasn't that just too damn good! I thought me that story up right as I was talking. Hell, my mama ain't never cleaned no houses for a living, not that there's anything wrong with that. My mama's name is Bernice, that Bessie Mae crap just sounded all old school washer woman to me. No, my mama was a first grade school teacher for a while. Then she got bored with that and opened up a pawn shop. She ran that Stop and Sell shop over there on Clearview Avenue for years. And she sure as hell ain't dead either! No Bernice closed up her pawn shop 'bout twenty years back now I guess and that's when she upped and moved off with that long haul, hairy fool, trucker, Burt. She and he course had a falling out soon enough but she ended up staying out there in Arizona, all retired now. Ain't that rich? She probably the only retired black sister out there in that Tucson. We can't figure out what she see in that place, but it's going on almost twenty years now so something must be right for her out there. And that Hoffman lady telling me she remembered my mama, how my mama polished they silver for the holidays! Oohhh I almost bit my cheeks off to keep from laughing."

Unreal but it worked and it was all so funny, such a relief that Wanda and I both burst into loud, hysterical nonstop laughter. The kind where your eyes tear up and your ribs ache. If we had been in any other restaurant or not known Mama personally I am sure they would have asked us to leave. Once we had calmed down, I called Sam and Richard and let them know things should be good, of course I wouldn't know for certain until the listing agent sent back the completed and signed around purchase and sale agreement and Marla had promised to email that to me by 9:00 p.m. I dialed up Percy while Wanda was digging into her piece of coconut cream pie. Percy was all aflutter, no word from Serenity but he had managed to locate Serenity's mother's contact information. She lives in Gary, Indiana and he spoke with her and told her about the situation. He said as we were speaking, Serenity's mother and sister were on a plane on their way to Clinton. He said he was going to pick them up at the airport in an hour and he wanted Wanda and me to stop by Serenity's house later on so we could speak with her mother and sister and hopefully figure out what was up. I said we'd be there in a couple of hours. We decided we would take my car and go to my house so I could check on the signed around offer and we could take Clyde out for a walk.

Once back at my little ranch I printed out the signed around offer and it was good, the Hoffmans had finally agreed and accepted. I called Sam and Richard and congratulated them, told them to schedule the inspection and let me know when it would be. Next, I called Doris Havlon and updated her and left a voice mail for Todd Blund so he would know all was okay. I filled out a Winterfrost transaction sheet and printed out another copy of the signed around deal. I'd stop by the office on my way to Serenity's to drop this deal in the office transaction box. PDF files are making my life a lot easier and my next purchase is going to be one of the new affordable printers that has a built in scanner and can create PDFs. Once I have that, I'll hardly ever have to step in the viper pit, a.k.a. Winterfrost. Wanda and I went out back to get Clyde and Black Panther drag or not, Clyde knew exactly who she was and they did their usual dance which looked even more stupid looking because of Wanda's skimpy dress.

Twenty-seven

On the way to Serenity's house, I dropped Wanda back by Mama Honey's so she could pick up her car. While she was unlocking it several men who were loitering started whistling at her and asking what her rates were. I suppose her retro look placed her in the street walker category. She gave them the finger and we both drove off for Capitol Heights. The lights were on and we rang the bell. Percy appeared and let us in. "Oh my Wanda, you have changed your look? It's very retro and all black, no colors."

Wanda nodded and put her arm up in a black power salute, "Right on baby! I'm a first class militant now. Naw, this here just a costume I put together to help out our clients earlier tonight." Percy looked confused and led us down the hall to Serenity's living room/kitchen.

There beached on the ocean liner sized sofa were two equally large, overweight, women all slumped in and quite comfy with the living room TV tuned in on a game show. They had their dingy fat feet propped up on the coffee table. One had poorly dyed red with black roots frizzed out hair. She was dressed in grubby, grey sweat pants and was slurping from a big gulp cup with a bucket of fast food take-out resting on top of her sizable belly. A cigarette burned on a make shift ash-tray (dinner plate) resting on the sofa's arm. The other younger woman with greasy and bushy brownish hair, was wearing stained grey sweat pants and an oversized, once white, Pepsi t-shirt. She was simultaneously puffing on a cigarette, drinking a sixteen ounce can of Schlitz beer and munching on a large bag of pork rinds. Percy looked out of place, "Alex, Wanda this is Serenity's mother, Darla, and her sister, Ronnie." They looked up, the mother let out a soda belch and the daughter squinted her eye while taking a long drag on her cancer stick as she reached for the remote and muted the TV set. "They ah, got here a little while ago and neither of them has heard from Serenity, so they came right away to help us find her."

The daughter, Ronnie, let out a cynical cackle, "Yeah, ain't that right Ma? We are concerned about Mona and her disappearing act! Not like she ain't pulled this shit before, huh?" The mother chuckled a bit. "Good thing we made Percy stop by that fast food place and the mini mart on the way over here. I knew Mona weren't gonna have jack shit to eat in her house. Percy says she sells them boxes of powder drinks over there. Looks like some nasty crap to me."

I piped in, "Nice to meet you, I am Alex Campbell and I am the listing agent for Serenity's house. None of us have heard from her since Saturday and the police won't let us file a missing person's report just yet. It's very odd that Serenity has not been in touch with anyone and all of her belongings seem to be here in the house."

Ronnie scooched up on the burgundy velvet sofa, her dirty grey sweat pants sticking to upholstery a bit. "Yeah, nice to meet ya' Alex. None of that Serenity crap around me and Ma. She's just plain old Mona to us and to anyone that really knows the bitch. I bet she's about busted your balls with sellin' her house, huh? Yup, Ma and me figured we best get out here and take it all in. She never invited us out here before. We didn't know how high she was livin' till we pulled up. Percy says that there white luxury car out front is hers? Well god

190

damn. He says she's a big time celebrity of sorts in this here town and on her way up to L.A. Does seem odd for her to just up and disappear. But you know this ain't the first time Mona's skipped out. Nope back in the 90s, once she lost all that weight, she sure skipped out of Gary, Indiana. Didn't she Ma? Yep, left Ma and me high and dry. Little bitch had herself a drug habit, must be what got all that weight off of her. Then she steals Ma's pension and that's just about the last we done seen of her. She'd send us a Christmas card every few years or so but she didn't want nothing to do with us. She denied knowing anything about Ma's pension fund being drained, claimed to know nothing about all that. Bank had a different story though. They showed us how Mona forged Ma's signature and had her on tape collecting the money from Ma's accounts. Ma here was too kind to file any charges. Told them it was a family matter, forbid them to do anything said she'd claim it was all a gift if they pursued charges. Me, I'd like to kick her ass."

I didn't know where to start. First, these greasy baby elephants are smoking inside my listing! Are they insane? Nobody smokes indoors anymore and in a house that is for sale! Second, it did not sound like they were too fond of Serenity. I can't say I blame them. But it didn't appear they were very upset or concerned about locating her. "Well Ronnie, sounds like Serenity does have a past. Our main goal now is to try and figure out where she is. If need be, you and your mother, as her next of kin, will need to file a missing person's report with the police. From what we can tell, Percy was the last one to speak with her on Saturday. She's missed her appointments and the classes she teaches. Her boyfriend hasn't seen her since Saturday either. Nothing adds up. I don't know any reason why she would be skipping town this time around. Her divorce settlement is done and the last piece of business she had was to sell this house and then she was on her way to L.A."

Darla moved around a bit, wiping her mouth on her stretched out, faded blue, Disney t-shirt, "Yeah, Mona's always been a handful. Done real good for herself though, this is one classy house she's shacked up in. You seen that big screen TV she got up in her bedroom? Ronnie says there's gold ducks for faucets in one of the bathrooms. Yup, me and her gotta talk, she needs to pay back that money 'cause Ronnie and me can't go on forever living off disability and unemployment. I guess we gotta find out where Mona is at, huh?"

Ronnie shook her head in agreement, "Yup we sure do. Hey you all wants a beer? There's more in the fridge, help yourselves. Me and Ma is kind of worn out from the plane ride and all. I figure you all know Serenity's world better than we do, so maybe you can figure out what to do. Ma and me will be here to file that report. Hey Percy, what's a good pizza delivery place? Me and Ma like to have our pizzas around midnight." With that she picked up the remote and the game show sounds came back on.

Wanda and Percy and I gave each other looks and I spoke up, "So ah Ronnie, Darla, you both know that Serenity's house is currently listed for sale and on the market. It is by appointment only, so anyone who wants to show it will call me first. It sounds as if you two are going to stay here? If so, then I'm afraid I'll have to ask that you only smoke outdoors, the cigarette odor is a big problem when a house in on the market. So outside on the patio or upstairs on the balcony off her bedroom would be the best places to smoke, make sure the butts are thrown out and not piled up in an ashtray or tossed on the ground. I guess we will leave you two to rest and we'll try and come up with a game plan and check back with you tomorrow?"

Ronnie was now staring at the TV and Darla appeared to be half way listening, she did look up, "Oh, okay then Alex that sounds good. We'll see what ya'll come up with tomorrow." She blew out a billow of cigarette smoke.

The three of us headed out and right over to Percy's. Kali was asleep on his living room floor with Hadley asleep above on the white sofa. Percy headed straight over to the bar nook built into his open kitchen and proceeded to fill the blender with ice. "Well hells bells, have you ever? I never would have thought that Serenity would descend from that side of the trailer park. Really!" He said while pouring whiskey and mixer in the blender. Wanda was leaning on the counter and nodded in agreement and said,

"You got that one right Percy. Lord them ladies be nothing like that Serenity. Don't seem too concerned about her not being around neither. Course they did say she stole her mama's money and all but still. Alex, we all got to come up with a plan." Percy turned the blender on high, took out three high-ball glasses, and cut up a lime.

He shut off the blender and began filling the glasses, "Here, this is a whiskey sour slushy, let's have them out by the pool and see if we can come up with something." He placed the glasses on a silver serving tray (monogrammed naturally), complete with blue linen napkins, a silver bowl of nuts and off he bustled, up to his pool area.

"Damn Percy, you didn't let me know when I was here the other day that you had no swimming pool hidden away up here. Now this is real nice, ahum, it's the bomb Percy! Look at the view from up here." He then showed her the electric privacy screens and boasted about his nude swimming activities.

"Ohh, Percy you a little devil now ain't ya? Now this the way to live, no doubt about it, you got it all going on in this here house Percy, cheers baby!" She toasted us and took a slug of her whiskey sour slushy.

We sat down on chaise lounges, watching the moon above and filled Percy in on why exactly Wanda was dressed the way she was and what had happened. Then we tried to figure out what to do with no Serenity, and a listing with smoking trailer trash hags now occupying it. We finally decided it would be best if Percy could search through Serenity's home office and see if there was a Will in there. He also volunteered to go over to TOTAL tomorrow and quiz Javier in person and try and figure out why he wasn't more concerned that Serenity is missing. I am sure Percy would also enjoy being near Javier, so not a bad assignment for him. I would try to find her ex-husband, Hayes and see what his story is and if he has any ideas as to Serenity's where-abouts. And Wanda would contact Detective Pete Davies and put the pressure on him to let us file a missing persons report for Serenity. Wanda was thinking aloud, "We also gonna need that Davies to get a court order so they can get a hold of her cell phone records and listen in on her voice mail messages. That takes some doing, so I'm gonna have to visit him in person tomorrow and put the squeeze on." I could only imagine, Wanda finds Detective Davies attractive and has a love crush and yell at him history (see Volume One) so this should be interesting.

Twenty-eight

The next morning I was up early and had walked Clyde, jumped into real estate clothes and was out the door by 8:30. Norman's inspection was scheduled for 9:00 a.m. and I pulled up at 8:50. Norman, Amy and his inspector were already there waiting. Actually the inspector had started evaluating the house's exterior. The inspection took about an hour and half and all was well, the only thing to try and ask for was a new hot water tank. I told Norman I would email that repair request form to him to sign and he could fax or email it back to me and I would get it to the listing agent by that evening. Norman's deal appeared to be on track and moving along. His mother called while we were doing the inspection and wanted to speak directly to the inspector, it sounded like what she heard calmed her down.

Just as I was about to wrap it up with Norman and company, Amy wanted to check out the back yard one more time to see about installing an above ground pool and hot tub, so to the back yard she went. As she went to the back yard, the next door neighbor pulled up in their drive in a grey Honda minivan. The ever-smiling mom, giving an upbeat toot-toot to us on her car horn. Out of the van came two younger girls in bathing suits and two young boys wearing Cub Scout uniforms. They all scampered over into the lawn where Norman and I were standing. "Hi there, I am Tammy Matthews and you must be our new neighbor!" She said while her crew of kids wiggled all around her, doing cartwheels and fidgeting.

"Oh, ahh, yes I am Norman Kluntz, it's nice to meet you." He said shaking Tammy's hand. Tammy was dressed in white Capri pants, flip-flops, a yellow polo shirt and had a sensible and perky mom hair cut. "Welcome Norman! We'll have to have a neighborhood party once you get moved in. So Mr. Agent, when's our big move-in day going to be for Mr. Norman?" She said smiling big and wide. I wondered if she was stoned on Prozac or if she too had an ever buzzing vibrator stuffed away in some obscure body cavity? However, before I could respond, Tammy's eager smile quickly faded and her face looked like she'd seen a ghost. Right on cue Amy returned, all decked out in her clear acrylic platform stripper heels, a barely there yellow fishnet dress with her enormous jugs barely concealed by a tiny lime green sports bra thing. She sidled up to Norman, placing her magenta talons on his neck which she began to knead and massage. "Hi, I'm Amy and Normie and I are sooo excited to be moving in, aren't we Normie? I was just checking out back to see where we could put an above ground pool and hot tub in. I get sooo hot you know? Normie is putting in my very own dance studio in the basement for me, so I can practice all my dance routines at home now before I go to work!"

Tammy looked like she was going to pass out on the lawn and her two cub scout boys' mouths were literally hanging open as their little eyes focused exclusively on Amy's tits. The girls stopped their cartwheels and perked up the minute they heard dance studio, "Ooohhh, Mom she's gonna have a dance studio and right next door to us! Ask her if we can come and do our routines there? We can have dance class right here Mom, no more of Miss Emily's Little Tinkerbell's classes! Ohhh, Amy can we come dance at your house, please?!" Tammy started to sputter and Amy lit up, "Why, girls of course you can! Oh Normie, I can teach them everything I know! Why I can train the next generation of stars for Scandals! Yes, girls, oh my you have inspired me! I'm going to have dance classes right here in my new home! Now you tell all your little friends and once my Normie has my pole installed and the little platform in, you and all your friends can just hop right on over for lessons. Oh, Normie this is great!" She squealed with excitement while kissing Norman's check. Norman turned beet red and Tammy's vibrator appeared to have lost all its battery power as she now looked like Satan himself had stopped by. She was sputtering when her girls shrieked in glee about dance classes and the boys began to ask if they too could come over. Amy was positively elated, "Of course boys, bring over your whole scout troop and your daddy and all of their daddies! We can bake cookies and have a swim party in my new pool out back. Tammy, you have to come over for hot tub cocktails as soon as we are moved in and have the pool and hot tub installed. It'll be great! So when's this neighborhood party you are going to have for us Tammy? Alex our agent here said we are all set to close and move in this place at the end of this month! I just can't wait to meet everybody; I just feel this is the perfect neighborhood." Before anyone could say another word, a green, four door Honda Accord pulled in the Matthews' drive, it too did a jaunty toot-toot at us. Out came a middle aged man in short sleeves wearing a blah tie. "Ohh, honey I forgot my laptop! Oh hey, are these the new neigh…" He stopped cold in mid-sentence as he was crossing over to us.

Amy lit up even brighter, "Oh my God! Ty it's you! My god it's been a while, what a year or so since you last saw me perform? Did you know I am now THE headliner at Scandals? I just started this weekend, you have got to get back there and check out my headliner act Ty. Damn, did you know we are going to be next door neighbors now, don't that just beat all? Ty and I used to be real close a few years back and he used to be one of my number one fans back when I was just starting out in dancing and all." Tammy now turned beet red as the color drained from Norman's face. Ty appeared to be in complete shock. Tammy found her voice again, "Tyler, do you know this woman? You were her number ONE fan just a few years back?" He started to sputter and Tammy started to walk towards him as he retreated. The kids were now even more excited, running between the yards and screaming in glee about a new pool and dance classes. I managed a lame nice to meet you as Tammy and Tyler walked away and I turned to Norman and Amy, "Well, looks like you already know your next door neighbor there and ah, that was a good inspection today Norman and I'll be sure to get this hot water tank request form to the sellers. So ah, you all have a great day and I'll be in touch." With that I went to my car and left. I noticed Tammy was yelling at Tyler outside their front door and the crew of kids was even more hysterical and running wild in their front yard. Ahh, suburbia.

Next, I had to figure out how to reach Hayes Brighton. I had looked in the phone book and online but there was no residential phone listing for him. I looked up his name in the property tax database and the last property he was on record for was Serenity's house. I could only assume he was now a renter. But where? I called his cell phone but it went straight to voice mail and the message machine at Wealth Creation Advisors and Imports did no good. I decided my best plan of action would be to roll over to TOTAL and see if anyone there could provide information as to where Hayes lived or his current whereabouts.

TOTAL gym is located on the business end of the Lee District and it occupies what once must have been a mid-sized grocery store chain building, most likely an old A&P building I suppose. The ample parking lot was three quarters full at 11:00 a.m., this place was booming. The building was painted black and had a large block letter green neon sign that read TOTAL. I parked and went inside and there was a spacious reception room with a seating area and a big front desk. Power Up Serenity promo materials and cardboard end cap displays of the powdered drink canisters in all the glorious flavors surrounded the ends of the reception desk. One end cap display even had a life size cardboard cutout photo of Serenity smiling big and wide, hands out to the side pointed toward the powder drink canisters. She was naturally outfitted in Lycra shorts and her barely there Power Up Serenity sports bra top. The copy bubble she was supposed to be saying read, "Live the Power Up Serenity Lifestyle!" In addition to a full line of TOTAL t-shirts and sweats on display behind the front desk, there was a mini store filled with TOTAL and Power Up Serenity goodies. Mugs, baseball hats, yoga mats, exercise balls, incense, key chains, mouse pads, gym towels, bumper stickers, notepads, journals, coasters, pedometers, on and on, it was all there and for sale. There was one class in progress to the left of the reception desk and through the glass wall I could see that Javier was leading it, his portable microphone hanging off his ear. It appeared to be a step class filled with various sized women and what appeared to be Percy in the front row. I could hear the boom of the music and Javier counting steps. A late thirty-something receptionist dressed in a green TOTAL sweat suit greeted me and asked if I was a member or interested in a guest pass. I explained who I was and what I was doing there. She looked a bit confused but said she'd buzz the office manager Joanne. I noted that she had short dark hair and was a bit brisk in her manner, certainly not all blonde and bubbly like Serenity. She went back to checking out a couple of women who were buying clothing items and a tanning booth pass. I noted that to the right of the reception desk was a large, lit up display board with "Serenity's Winner Circle" members of the month listed, along with their mug shots. I quickly spotted RG's mug shot. She looked like a gloating and smug little pig. There were other groups and "winners" listed for Javier and other teachers and all this filled a very large wall. I noticed the other female teachers and coaches, whose mug shots were posted on the instructors' part of the wall, were all dark haired and a bit older for what you would expect in the industry. They too, all looked very no-nonsense. Sort of like girls high school field hockey team coaches except not as chunky as that stereotype. Joanne appeared and asked me to follow her back to the office. She was a middle aged brunette wearing a green TOTAL track suit and jogging shoes. She had a more housewife/den mother demeanor than the other female staff members. We reached her office just off the hallway which led to the weight room and saunas. It was a medium sized room, with a couple of small windows and fluorescent lights. She rang the front desk and asked the woman who picked up to bring her a mango Power Up Serenity shake and then asked me what flavor I would like. I didn't want any but figured I'd play along, so I asked for vanilla.

Joanne indicated a chair for me to sit in next to her desk, "I understand you are Serenity's real estate agent and you are trying to start a search for Serenity? We are very concerned. She's never missed a class once and has never ever not checked in a couple of times a day, at least by phone. The last we heard from Serenity was Saturday morning." A brunette and brisk woman walked in and gave us our Power Up Serenity drinks, we thanked her. I quickly explained what the situation was with the police and a missing person's report and that her mom and sister arrived last night. I told her our various assignments for today to find Serenity. Joanne thanked me for helping out. She showed me a missing person's flyer she had created on her computer's screen and asked if she could start handing those out. I said I thought it was a great idea and asked if she would print some for me and I could pass some along to Wanda and Percy.

"Done. I just hit print for five hundred copies and those should be ready for you at the front desk on your way out. Now, I haven't seen Hayes, Serenity's ex, in almost nine months. You know that divorce was really bitter and they had quite the battle to see who was going to end up owning and running TOTAL. They started it together but in fairness over the years it had become Serenity's baby.

She's made this gym what it is today with her coaching and lifestyle business and now of course with her protein shake line. Aren't these just delicious? They just clear your energy meridians out and give you such pep and focus." I managed to gulp a sip without grimacing and gave a feeble, yum sound.

I quizzed Joanne about the company finances, anything weird in the past few months, or any money missing since this weekend? Nothing odd on that front. Joanne said she'd checked the accounts first thing this morning and no unusual activity. So Serenity had not apparently emptied the business accounts. Joanne said Hayes was now completely out of the business picture, it had all been transferred over into Serenity's name and control when the divorce was finalized. She hesitated a bit and I asked her what she was holding back, I reminded her it could be crucial for Serenity's well being.

"Well I don't like gossip, but the past couple of months around here, well it has been obvious that Javier and Serenity have been at odds a bit. I think he wants to have more input and control and I know he wants her to make him a legal partner in the business, give him check signing and cashing authority. She has said no every time and he's clearly not happy about that." I asked her how their relationship was going.

She took a pull on her shake, "She is just head over heels in for him and really who could blame her? I mean Javier looks like a model and from the moment he started teaching here, she clearly had her sights on him. You know he is significantly younger than she is and it is clear that she is working really hard to, you know, keep up with the younger girls and all. Personally, I think Hayes was a better match for Serenity, same age and all but she treated him like trash, especially towards the end. He ended up really despising her and for good reason as far as I am concerned. I always felt Serenity sees Javier as someone who can take all of this to the next level for her, you know in L.A. and nationally. He has movie star looks, not that Hayes is any strain on the eyes mind you. But Javier has that ladies man appeal." I asked if she ever suspected Javier was fooling around with other women. She went pale.

"This really is getting gossipy. But you know there have been some rumors around here with certain clients and one young instructor was fired by Serenity a few months ago, for no real reason at all except well we suspected she and Javier might have had a thing. He was really furious with Serenity when she did that. Actually, she really cleaned house a few months back. If you look around, all of the female instructors and coaches here are now dark haired and older and well how to say this, ahh more manly? I think Serenity felt very threatened by any female who was a natural blonde or younger or more feminine that she, so she slowly got rid of all of those that were like that and phased in what we have here now. I mean I can't say I completely blame her what with Javier on the prowl and she probably wants to make sure she has the best image here, what with the promotion of her drink line. She's made herself the brand icon so to speak and I guess she wants to maintain the lead in the looks and persona department. As I said, this really irked Javier. I found it a bit funny, you know these new women instructors here don't fall for his bare-chested, rooster strutting about routine. Oh, now I've gone and said too much, here bottoms up!" With that she toasted me and I was obliged to gulp down the gritty nasty tasting vanilla glop. Joanne then gave me the last address she had on file for Hayes, a rental over near his office. She wasn't sure if he still lived there or not. We then promised to be in touch with each other and I picked up the black and white missing flyers on the way out.

Serenity was so threatened by the other pretty girls that she replaced her staff with older, efficient lesbians or well, possibly straight women who didn't bother with fake bakes and inflating their girls. Interesting, just confirms what an insecure bitch I already thought she was. I drove over to the southeast area of Clinton's downtown, where Hayes' office is. This area is sometimes referred to as Laughton and it is mostly crappy, half in-business, half abandoned strip malls like where Hayes' office is. There are some older brick apartment buildings and warehouses, with a few smaller manufacturing buildings as well. It lies to the east of my no-name neighborhood and was part of the industrial sprawl from back when Clinton was a booming port. First, I stopped by Wealth Creation Advisors and Imports but the shades were all drawn and nobody answered the locked door. I gave the business number a call and could hear the lonely landline echoing inside. Next, I drove up the hill to a flat top area where there are a few red brick apartment buildings. I went down a side street and located the address for Hayes' apartment building. It was a six unit, rectangular, three story, red brick building and according to the yellow bricked corner stone was completed in 1921. It was not attractive now and I doubt it had been a looker when it was first constructed. They had put a sort of faux castle like trim around the top of the flat roofed building with a few yellow bricks put in for a minimal pattern, but that had been the extent of any attempt at architectural allure. This was clearly housing that had been built in a hurry to accommodate the influx of workers for the booming port. It was a stepping stone place, where someone would start out on their way up or end up on their way down. Nothing horrific but no frills either. I parked by the curb and went in the front door. There was a dirty white tiled foyer, two units on each floor with a central dark wooden staircase. A row of six brass, locked mailboxes lay directly in front of the entry door, right in the stairwell nook. I noted Hayes' last name "Brighton" was written on a name tape for *Apt. 6.* Hayes was on the top floor and a moss covered skylight at the top had once let natural light shine down on the now dark stairwell. Once I reached the third floor, I knocked on number six but no answer. I looked out the little vestibule window and noted the cracking sidewalks, the grass out front that needed mowing and zero street life. I called Hayes' cell phone again but it went to straight to voice mail. I went down and decided to walk around the building to check out the back.

The back had screened porches on each level and a wooden stairwell in the center that led up. There were six parking spaces, a bank of rusting green trash bins and a potholed gravel access road that bordered a lot of scrub trees and a few old oaks. I walked up the wooden stairs and once at the top I found the screen door to apartment six's porch open. The porch slanted a bit but it was fairly roomy. There wasn't a stick of furniture on it; it was completely empty, no potted plants, old bottles, absolutely nothing. There was a back door with a single window pane in its center. I rapped on the door and no answer. I turned the black brass door knob and it opened. I used my real estate agent voice and called out for Hayes, asking if anyone was home? Nothing, just the hum of the aging avocado green refrigerator. The kitchen was painted white with old white metal cabinets. A small eat-in nook was to the left of the door. A central hallway led to the rest of the apartment. Next to the kitchen off of the hallway was a powder blue and black tiled bathroom, just a dripping shower faucet in there. I took the door from the bathroom that led into a bedroom. It was nothing to write home about; full size bed with a navy bedspread, a bedside table and white metal lamp, running shoes on the floor, a basic chest of drawers. I went back into the hallway and continued up front. There was a smaller room on the right; it had a desk, black filing cabinet, a computer and some Power Up Serenity boxes in it. Finally the front room, the living room. It was fairly large, nice windows, a standard sized TV, a green leather sofa, maple coffee table with a green bottle of Heineken beer and what appeared to be a very dead Hayes in a grey recliner chair. His blue eyes were open and there was clearly a bullet hole in his forehead. His skin looked grey; I didn't even bother to walk any closer. I quickly turned around and high tailed it down the hall and out onto the screen porch. I was completely freaked out. I fumbled through my wallet, found Detective Davies card and dialed my cell phone. He actually picked up on the first ring and I tried to catch my breath and explain what I had found.

Twenty-nine

Detective Davies called the police response team, per procedure and he arrived about the same time they did. I was waiting on the front stoop to Hayes' building. Even when the police cars arrived, not a soul peeked out of their windows much less came outside to have a look. Not exactly a stellar Community Watch neighborhood, McGruff the crime dog would be very disappointed. I showed the police and Detective Davies to the back door and they all set about doing their work. A crime/homicide unit was called in. While we were waiting for them to arrive Pete Davies said he had spoken with Wanda this morning and once this work was completed he planned to stop by Serenity's house and take a missing person's report from Darla and Ronnie.

Obviously Wanda had somehow made her point with Davies et al. because getting a missing person's report filed is no small feat. However, I guess now that her ex-husband is dead with a bullet in his head it might drive the point home a bit more to the cops that something is up and things are not right. I asked him if he planned to interview her boyfriend and the staff at TOTAL. He gave me a quizzical look, "Something makes me think you and your co-junior detective Ms Billings are already on this case? Have you all talked with her boyfriend or the people at her gym?" I quickly filled him in on that morning's events and I let him know that we had spied Javier at Scandal's on Saturday night obviously enjoying himself. "Well good work and that is off the record. I won't even bother to ask what you two were doing at Scandal's on Saturday night. Heck, if you two had not started your detective work up, regardless of how amateur it is, we probably wouldn't know about the dead ex in the living room yet. So again, off the record, thanks. Now we'll take over all of this and you and Ms Billings can go back to work doing the house selling, running that hair place or whatever it is you two exactly do. I will say that I doubt we are going to get anything from this scene, it appears squeaky clean. That back door, you said was unlocked when you arrived? Could be the victim left it unlocked but I'm betting this was done by a professional hit man. Judging from the body, I'd say this happened yesterday or the day before. He was hit real clean, like a pro would do. If the back door had been locked, any pro would be able to pick that old lock in no time. We'll know more once the coroner has a look. But now that her ex is officially dead, it does increase the scrutiny and urgency to find Serenity. I might have some more questions for you about her but in the meantime you are free to go. We'll finish this up here and as I mentioned, I'll be stopping by to get a missing person's report later today." I thanked Detective Davies and went down the back stairs and headed off in my two door beater.

I had one voice mail from Sam letting me know they had scheduled their home inspection for the following day, so I confirmed and notified Larry, the whiz listing agent, who would hopefully make sure the Hoffman's were not in the house when we did our inspection. There is nothing worse than arriving with clients and their home inspector and finding the seller there hovering around. It is technically a legal gray area. An argument could be made, I suppose, that the seller has a right to observe a buyer's inspection. However, the norm is that the listing agent lets the seller know the time and date of the buyer's home inspection and advises that they vacate the property until it is complete. I've asked some sellers who have stayed to leave and all have complied. I suppose if a seller insisted on staying then I'd make sure the inspector wrote the report and spoke with the buyer in a separate room so the seller could not overhear their discussion. Wanda called me to see if I wanted to have lunch with her at the Rusty Nail. I halfheartedly agreed and she said she would meet me there in fifteen. The Rusty Nail is located at the southern edge of Highmont and the northern tip of Laughton. So it was close by for both of us. Wanda likes this place and I am not so fond. The name alone does not do anything to make me hungry and I think of tetanus shots.

The Rusty Nail has been around forever and is located in a one story, standalone clapboard house with a huge deck added on in back for outdoor dining. It is a popular place for lunch and the gravel parking lot was almost completely full when I arrived. It started way back in 1940s when it was run out of a contractor's house; his wife started feeding the day laborers and as time passed, their home became a full time restaurant. It was called the Rusty Nail because the laborers did construction work and I guess maybe it was a rusty nail as a play on words? Who knows, but the name stuck and they've been slinging hash for lunch full time for many a decade now. I went in and the place was wall to wall people, some construction types, some in business suits, a very mixed crowd. The Rusty Nail is known for its homemade pork barbeque and fried fish sandwiches, neither of which floats my boat very much. The tables inside are all picnic style and the open beam ceiling makes the place very noisy. I hate eating in a noisy restaurant. Fortunately, Wanda had already arrived and was seated at a table out on the deck which is much quieter. Her Angela Davis/Black Panther costume had been decommissioned. Today she had her hair pulled back in a tight pony tail with some kind of rhinestone clip. She had on shimmering multi colored earrings which dangled almost to her shoulders, an orange peasant style top and aqua blue Capri pants with uncomfortable looking hot pink spiky sandal things. Just another day in the staid mortgage world. "Hey baby, I ordered us both some iced tea for a change and I made sure yours is the unsweetened kind. Don't make no sense to me, tea without no sugar, but hey to each his own, huh? Now I met with Davies and he's gonna…"

"I already know Wanda. You see I am coming from a crime scene." Her eyes bugged out and I filled her in on Hayes' body and what Detective Davies had told me. "Damn straight if we ain't got us another one Alex! Ain't that too much? You and me on another case."

"Ahh, Wanda the last time I checked, private investigator or detective were not boxes either us checked when filling out occupation forms. I sell real estate and you do home loans. Boring but necessary and hopefully lucrative."

Our teas arrived and Wanda ordered a pork barbeque sandwich, I grimaced at the menu and finally chose the children's menu grilled cheese, on rye with pickles, just to be grown up. Wanda took a pull on her tea, "Now we gotta brain storm this one and meet up with Percy and plan what we are gonna do. I'm thinking with Serenity's ex

211

now shot dead through the forehead, we in for a ride with this here. No doubt about it, I wouldn't be surprised if Serenity had him killed or maybe she's been off-ed too and ain't nobody found the body yet?"

Sigh, "Yes, inquiring minds do want to know Wanda. But that's what Detective Davies and his cop pals are going to do. That is their job and as I mentioned, our jobs are…"

She put her hand up, "Talk to the hand honey, I ain't even gonna hear this bunk. Nope, we got us a killer on the loose here and a missing bitch who happens to be your client. So let's just zip the lip, pop the cherry on top of the car, and get to work."

Thirty

Work turned out to be a two hour lunch with more speculating on Wanda's part. Then Percy called and wanted us both to come by his house. I left my car and piled into Wanda's and we went over to Percy's. Percy practically pounced on us when he opened his front door.

"Oh, I am glad you all are here, just leave your shoes there by the door," he said as he led us up the steps into his living room. He had his lap top opened on the mirrored coffee table and Hadley was perched on the edge of the stark white sofa. Percy swatted him down, "Now move Hadley, I want Wanda and Alex to sit here and take a look." He plopped in front the of the computer and we sat next to him, peering at the screen. "I went ahead and copied Serenity's entire computer files and her emails to my scan disk here. I thought we might want to preserve it, have a look through and see if we can figure out where she might be, get some clues." I let Percy know about Serenity's ex husband and that Detective Davies was going to stop by next door to file a missing person's report with Darla and Ronnie. Wanda said the police might take Serenity's computer with them then, so it was good Percy had copied everything. Percy was all a flutter about Serenity's ex and me finding the body. "Oh that is just too gross, you saw the dead body! My god, I wonder if she did have him killed? What if she's a killer on the lam? Why this would just be straight out of a made for TV movie, they'd call her the 'Serenity Killer.' What if she's out there lurking and waiting to kill more, oh my! Well it's a good thing I had Arnie take Kali out to her place today, I wouldn't want a killer coming back for her dog or something. Ohhh, just gives me the willies!" He probably hadn't been this excited since Ethan Allen came out with a non-traditional furniture line.

"Well, Percy it is important not to leap to conclusions. You know I hate Serenity but could she have had her ex killed? What would be the pay-off for her to do that? Her divorce was final, the settlement had been disbursed, she got the gym and they were both in agreement to sell the house and split the proceeds. Granted she did try to sell it without his knowledge or consent but she's so stupid that could have been an innocent mistake I suppose. So where is she and why is Hayes dead?"

Percy narrowed his eyes as he thought aloud, "You know I found Serenity's Will in her office and naturally I made a copy of it. Well I read it and originally she had everything going to Hayes if she passed away but then it was changed to Javier recently. But her interest in that house was always willed to Darla. So if Serenity has died, then Darla gets that house or at least Serenity's interest in it. I wonder who Hayes willed his interest in that house to?"

"Those are good questions Percy. And if you will excuse me I am going to call Doris Havlon and update her on these events. Per my listing, one of the sellers is now dead so is my listing still valid? She'll have to find out exactly what you are asking Percy." I stepped out on the patio area and called. I also left a voice mail for Todd Blund, my designated broker at Winterfrost to see his take on these events, although I doubted he would have an opinion, it's just all sell and make it happen somehow with him, no plan ahead and avoid problems. I could hear music coming from Serenity's yard. It was a fairly loud Shania Twain song. Country music blaring in Capitol Heights, that put a nice ironic twist on things. When I went back inside, Wanda was scrolling on Percy's laptop. "Humph, this woman gets something like two hundred emails every day, it's crazy. Nothing so far indicates she was going away or planning on killing nobody. Lots of emails in here about those drinks. She keep emailing Hayes telling him she needs more product for the drinks, seems very pissed. Looks like he finally told her to solve her product problem herself. He still claiming that he has an interest in those drinks' profits though and she does not sound real happy about that reminder. Must be from the looks of it, he got himself some legal rights to those drinks' profits in the divorce settlement. Ohh, in this email she whining to Javier about Hayes and the drink and Javier is telling her he'll make it all happen, the product will be good. But he's wanting himself a cut on them drinks' profits now, saying if he has to work and get involved in the drinks then he should be entitled to a share, especially since Hayes ain't doing nothing no more about the product. Humph."

Percy was bustling around in his open kitchen and set to work making a batch of slushy drinks. Again it was the monogrammed silver serving tray, pale yellow linen cocktail napkins this time, silver bowl of nuts and tongs, and a crystal pitcher full of margaritas. "Here, let's all go sit up on the pool deck now and relax. All this dead and missing people is just making me a wreck." He led the way out and up with Hadley's short little legs moving double time following in his wake. Up top, Percy set up the drinks on the round glass table and we sat in chairs around it and took in the view while sipping our drinks. "Oh thank the lord!" Percy exclaimed, "That damn hill-billy music is off. I am telling you Alex those two are going to destroy Serenity's house. I still can't really believe she is related to those slobs much less is the daughter and sister of them! Really, it's no wonder she never had them out to visit. They make Rosanne Barr look like June Cleaver in comparison. And I am telling you Alex, they are still smoking inside the house. Not that the tobacco stains will do any harm to the hideous wall colors. I seriously wonder if Serenity was adopted or something but she never mentioned that, so I suppose she is related. Look, they are out on the patio down there and there is a man with a badge. Alex, they are filing that missing person's report. You didn't say a peep about how hot the detective was, oh my lord look at him."

Oh Christ, not another one who has the hots for a man with a badge or wearing a uniform. "Humpf, move let me look down there Percy. Oh yeah, that's Davies down there. Ain't he just something to look at Percy? You oughta see him up close, got huge man titties on him and…"

"Enough!" I said. "Really, this is not the ninth grade girls lunch table. Yes, he is attractive but do you have to obsess on it?"

Wanda gave Percy a knowing look, "You hear that Percy? Our fudge ripple got himself a man crush going on but he don't even know it. Course when you swimming at both ends of the pond, I guess it get a little confusing." They smirked and I was ready to belt them both. I did not have the hots for Detective Davies and why Wanda could not get over the fact that bisexual people exist and be done with it is

216

beyond me. "See there Percy, right now he sittin' there thinking mean things. I can tell cause his eye brows twitch up a bit, see that?" I was getting ready to let my claws out and reply when my cell phone interrupted.

"This is RG with Cooper's Hawk Mortgage. I was just at TOTAL and one of the women there told me that Serenity is missing. This is not true, is it? I am one of her VIP clients and in her Winners Circle so I think I would know before anyone else if in fact Serenity was missing. They said that her groups were going to be covered by a sub this week, as she was away on important business. But then Eddie just got a missing person flyer over there with her on it."

Welcome relief, odd to associate that thought with RG, but so what. "Yes, RG I am afraid it is true. Serenity has been missing since Saturday and the police are actually taking a missing person's report from her mother and sister as we speak." With that, RG let out a wail and started blubbering. Eddie took the phone and said she was too upset to talk. I filled him in on what was happening and suggested he and RG might want to get some copies of the missing Serenity flyers and hand them out. He thanked me while RG's crying and wailing became very loud in the background, I suppose that was his cue to end the call.

I hung up and Wanda stood up, "Okay I think we all got to get on over next door, so we can make sure Davies be filing that report pronto. Plus, it'll give you a chance to see the man up close for yourself Percy. See if Alex don't blush when he's around that man." She let out a cackle and thus it was decided to go next door.

I rang the bell with Percy and Wanda practically crushing me. After a long pause, Ronnie waddled up to the front door and opened it. "Oh, it's you guys, come on in, we gots the cops out back. Ma' filing that report and all. We didn't realize she was still using ex hubby number three's last name, Silvano. That's a joke. Micky Silvano could be the one who offed her, he hates her so much. Don't know why she stopped at that last name but guess she liked it or got tired of changing 'em." This she said while exhaling a large plume of cigarette smoke. The house reeked of cigarettes and the dingy baby elephants had certainly made themselves at home in the kitchen/living room. It was covered with fast food containers and empty micro-waved plastic food containers. The sink was filled with dirty dishes, greasy hand prints were all over the refrigerator and stove. It appeared someone had fried up something really greasy, the crusty pan was left on the range next to an opened can of Crisco shortening. Naturally the TV was on and some home shopping channel was currently tuned in. The plank coffee table was now littered with empty Schlitz beer cans, half drunk two liter bottles of orange soda and some generic brand of Mountain Dew, a half eaten Little Debbie blob and Twinkie wrappers tossed all about. An open box of two thirds eaten Krispy Kreme jelly glazed doughnuts was perched on one arm of the enormous sofa. A dinner plate was overflowing with cigarette butts on the other arm of the sofa and the cushions were askew and had food crumbs all over their burgundy velvet fabric. A pair of dirty, once pink, socks lay on the kitchen bar counter top, along with plastic bags filled with junk food from some local mini mart. Well, at least they made themselves at home. A couple of rusted out cars on blocks added out back and used tires stacked up out front and they'd be completely in their nesting zone. When we walked out to the patio, I noticed neither Darla nor Ronnie appeared to have changed their grubby sweats much less taken a bath. Ewweeee, smelly, baby elephants.

Thirty-one

Darla signed the paperwork that Detective Davies had for the missing person's report. He listened and took notes as Percy filled him in on what he had learned. Ronnie gave a sarcastic laugh, "Sounds to me like Mona is up to her old scamming life." She looked up at Detective Davies and exhaled another cloud of smoke, "Yup, we done filled you in on what she's gone and done back in Gary and I wouldn't be none surprised if she and that Hav-yer guy was up to some kind of scam. Sounds to me like he might have been getting tired of Mona and her ways. Maybe he done offed her to shut her up? I can tell you fer sure that Mona ain't gonna walk away from no money and this she gots here going on is one serious cash cow. So I'm placing my bets Mona's been offed or maybe they done kidnapped her." Darla looked a bit sad and shook her head in agreement. "Damn Ma, look at the time! Is ya'll done with this here interviewing? We got ourselves some appointment TV to watch. Don't wanna rush this here or nothing but we already missed all our shows on Monday due to the travelin' and with all the stress, the TV is a great way to relax your mind." You mean you have a mind that is actively in use that needs to be relaxed?

"Nope, we are done here ladies and thank you for your time. I'll get this report filed right away and update you on anything we find. I gave you my card, so if you learn anything new please call me." Detective Davies stood up and the baby elephants led us inside. Once in, we showed ourselves out as Darla and Ronnie got the right channel tuned in, and started getting their foods nuked and unwrapped in preparation for a big night of TV. Outside I asked Pete if he thought it odd how Darla and Ronnie did not seem too concerned or really that helpful. He shook his head, "Well it is a bit strange but people react differently to stress and they are so estranged from Serenity and have such a bad history with her that their lack of enthusiasm could be a defensive reaction against dredging up past hurts. Anyway, I'm going to file this report and speak with Javier and the people at the gym. Now that we are officially on this case, I would appreciate if you all would put away your junior detective badges and leave the investigative work to us." I nodded in agreement while Wanda just "humpfed" quietly to herself and Percy twisted a green monogrammed handkerchief in his hands and lamented, "Oh my, who ever would have thought all of this and in Capitol Heights? I mean she is such a star and I never would have guessed that those people would be staying in her house much less related to her."

Wanda drove me back to my car and I went home to walk Clyde and then I had a quick condo showing for a new client. After that I went home and attempted to pay my bills and do the necessary accounting work, always a thrill. The next morning I was off to attend Sam and Richards' inspection and thankfully the Hoffmans were not at home while we were there. There was nothing of significance found in the inspection; the house had been superbly maintained. Therefore, with nothing to ask the sellers to fix, Sam and Richard signed the inspection response form, thus waiving the inspection contingency and now moving us along to the appraisal and then on to signing and closing. I spent time putting up and passing out some of the Serenity

221

flyers. Doris called and said she thought it would be best if I had Darla come in and sign the power of attorney for Serenity's listing. Since there was now a missing person's report she could put Darla down as having legal authority to sell the property. The Hayes end of things was not so clear. His Will would need to be located and go through probate and then they would have the appropriate person on that end sign for his ownership interest in the house. So right now, the listing was in limbo as I did not have sellers to review or sign any offers. I was inclined to temporarily take the listing off the market or cancel it. Doris thought if Darla signed that paperwork it would legally suffice. A listing cannot just be pulled without the written consent of the seller. So Darla could sign for that. The other seller, Hayes, was now deceased and no Will or ownership for his part of the house had been determined yet. I called Todd and filled him in. He thought the listing should just stay live and then if an offer came in we could try and figure it out, make it happen. This made no sense to me, how can you offer something for sale if the legal end of the sellers' side is not current or in alignment? Todd reluctantly agreed and said to have Darla sign the temporarily-off-the-market paperwork, remove the key box but keep the Winterfrost sign in the yard, "We want to keep that yard sign name exposure." is how he put it. I called Percy and had him email me the copy of Serenity's Will which I then forwarded to Doris. She would then contact the attorney who had prepared the Will and arrange to meet with Darla and get the activation of the power of attorney in place. She said she would let me know once this was accomplished and then I could meet with Darla and get her to sign the temporarily-off-the-market paperwork. Such a maze to go through.

Thirty-two

By the afternoon I had previewed seven new listings and shown another condo to my condo buyer. This one would not work out because the balcony was not wide enough to place a full size chaise lounge and outdoor furniture set on it. I tried to politely explain that most downtown condos do not come with balconies that are wide enough to accommodate a full size chaise lounge and outdoor furniture set, but that fell on deaf ears. I was taking Clyde for a walk along the rotting piers when my cell rang. It was Katie Katori from News Four. She was putting together a special segment for the local evening news about Serenity being an official missing person. She had spoken with the police and others and wanted to know what I knew and or what I had to add. I basically let her know I had nothing to add but I hoped Serenity would be found alive and well. I suppose that was mostly true, the alive part anyway. She tried to push for more details and to see if I had any additional information but I stone-walled. She then said she had heard that I was the person who discovered her ex husband's body. I declined again to comment. She sounded perturbed but years of kiss ass training kicked in and she ended on an artificially upbeat note, thanking me profusely for my time and telling me to tune in at 6:00 p.m. to watch her segment. She also gave me her personal contact number just in case I wanted to talk or thought of something else she should know. She had peaked my curiosity and since I do not own a television I called up Wanda to see if I could pop over and watch Katie's report. Wanda was up for it if I promised to bring Clyde. She decided she would invite Lexi and make it a dinner. She told me to bring a cake from Sasser's and be there at 5:45. Clyde and I diligently stopped by and visited with Daynia, I purchased a lemon something or other cake, sounded kind of summery to me.

We rolled up to Wanda's right on time, cake box in hand. Wanda's front door was now a vivid orange and today's music choice was the ever cheerful Amy Winehouse. Wanda greeted Clyde and took the cake box from me, "There's some slushy on the counter, put this cake on that green cake dish that's over my sink, I'm gonna get this here platter of chicken out to my grill. Lexi should be here any minute and let's pray she ain't bringing no food she done cooked up for us. I told her we had the bases all covered, but you know how she gets sometimes. Humpf, I'm telling you that potato salad of hers is just plain nasty."

"How are we barbequing on your deck Wanda? You haven't let anyone out there in some time."

"Yeah, well that Arnie done shored up the whole deck and it is all safe now. She gonna come back in a couple of weeks and add on a staircase down to the back yard from the deck for me. Now won't that be nice? No more going out the laundry porch side door to get back there. I'm gonna let this chicken slow cook out there on the grill, go ahead and turn on that TV so we are ready to see what that Katie Katori has to say."

I did and Lexi arrived, thankfully with no potato salad or other homemade goodies in hand. She tossed her green floppy hat on the counter, "Hey shark, sold any houses today? Pour me one of those and add some extra rum to mine. Damn I tell you those city art board shits are going to be the death of me Alex. I had the first phase meeting with them this afternoon to review the new installation I am putting in at the Muni building. They wanted to review once again the two design proposals I came up with. I thought they had decided on option two last month. Well, not so, now they voted to go with option one and that means I have to procure a lot more steel. They have no comprehension of how one gets the sculpting supplies, how long it takes to get everything lined up before you can actually start the work. They said they would prefer everything be completely finished by next spring so it can be officially unveiled in time to coincide with the city bond levy campaign. Such idiots, like an artist can just produce a major piece of art like that on their ridiculous money raising time line."

I was tempted to point out that those fund raising levees were in part what kept artists such as Lexi in municipal commissions, but I chose to keep my trap shut. Wanda came in from the deck, greeted Lexi and then turned up the sound on the kitchen's TV set. After an obnoxious local car dealership commercial they were back in the newsroom and there was Katie. The anchor introduced her as the *Clinton AM* anchor and said she was doing this special News Four exclusive report because of her personal connection to the story.

"That's right Chip, everyone knows me from the morning show but I have had to go back to my cub reporter days to personally cover this story and News Four exclusive report. Everyone who watches knows, that I am a huge fan of Clinton's Serenity and in fact she was just recently on our morning show, Chip. Well, as we'll see in my exclusive report, Serenity is now officially a missing person." She then turned her head to mime watching the taped report. The tape rolled and Katie was outside Serenity's house with Darla and Ronnie standing next to her. Apparently they still hadn't taken a bath or changed their grubby sweats. Katie asked who they were and if they had any idea of where Serenity might be, etc.… Darla shook her head no and Ronnie piped up, "No we don't know where she's at, heck we ain't even heard from her in more than a year. But the police got a report on her now and that's what brang Ma and me out here. If she's listening out there, Mona you need to get your butt back home and now, cause you is causing Ma a world of grief."

Katie appeared a bit taken aback then joined right in, "Yes, your mother does appear to be quite upset and only a mother can feel such a pain so deeply. Well, we are all concerned about Serenity and in fact there is going to be a vigil for her at her gym TOTAL tonight which I believe you ladies are planning on attending." The camera then did a cut to just Katie alone in front of Serenity's house as she did a story run down and filled those who were clueless in on exactly who Serenity is and that her ex-husband had been found shot to death just yesterday. Next, they were live in the studio again and Katie said they were going to go live to hear a report from Mandy Bowers who was at TOTAL. "Mandy, you are there live at the gym, what can you tell us?"

Mandy the ever perky brown haired twenty-something ace reporter was standing in the parking lot outside of TOTAL, "Yes Katie we are live here at TOTAL which as many viewers know is *the* gym for Clinton's powerful and elite. And as you reported Katie, the owner and growing celebrity Serenity is now officially missing. I have here live with me one of Serenity's top circle clients who was just on your *AM* show with Serenity last week. This is RG Boysun. RG can you tell me what this vigil is all about, I understand that you spearheaded this important event?"

There in her white men's suit was RG, her meaty paw clasping on to Mandy's hand held microphone, she cleared her throat and spoke up in her deep baritone, "Yes Mandy I am RG Boysun of Cooper's Hawk Mortgage and an exclusive VIP member of Serenity's Winner's Circle. I am a long time coaching client and personal friend of Serenity. I felt I had to set up this vigil in order to help get the word out and hopefully bring Serenity back to us. This is so out of character for her to just disappear, she's never ever missed a class or coaching session."

Mandy bobbed her head in agreement and then asked RG what the ribbon was on her suit's lapel, "Ohh, this the green ribbon symbol that I personally created to signify that Serenity is missing and that we need to find her."

"I see, and the gym's logo and name is in green, is that how you got this unique idea RG?"

"Ohh, yes this an original idea of mine that I just came up with and I wanted the green to represent the TOTAL logo. So everyone who is a gym member now has a green ribbon to wear and we are selling them here tonight at the vigil so the general public can wear them as well. We need everyone to know that Serenity is missing and this ribbon will help with that."

"You say the ribbons are on sale tonight here at the vigil and will that money raised go towards helping find Serenity?"

"Absolutely, my husband Eddie will be collecting the ribbon proceeds. I might also add, that I personally have pledged one hundred dollars of my own money as a reward for any tip that leads to us finding Serenity. And in addition to that generous reward that I personally am offering, I am also offering to the public to review for free their current home loan and see if a home equity line of credit is available for them to use. Anyone who opens a home equity line of credit with me in the next thirty days, I will personally contribute ten dollars to the find Serenity fund."

Mandy put on her care bear smile, "That is just so generous of you RG and I am sure all of Serenity's loved ones greatly appreciate your help. I understand that you have decided to have your cell phone line be the official find Serenity hot line and we are going to post that number on the screen now for our viewers. Anyone who wants to purchase a green ribbon or might have some information about Serenity can call the number below."

RG pulled the microphone back, pursing her thin lips, "Yes Mandy, we'll set them up with a ribbon, put them on a list to help us with our search for Serenity and of course they can leave a message there for me to review their current home loans. So they can help contribute to the missing Serenity fund by taking advantage of my generous loan review and home equity line of credit offer."

Mandy subtly jerked her microphone back and the camera zoomed in on her, "So Katie, there you have it, friends are jumping in and Clinton is coming together as a caring community to help locate one of its very own missing celebrity members. I should add that anyone with information about Serenity's where-abouts can also call the Clinton police department, their number is listed below. And a candlelight vigil for Serenity will be getting underway here at TOTAL tonight around 8:00 p.m. Once it is dark they will light candles here in the parking lot and of course they'll be passing out these missing flyers. They are going to be selling the green ribbons and have some drumming and singing to help boost everyone's spirits. As we go back to you Katie, I've asked the group that is already gathered here to give us a sampling of some of the singing they will be doing here later on this evening at the vigil, sort of taste if you will to get the public out here tonight." With that the camera panned to a small crowd which was mostly the ex girls hockey coaches in green sweats along with RG in white in the center and Eddie beating on a drum. There was a brief silence until RG realized the camera was focusing on them and then RG bellowed out "hit it" and they all began to sing to the tune of an old civil rights march ballad, "We shall find Serenity. We shall find Serenity , some—daaayyy. Deep in our hearts, we still believe...."

Back in the studio, Katie spoke, "That was Mandy Bowers reporting live from TOTAL. Chip, I know our viewers will want to get out there tonight and help support this important effort to locate Serenity. While we were listening to Mandy's touching and important report, we got a new development in this story! We are going to go live now with a News Four exclusive report from the Clinton Police Station with Chet Hamericks our live action reporter. Chet what can you tell us?"

"Yes, Katie and Chip, we just learned that the police have taken in one of the gym's co-owners a Javier Arnez for questioning. He is a popular instructor and coach there at TOTAL and reportedly was personally involved with Serenity. We have no official word on what the police are talking with him about but it could be significant that they are speaking with him now and at the station. We hope to know more about this important development and will report back to you as soon as we know more. Chip and Katie, back to you."

The camera panned in on Chip, a generic, graying news anchor, "Well that certainly is a developing story to watch out for that you have brought to us Katie, thank you. Next on news at six, we are going to get another report on that local nail salon that is allegedly spreading toenail fungus in our community and then our own Trent Zandy is going to be here to give us an exclusive run down on how our Clinton high school football teams' late summer trainings are going."

Riveting! Now I know why I never bothered to buy a new TV set when I moved into my current house or why I don't stay up late at night pining away because I am unable to watch the local news.

Lexi pointed the remote and turned off the TV. "Box of crap. Geesh, that RG sure promotes herself doesn't she? You two were not overdoing it when you described her to me, god!"

Wanda responded, "Ahh, humm. You got that one right Lexi. That ole man/woman don't miss a beat and she on the TV promoting them home equity line of credits. Damn, anyone in the biz knows that ain't no way to go, especially right now. What with the national home market starting to dip. I've never been a big fan of people taking out money on their houses, treating the house like some ATM. Don't make any sense, they spending all this money on trips and what not and acting like the equity line don't ever have to be paid back. Hell, there's people out there, probably like old RG there, who tell people not to worry 'bout paying them lines of credit back, because their house gonna sell for way more and cover it all when they sell. That's just crazy, no market just keeps on going up forever. I'm telling you this here is a time bomb just waiting to go off but nobody wants to hear that right now, no sir. Humpf. Here, let me go out and check on our chicken."

Thirty-three

After dinner, we sat around eating the lemon cake and Wanda let on to Lexi and me, officially, that she and the appliance salesman boyfriend were over. "Humpf, he's enough to just turn you off men. Telling me how much he love himself a full figure woman and how he love my cooking and carrying on about how mature and successful I am and then I go and hear tell that pig going out with some twenty-two year old, thin as rail, woman that also be selling in his showroom. Well I can tell you this, old skinny ain't gonna be cooking him nothing in her kitchen. Hell, she probably serve him one of them nasty Serenity power drinks and call it good. Damn fool that man is but least I got me a new kitchen!"

Lexi and I nodded. Then Lexi announced she had to get going and that she was stopping by the Wharf Rat to see if she could find Tony and increase her order of steel for the Muni project. Wanda perked up, "Oh, you know me and Alex should follow along behind you down there. We could see if Tony got any inside information about Serenity and her husband's killing." I tried to interject and protest but Wanda was on a roll, "Yeah, come on Alex let's get down there and see what we can find out, I'm gonna wrap the rest of this chicken up and put it in the fridge and then we can go. We'll take your car Alex and Clyde can stay here and keep an eye on my place. Don't let no ex in my house Clyde, just bite that pig's ass if he bother to show up pleading for mercy."

Down to Dock Street we went, following Lexi's aging yellow Bronco. We easily found curbside parking, as no one frequents this part of Clinton's forgotten waterfront. The red neon sign flickered a pale red hued *W*, the other neon letters had long ago burned out. In we went. The cement floors were as sticky as ever and my shoes made ripping sounds with each step. The jukebox was playing an old Frankie Valli and the Four Seasons song. They sounded way too cheerful and castrated for this crypt. Three run down old men were attempting a feeble game of pool underneath a single swinging light bulb and a fog of blue cigarette smoke. The fog of nicotine was prevelent, despite the fact that Clinton banned smoking indoors in public venues almost five years ago. One lone man sat at one of the rusty metal tables and appeared to be reading horse race results or some kind of gambling numbers. The large bar was empty. Leo the one eyed bar tender was parked by an ancient beige, key punch, cash register. The dusty gold flecked, spidery mirror behind him was hardly providing any reflection. A dingy gray dishcloth sat on the bar's counter top and as we sat down on dubious red vinyl stools, Leo the pirate made a weak attempt to swab the countertop. Lexi greeted him and ordered us three bottled beers, which he promptly slid down the bar's counter top. They only sell one kind of non-tap beer at the Wharf Rat and that is bottled Budweiser. Lexi insists on bottled beer only. She swears the bar glasses are never washed, just rubbed out with Leo's grubby dish rag and set back on the shelf; and this from Lexi, a notable slob herself. We were perched on our bar stools when behind us came a raspy, cigarette deep voice,

"Well, well, look what the cat dragged in here tonight Leo! We got company, it's Lexi right? And you are the real estate agent and the

234

hair/mortgage person I met here a while back? Damn it's good to see some life in here, hey Leo! Pour me another one son and empty my ash-tray, it's full!" Leo gave a grimace but slowly moved to pull down a bottle of Crème de Menthe and fill the empty shot glass on the bar top. He also tilted the aluminum ash tray and let the butts fall on the floor behind the bar. Now how's that for first class service? I'd love to take Percy here.

I turned to the side and sure enough there was Sandy, an unlit Kent cigarette between her overdrawn ruby red lips. Sandy has been a regular at the Wharf Rat at least since the early 1960s. She runs a tab and from what I can tell never misses a night, front and center at the Rat. She looks like a twin of Judy Garland circa right before her death. Sandy had on her usual pajama looking pants suit, this one with short sleeves to account for summertime I guess. Same swirling purple patterns though. Her pants suits look like vintage lounge wear circa 1968 and probably are that old. She flipped open her butane lighter and lit up her Kent, inhaling deeply and exhaling without removing the cigarette from her lips all the while talking, "So what brings you fellows down to our corner of the world tonight? You all are looking to talk to Tony I am sure, hell everybody that comes in here is! Not like it used to be, no sir-ee. This here was a respectable place." With that she let out a loud cackle and raspy smoker's cough. Lexi chatted up Sandy and let her know we were indeed looking for Tony. "Well, that's too bad for you folks. Tony has already been here and dashed. He's making his rounds tonight, got to hit all his places. But I know for a fact he was headed over to the new place he is helping to run. It's that old sportsman bar just shy of Laughton on Timber Lane. You know the one, the Hairy Beav?" We all gave Sandy blank looks. "Lord you kids don't get out much do ya? The Hairy Beav is a real old watering hole originally for the workers and sportsmen down that way. It's been under for a while now. But Tony and company helped reopen it, only now the Hairy Beav is different. That's where you are going to find Mr. Tony tonight, checking up on things out there."

With that, Lexi and Sandy started chatting about a mutual artist they both know who hangs out at the Rat from time to time. Wanda and I decided to take off and find the Hairy Beav. Well, in truth Wanda decided. I would have much preferred going back to her place and play games or just going home to bed. We drove from the Wharf Rat into the lower part of downtown, headed south from there, where we just skirted the edge of the no-name area where I live and then went north towards Laughton. Wanda is good with street names and had us on Timber Lane in no time. I go by visuals and street names are almost unknown to me. I know Timber Lane because it winds around the edge of Laughton and then heads out towards the green belt, where it is a beautiful forgotten drive, with old trees on each side, and a large tributary stream which feeds into Warner Sound. It eventually ducks under the interstate where it peters out on the outskirts of Clinton, sort of near Lexi's. It is by no means a good short cut as the road winds and meanders all over the place. It got its name because at one time timber was brought in and loaded onto waiting railroad cars on Timber Lane. Then the timber was taken by the railroad cars down to the loading docks and the ships below. It's been well over one hundred years since this has happened but Timber Lane is still here. I spotted a faded sign with a cartoon beaver and *Hairy Beav* was lit up in flickering blue neon, the "*er*" of beaver had burned out long ago I suppose. The graveled parking lot was about half way full. It was a one story red brick building probably originally built at the turn of the last century.

Wanda and I got out and approached the single entrance door. Just inside the black wooden door was an entry hall of sorts dimly lit by a single light bulb. The walls were all painted black and a black curtain kept us from the bar. A vacant stool was next to the entry door; apparently the bouncer was not on duty tonight. So in through the black curtain we walked. Once inside it was a fairly well lit room for a bar, with exposed brick walls, some old wooden booths, a medium sized wooden bar and two pool tables near the back. No gross sticky floors here. There were several large TV screens positioned throughout with various sports channels tuned in and some aging taxidermy heads of elk, bear, and antlers were tacked on the walls. Most of the patrons appeared to favor flannel shirts and had very short hair. I was just taking that in when a powerful hand clamped down on my arm.

"Okay fellow the shows over. OUT! Don't know how you got in past TJ but this is for womyn only!" I looked up and a very stout and scowling woman wearing a red flannel shirt with the sleeves ripped off and sporting tattoos down her sizable arms was glaring at me, her large nose ring glimmering in the light. I started to try and explain and managed to say we were looking for Tony but her grip tightened and she yelled into a little microphone clipped to her torn up flannel shirt,

"PK I need back up we've got an incident—there's a male on the premises. Repeat a MALE offender in the bar, over!" Instantly it was like the steel toe brigade descended on me and before I could say a word, a tall, gruff billy goat looking female, hoisted me over her shoulders and started to turn towards the door. Wanda let out a yelp and the stout one with the microphone, touched her arm, "He ain't hurt you or done nothing has he honey?"

Wanda pulled on my pant leg, "Hell no fool! He is with me! We here visiting to see Mr. Tony. Put that man down now, ya'll is something crazy!"

The stout one smirked and patted Wanda's arm, "Here my cup of mocha, come sit at the bar and we'll take care of this offender. I'm sure he didn't come with you, there's no need to be afraid. This is your first time here I bet. It took a lot of courage for you to come out here tonight now didn't it? This is a womyn's only place, no penis is allowed to corrupt our safe place. Here little sister," she said wrapping her arm around Wanda's shoulders, "let's get you a cold one, the Hairy Beav is an official safe place. No need for you to worry, you are among your sisters now. We have collectively reclaimed this former male pig, bar and subverted their perverted male paradigm. The Hairy Beav is now an official penis-free zone and a reclaimed safe space!" Wanda pulled herself away, "Oh no baby, I don't swim in no lady pond, no not me! Now him there, he be swimming on both sides the pond, but me I only swim in the man pool. The stout woman gave Wanda a knowing and leering grin, "Oh sure, that's what they all say 'till they've had one night with me!" she flexed her double jointed thumb in the air with great pride and flourish. Meanwhile, I was being carried out like a sack of potatoes when a deep baritone voice I recognized, yelled.

"HOLD IT PK! Stop where you are! That man is a personal friend of mine. You put him down NOW! These two are with me and that includes him, now put him down!" PK stopped, turned around, snorted a bit and then reluctantly slammed me down on the floor. Wanda leapt over to where I landed and helped me up. "Hell, we getting' out of this here crazy-ass lezzy bar! We can find Tony another time. Come on let's go."

RG quickly barged over, "No, no, no, there is no need to leave. I am a VIP here and the ladies here all know that my word goes. Isn't that right PK?" RG said glaring at PK, her white men's suit almost shining in the bar's dim lighting. PK responded by snorting, kicking her steel toed boot on the floor and gruffly pulling back the entry curtain and storming off. There was a brief silence then the bar noise resumed, conversations, pool balls clacking, a KD Lang song started up on the jukebox. "Here, come on over to my booth, I'll make sure you all get a nice drink. I am sorry the ladies here are so rude but I suppose some of them over-react for good reasons." RG led us over to a booth where she sat down and snapped her fingers, calling over a snarly bald waitress. She wore a black tank top, with metal clips pierced through where her shaved off eyebrows belonged. "Having?" She gruffly snarled, pen poised over her order tablet.

Wanda looked at me, and RG translated, "Oh Chris here wants to know what you would like to drink. I'll have another Pink Lady

Chris and you?" She said looking across the table at us. Wanda sputtered a bit then said, "Pina Colada" and I stammered, "I'll have a Coke please." Chris slapped her order pad shut and sneered at me, "A Coke, typical, fuck----ing male pig in action." And then she stomped off, her heavy steel toed boots probably leaving dents in the wooden floor boards.

RG sat up straight, fingering the green ribbon on her suit's lapel, "Did I hear you two are here to see Tony? Very odd you would know him but he is in the back right now going over some business with the manager. I am a partial investor here at the Hairy Beav, a VIP in on the ground floor. It was such a pity when Puss-n-Boots closed last year. The worst part was there was no longer any place I could watch the Lady Seadogs play their away games and all the other women's league sports teams that I follow. Boots was the only bar to carry the women's sports channels. So when this opportunity arose for me to help reformat this old bar into its current venue, well I jumped right on board. Now I have my very own VIP lounge here to unwind and watch my teams play. And of course, the ladies here are a big portion of my loan business so I needed to help out their community too." She pointed at the TV screen mounted above our booth which had women's roller derby playing, "See there, the Rabid Rats are totally acing the Dirt City Ladies."

Snarly returned, putting cocktail napkins down in front of RG and Wanda, carefully placing RG's Pink Lady down and going into a major Pepe Le Pew routine wiping down Wanda's glass, arranging the umbrella just so and delicately placing her Pina Colada on the cocktail napkin, "For the *new* lady." She said in a courting lilt, her metal eyebrow things going up like Groucho Marx. Then she slammed an unopened, warm Coke can down in front of me, glared and stomped off. My, I felt so welcome and at home. I couldn't wait to find a guitar and sing some community building, solidarity songs about bisexual and lesbian togetherness. RG's eyes grew narrow and her thin lips pursed into almost non-existence as her face grew red, she put her fingers up to her thin lips and let out an enormously loud whistle.

"Chris!" She yelled out causing the entire bar to stop. "Bring a glass of ice and cocktail napkin over here right now!" There was a commotion at the bar and Chris reluctantly brought over the glass of ice and set a napkin down in the middle of the table. RG grew redder, "Open that can and pour that Coke and get a swizzle stick for the glass along with a lime wedge. You get this done right now and with a smile on your face or you can just leave right now, do you HEAR me?" RG looked like she was going to literally explode. I tried to murmur it is okay or something but RG just stared at Chris and the bar like Joan Crawford with a wire coat hanger in hand. Chris rushed off for the swizzle stick and lime wedge, the bar tender came over as well, pouring my Coke while profusely apologizing to RG. "Don't you apologize to me, you apologize to my guests here and this better not EVER happen again. RG is definitely NOT happy! Do you hear me, Reece?!" The short haired, bar tender gave quick apologies to me and Wanda and wiped off the table, major ass kissing. I suppose RG invested quite a bit in this delightful and welcoming lady love venue. Just don't bother stopping by if you happen to have a penis hanging between your legs.

RG filled us in on how upset she was about Serenity's missing status. How worried she was about the gym, her groups. Wanda let her know we were out looking into things, trying to find her. RG then mentioned her interview on News Four earlier and told us the vigil had been a great success, "We sold at least two hundred ribbons, I have Eddie tallying up a final count as I speak." Then RG nodded and said it looked like Tony was finished with his meeting in back with the bar's manager, she pointed where we should go to find him. Wanda and I walked past the bar and pool tables, heading into the narrow hall where the restrooms were and an open office door at the back. Along the way, Wanda caught approving and leering glances from various bar patrons. I got snarls, glares and one patron hit her fist in her palm as if she couldn't wait to kick my ass into next week. I felt like a cat walking down a row of caged dogs at the animal shelter. I noted the men's room door had been removed and the urinal now had a large fern growing in it. The women's rest room had a door but a new sign read, "Womyn." A fluorescent light shined from the partly opened office door into the dimly lit, dark red hallway. I rapped lightly and in we went. Tony was sitting behind an ancient steel desk, looking over what appeared to be accounting spreadsheets. His burning cigar was parked in an ancient ruby red glass ash-tray which probably weighed ten pounds or more.

"Whoa, if it ain't my two P.I.'s coming ta visit wid me! Youze guys get out to some of the strangest places. I wouldn't expect to meet up with youze two in this here bar. I knows youze a fairy Alex and hey youze know my brother in Miami, the fairy I told you about before?

He's gonna be visiting Clinton soon, so's I'll make sure youze two get set up, ya know what I mean? But youze, Wanda ain't it? What is youze doing here? Youze don't strike me as the type who dates lady lumberjacks."

Wanda looked taken aback, "Oh hell no, not me Mr. Tony. I already done told them women out there that I don't swim in no lady pond." Wanda then proceeded to fill Tony in on what was going on and why we were there. She let him know about my listing, Serenity missing, her ex-husband's death, all the while he leaned back in his swivel chair puffing on his cigar.

"Youze two guys sure end up in some of the strangest situations now don't cha? Youze know from the last time when we helped each other out, I'm always happy to help along these investigations youze do in my own quiet way. Youze helped me out wid the computer last time and kept me outta the whole law part of that situation and as youze know I appreciated that. So's here's what I can tell youze about what I do know about this here. First, the cops ain't gonna find nothing with that dead husband of hers. That was professional all the way, no one's gonna get a rap for that. Nows I didn't have nothing to do with that man's death, he wasn't in my business if you know what I mean. I do knows he was stepping on some big toes in the narcotics end of things. He shudda known better. Youze can see, those folks put an end to things that don't go their way. Now the Serenity chick, I don't know nothing about where she is. I heard about her missing and her gym but that's it. I do know her boyfriend has been asking around, making some contacts to try and get himself set up in well let's say a line of some illegal substances. He actually met wid me and tried to get me to help him out. I told him I don't handle that line of things, the drugs is not my bag or business. Everyone seems to think big Tony here is into everything just because I run me some clubs and all but I stay out of the street drug line of work. This sure seemed to surprise that Jav guy but so be it."

I politely cut in and asked what kind of drugs Javier was trying to procure. Tony puffed and smiled, "Youze don't miss a beat. Well I'll tell youze cause youze helped me out but I ain't telling this to nobody else so youze didn't hear nothing by me. That Jav was trying to get a good source of cocaine and amphetamine, said he had to have it for that woman's drinks. I don't know about all that but I do know her ex was running some serious coke and amps through his shell biz and he crossed his source one too many times. I guess the Jav guy is trying to take over now that the ex hubby is dead. But that Serenity chick, I don't know nothing 'bout where she is now. I know she has a real history of running in the drug circles here and her whole gym there was a front when it first started. Then it took off and she made herself into a celebrity. It all went to her head, she started to think she was the real thing, all legit, ya know? Could be she hired out to have her ex offed, could be somebody has offed her along with the ex, who knows? Only thing I do know is her boyfriend is under the police microscope now and it don't look good for him, now does it?"

With that Tony ended our meeting, stood up and showed us to the door. Wanda led the way back to RG's booth. "Thank you for the drinks, we had our meeting with Tony, so we on our way now."

Wanda said. RG looked up from the TV monitor, "You have to leave already? You could stay here and unwind with me, I can get us another round." We deferred. "Okay then, here let me call Eddie real quick and have him set you two up with some green ribbons." While dialing she whistled for Chris and ordered a Sprite. "E-eeeee, I'm sending Alex and Wanda out with a drink for you and I want you to set them up with ribbons. What? No Eddie, Sprite. No! I don't want to hear another word about it, you know you get too animated when you have any caffeine; you are having a Sprite period. Huh? Look, I'll be out there when I'm done. You sit there and enjoy your drink, get those tallies completed. You know you are not allowed in the bar Eddie, we've been through this before. I don't care if you are tired, I have another derby round to watch. You can nap in the car until I'm ready to leave." With that she clicked off her cell phone. Chris put a glass of Sprite on the table. "Here, take that Eddie. He's in the rear of the parking lot, under the street lamp, in my beautiful white Escalade pickup which is hard to miss."

Out we went with Eddie's Sprite. I could practically feel the collective steel toe boot kicking my ass out the door. We found RG's pickup and Eddie opened the driver's door, there was a side step thing attached to the running side board to help him down to the ground. I noted a phone book on the driver's seat, I suppose it was to help Eddie see above the steering wheel. I handed him his Sprite and he thanked me. He had two ribbons in his little hand and said it would be twenty bucks each. Wanda balked, "Twenty dollars for a small piece of green ribbon and a safety pin? Have you lost yo' mind? I ain't paying

245

nothing for that there. No ribbon gonna find Serenity no how. What you all doing with that ribbon money anyway?"

Eddie became very nervous and stammered then he pleaded with us to buy the ribbons, "If you don't, when RG gets out here and checks the tallies she's gonna know you two didn't pay and she'll blame me! Please, you have to do this just for me, you have no idea how mean she can...."

I opened my wallet and handed two twenties to Eddie, "Here enjoy your Sprite and hopefully you'll be heading home soon." I really wanted to say here's a spouse abuse hotline card, give it a call.

Thirty-four

The next day, Wanda and I jumped into motion. We decided she would contact Detective Davies and fill him in about the possible drugs in the Power Up Serenity drinks and I would take a sample of the drink powder to Norman who could analyze it and see what he found. I figured Norman could probably make it happen faster than the police were going to be able to. I dropped off sample powders to Norman at Clinton Chem Labs and he was very excited to test them. "It's ahh, important though that I maintain a clinical neutral stance when evaluating this substance, you do understand that don't you Alex?" I assured him I did but let him know I'd be most appreciative if he could run his tests as quickly as possible as the public's health could potentially be at stake. I told him to look for any substances which are energizing to the human system.

On my way through town, I stopped at Serenity's house and Darla signed as power of attorney to temporarily suspend the listing. I then went by the Winterfrost office to drop off a copy of the temporarily-off-the-market paperwork for Serenity's house. Probably best, seeing how it did not appear Serenity was going to reemerge anytime soon and the house had become an absolute burgundy, smoke filled, pig sty. I parked my aging clunker between two enormous, shiny SUV's and went in the Viper Pit, a.k.a. Winterfrost. Inside was the usual klatch of non-selling agents who hang around the coffee pot and complain all day. Todd was all a flutter when I handed him the paperwork. "Have you heard Alex? There is a very good chance we are going to have Tiger Conley join our office! Can you believe it?" I nodded and smiled agreeably, not having the faintest idea who in the hell he was talking about. I left him sputtering with glee and was walking out when who should I smell? Today's ensemble was flaming red from head to toe; red pointy bitch boots, flared red pants and a silk red blouse with gold buttons. However, Share appeared to be a bit off her game today. She saw me and grasped my arm, all her various bracelets clanking away. "Well, how's it going with you today Alex? I heard you have to take your little Serenity listing off the market. Any word on where the owner is yet? You know I had my strong doubts about her when I interviewed her for that listing, my sixth sense said no. That's why I refused to list it." Yeah right, like you refused a listing Stinky, not quite. "Anyhow, looks like it didn't work out for you. Well, at least the Winterfrost name got some good exposure.

Did Todd tell you who might be coming to our office? I personally cannot see that remotely working out, even if it is true which I strongly doubt." She pulled out an atomizer from her red purse and proceeded to spray more stink in her freckled tit valley. "Well you know how this biz goes, newbies every other day, right Alex? I mean Todd does not have another anchor and mainstay agent like myself, now does he? I practically put Winterfrost on the map single handedly, not that I am one to brag but as everyone knows I do have a following." She put her atomizer away, pulled at her spiky orange hair with her blood red talons, trying to make it somehow reach new heights. "Anyhow, it's been great catching up with you, I'm sure your little owner is going to turn up one way or another. I've got to get cracking, lots of things to do for clients and what not. We'll just have to wait until Todd comes to his senses about that whole Tiger rumor thing, huh?" With that the red devil hoofed off, her vapor trail lingering strong and wide in her wake. What the hell had she just babbled to me about? It was over my head. However, something sure yanked Stinky's chain because for Share Shelton, that was an unusually friendly and collegiate "conversation." Just then my phone let out its boring ring tone and I picked up. It was Wanda.

"I just let Davies know about the drink tip we got. You know that man is starting to appreciate us Alex. He actually wondered if there were some way we could maybe get it tested because we can probably get it done faster than he can. He is putting in the request and doing the paperwork but he says it will take a while for them to get to it. I told him not to worry because we have our very own chemist looking into the matter as we speak. I think he's starting to realize that we are force to be recognized and…"

"And Wanda, we are not private investigators or detectives so just stop the spin and whirl right there. Norman is looking at it and says he'll call me as soon as he knows anything. What did Davies have to say about the other tips Tony gave us?"

"Oh, they already know that was a professional hit her ex took. Seems to me like they were already fishing around his business maybe and checking out what was up over there at Wealth Creation Advisors and Imports. Not that he told me that mind you. Don't sound like they plan to try and even solve that murder. But they are still questioning Javier about things and it doesn't sound like they have any information or word on Serenity at all. It's a good thing you took that listing off, cause I'm thinking she ain't gonna be found alive. I don't think they believe that either. Sounds like they are trying to figure out if boyfriend had anything to do with the ex's hit and her disappearance. I think they are betting on pinning things on him." Wanda and I chatted a bit more and then I had to go show another condo to my buyer that refuses to be realistic. This time the condo had a balcony large enough to accommodate a chaise lounge and table and chairs but now the cabinets in the open kitchen were not big enough. This from someone who does not appear to cook at home. Also, I pointed out it would be very easy to install more cabinets on the large open wall next to the kitchen, but that was not acceptable. I spent the rest of the day previewing and running errands.

The next day, I worked in my back yard and was getting closer to completing a fountain of sorts but still no gushing Valium inducing geyser, so more work to do. Around 2:00 p.m. I had a call from Norman. He told me that the sample powders I had provided him definitely contained cocaine and various amphetamines in them. In fact, he suggested re-running other samples and alerting the FDA and police. Norman said these powders would definitely affect anyone who consumed them, i.e. providing a lot of energy, suppressing their appetite. Ah-ha, the secret of the Power Up Serenity drinks and Serenity's loyal groups might lie in her laced protein powders! I quickly called Detective Davies and put him in touch with Norman. He said he would be contacting the county health department and the local FDA contact. He would request all Power Up Serenity drinks be voluntarily removed immediately from any local stores selling them until conclusive tests were run again and results were final. And that is exactly what happened. By early evening I had two calls from Katie Katori at News Four requesting to speak with me. The word had gotten out very quickly. I drove over with Clyde to Wanda's house to watch the local news.

Upon my arrival, I had a call from RG. "I just went by TOTAL and they tell me all the Power Up Serenity drinks have been voluntarily recalled until further notice and testing. What do you know about this? How can this happen without Serenity's approval? Do you know where I can send Eddie to get some extra powder drinks until this blows over? I have to keep up with Serenity's daily regime or I might not keep my place in the Winner's Circle. The gym is in complete chaos, no one knows anything over there. And they say the police are still questioning Javier, so no one is on site and officially in charge. This is all most unprofessional and I'd like to know what they think they are doing messing with Serenity's drinks and the gym and why they have not found her yet?" I filled RG in on what I did know and told her I could not help her with any additional drink powder. She sounded very annoyed and edgy. Coming down off her uppers I suppose? Wanda had her kitchen TV tuned to News Four and was cooking what smelled like a tasty spaghetti and meatball dinner. I let Clyde dance with her and then he took off to sack out on the brown leather sofa in her living room. I suppose the summer heat was making him lazy this evening. Wanda turned the TV volume up when they came back from commercial and there was our good friend and ace reporter, Katie Katori. She appeared a bit edgy as well, perhaps her drink source was drying up too or the thought of no Power Up Serenity was unhinging her?

Another graying and generic news anchor, Kent, introduced her, "Thanks Kent. I am back here tonight to do a special News Four exclusive follow up report on the missing Serenity story. I spoke with the police this afternoon and they still have no clear leads in the missing case of TOTAL's owner, Serenity. Police say they are still actively questioning her business partner and alleged boyfriend Javier Arnez. Police are also now stating he is an official person of interest in this case. They also have stated they believe Serenity's ex-husband's death earlier this week that of Hayes Brighton was a murder and was a professional execution, though they have no leads in that case. Some are speculating that Serenity's disappearance and the murder of her ex-husband and co-founder of TOTAL may have a link to her current business partner, Javier Arnez.

In a very odd twist, today the police got reports that the locally popular protein powder drinks called Power Up Serenity sold exclusively by Serenity's gym TOTAL have been voluntarily recalled until further testing can be done and the FDA can investigate. Apparently traces of cocaine and amphetamines have been found in the powders. Police have asked any local merchants who may be selling these powder drinks to remove them from their shelves immediately as there could be a public safety risk. News Four determined that the drinks thus far have been sold exclusively at TOTAL and no other local merchants appear to have sold the drinks. However, starting next month the drinks were set to go national and distributers had planned to launch and sell the protein powder drinks at various health food venues and gyms across the country. Those plans are now obviously on hold now, pending more investigation. Meanwhile, the police and local health department authorities have advised any local resident who may have any of the following Power Up Serenity protein drinks in their possession to discard them immediately. They say they should not be consumed under any circumstances until definitive testing is completed by the FDA and other authorities. Now here on your screen are the names of the Power Up Serenity drinks that are being voluntarily recalled. As everyone already knows Kent, I have been huge fan of Serenity and of these Power Up Serenity drinks. I personally discarded my stock of Power Up Serenity drinks and will be waiting to hear more. In this next report, you will see what local physicians have to say about the possible health risks persons such as myself may have run by consuming such drinks laced with the alleged substances found in them."

They then cut to her physician report. Wanda stirred the sauce pot, "See that's how Serenity got all them skinny people and wanna be skinnies to join her groups and gym. Bitch done drugged 'em plain and simple. Alex, we gotta figure out who has offed her, cause it's clear she ain't coming home and I don't think she's run. No money is missing and she ain't the type to flee without the money with her."

After the doctor interview, Katie was back and said she'd spoken exclusively with Serenity's mother and sister and they cut to that report. There on Serenity's ocean liner sized burgundy sofa were

Darla and Ronnie. They still appeared to have on the exact same clothes as when I first met them, even grungier now. Katie was asking them about the latest developments; Darla just shook her head in sadness and showed no real surprise. Ronnie responded, "Well Katie you can just see for yerself by this here what Mona is all about. I already done told you about what she did to Ma here several years back, so this drug stuff and her drinks, it all makes complete sense. What don't make no sense is that none of the money is missing from her accounts and I can assure you Mona wouldn't be leaving town without the cash." Katie tilted her head a bit to appear concerned and asked Darla if she agreed with Ronnie and she did. She then asked about Hayes' murder and Ronnie said, "Ya know I wouldn't put nothing past Mona, not even murder. I can tell you if she thought her ex was in her way, then she'd do whatever it took to get rid of that problem." Katie acted astonished and asked Ronnie to restate what she'd just said and Ronnie repeated her accusation. "You can see here, from the family of Serenity that there are some very strong questions and doubts about why and how she is missing and most importantly who murdered her ex-husband and former business partner, Hayes Brighton." Back in the studio Katie and Kent bantered back and forth about the interview and Kent then assured everyone that News Four would be staying on top of this breaking story and Katie would keep everyone up-to-date on any new developments.

Then, it was time to plug the next segment, the lighter, kittens and bunnies, feel good side of the "news." The daily story that makes everyone try and think humans aren't a lost cause after all. Tonight's feel good segment was a story about a local third grader Timmy Todden who was apparently walking across the state to raise awareness and funds for hamsters, or some such, with mental disabilities. I better call the cable company now and have a TV and cable installed immediately in my home.

Thirty-five

Wanda and I ate the spaghetti and meatballs, Clyde naturally got his own plate with meatballs, much to my disapproval. He gave me a smug look in response to my protestations to Wanda. My cell had rung once but I was ignoring it, nothing interrupts my dinner. Wanda's cell let out her "Respect" jingle and she picked up right away. I suppose that is the sign of a true type A success story. Between bites she let me know it was our friend Percy. "Ahhum, humpf, yep. Okay then baby, we'll come on over soon as we done eating our dinner." She hung up. "Percy say he found some interesting emails in Serenity's mailbox that he copied. He wants us to come on over and have a look, says he's making us some slushies and has an avocado dip he wants us to taste." I really didn't want to go to Percy's house but the intrigue of what was in Serenity's emails got the better of me. So after dinner, with Clyde in tow, off we went in my car.

We pulled up just as it was beginning to get dark. Percy must have a sixth sense as to when guests or visitors are approaching because once again there he was right at the front door waiting for us, telling us to remove our shoes. He ohhed and ahhed over Clyde who gave Percy an enormous and sloppy lick right up his fat face. Out came the monogrammed hanky as he sputtered and tried not to let on that Clyde had pissed him off. Instead Percy went into dog baby talk (which in my opinion is even more nauseating than human baby talk), "Ohhhh, wee have our widdle friend Clyde here Hadley. Hadley wadley has a playmate. Why your guest is here too Mr. Hadley! Are you gonna let him pway wid your widdle toys Hadley?" Hadley promptly picked up the nearest toy and headed out for the patio. This peeved Percy, "Now you get right back in here Hadley! NOW! You share your toys you spoiled little boo!" He caught up with Hadley and wrenched the blue plastic toy from his jaws bringing it back inside to Clyde and presenting it to him with great fanfare. Clyde promptly sniffed it, and looked up to me as if to say, *what the hell is this? I don't play with toys.* This Percy ignored as he bustled into the open kitchen and turned his blender on high. He was making us Pina Coladas and had out his silver monogrammed serving tray and yet another serving pitcher. This one appeared to be antique amethyst colored glass, quite nice actually. Turquoise linen napkins and crystal daiquiri glasses were set out on the tray. Off Percy bustled to the patio seating area with the tray in hand. He had his laptop set up on the coffee table along with a crystal bowl full of avocado dip and a sliver bowl with chips. There was a stack of printed out pages as well.

He poured our drinks and then handed Wanda the print outs. "Here take a look at these emails that I found. I have to say I am just absolutely blown away with our Miss Serenity. First, I never would have imagined she'd be remotely related to the creatures who are now inhabiting and wrecking her house next door. I mean really, all we need next are some confederate flags and NASCAR stickers out front and those two will be right at home. Serenity's décor was one thing but those two, aghh! Adele would just die, simply die of disgust knowing those cretins are occupying HER house! Really, *who* is actually *from* Gary, Indiana, just imagine!" He said while plumping himself up on the white canvas sofa cushions and wiping his brow with a pale yellow monogrammed handkerchief. I could see Percy's point but then *who* is from eastern blue blood stock, *really*!

Wanda was already reading the second print out and sipping her drink. "Humph, you done hit the gold mine Percy! Damn, check this out, that bitch actually almost spelling it out to this here person how she wants her ex killed. What fool hires a hit man and spells it out in writing? Guess we all know who that fool is now! Here she's talking about making the cash payment, down by that interstate rest stop south of Lexi's. They telling her it's best not to write this all out but the hell if she's listening! Saying she prefers they use a gun and be quick. Like she the execution pro. Damn that woman is seriously insane!"

I asked how easy these emails were to find and Percy said they had been set aside in her email program under a file folder entitled *tasks*. "I guess she thought putting them in a separate file would keep it all secret and safe." Percy said, "But if this does show she had her ex killed then where is she now? No money has been removed or moved in any of her known accounts. Do you think Javier could have been in on this or found out about it and had her taken out? There wouldn't be any benefit to him if she did because her Will doesn't leave him anything."

Wanda and I nodded in agreement and I reviewed the emails. I pondered out loud, "There is no real motive for Javier to get rid of Serenity. She really is his meal ticket; he's not the sharpest tack on the board. Sure he's got looks and girls galore but I don't think he has the necessary mental power to plan something so elaborate and get rid of Serenity. Besides, if he did he was too stupid to get her Will changed first, so getting rid of her would do him no good in terms of the business and money. Also, Serenity was the force behind everything, she was the rising media star not him. Makes no sense for Javier to want Serenity gone. From these emails it doesn't appear he had a clue she was putting out a contract on her ex. I am guessing she wanted Hayes out of the picture and she was pissed because Hayes was no longer supplying a steady stream of drugs to lace her protein drinks with. I bet Serenity put boy toy up to securing some uppers on the street to put in the Power Up Serenity drinks. She was probably stupid enough to think Javier could handle that part of the biz and she could get Hayes completely out of the picture and have it all for herself. Sounds plausible, doesn't it? Especially in light of how narcissistic and selfish she is. But even with this theory, where is Serenity?"

Wanda took another sip, "Well I guess you know who we need to speed dial now? Percy you gonna be able to control yo'self when that Detective Davies shows up? Humph, I tell you what, I'll just let you have him Percy. Me, I'm just about off men for now. Just had enough, well not enough to go swimming with the ladies Alex and I met last night, but enough to rest my dawgs and focus on my career. Yeah, that's what I'm gonna do now is just focus on my businesses." I called Davies and left a message about what we'd found and then Wanda and I filled Percy in on last night's fun at the Hairy Beav.

Thirty-six

The next day Wanda and I arranged to go and meet Detective Davies and provided him with Serenity's emails. He agreed, off the record, it looked like she was the one responsible for having her ex husband killed. We mentioned our theory on Javier and that we didn't think he had the smarts to pull off a murder and apparently had nothing to gain by doing so. Davies concurred, again off the record, and said they'd take the information we provided and go from there. "I guess I have to thank you two again, unofficially, for helping with this on-going investigation. We obviously would have discovered these emails but with budget constraints it is great you were able to help speed this along and speed along the Power Up Serenity drinks test results. Our labs are confirming what your client Norman found. However, I will say again that I wish you two would stop this junior detecting hobby."

Wanda looked peeved with that comment, "Ah-hum is that right? Well let me just remind you that we are acting like responsible citizens and helping out the po-po with their investigation. Last I checked, I didn't see me or Alex going all media and claiming credit for none of this. So I think you should thank us unofficially and keep your fat mouth shut Davies." He muttered something like *always a charm* and we saw ourselves out of the Clinton police department's administrative building. Outside, Wanda grew even more irate when she discovered Miss Emerald had a parking ticket. "Damn, I come all the way down here to help out the fool po-po's and they can't thank me properly and then have to add this here ticket for my troubles. I tell you, this calls for a big lunch with a pitcher of slushy. After lunch at Barnacles, I went off to preview some listings and to show the reluctant condo buyer yet another new listing that apparently had a wide balcony and lots of kitchen storage. This too failed because now the entry hall was too long and narrow. I tried to politely bring up my diatribe about how when you purchase a place it is about compromise, not everyone gets every single item on their wish list, even those with millions to spend have to compromise on certain things. This fell on deaf ears. I was contemplating calling it quits, then I looked at my current balance on the ATM receipt and decided patience was in fact still a virtue.

The sun was out in full force and it was a perfect late summer afternoon, boats bobbing all around in Warner Sound. I took Clyde out for a walk through the green belt and when I returned Wanda phoned. "Hey, I'm over here at Percy's and we having us a pool party. Get your bony ass in a swim suit and come on over baby, this pool top patio here is the bomb!" I was a bit taken aback. Since when did Wanda go off and "party" with Percy? When did he become part of her inner circle? I felt a tinge of jealousy; I thought I was Wanda's best cohort? My inner three year old was way pissed, she'd gone to play in Percy's sandbox without telling me first, how dare she! I did come around and decided I'd go over to Percy's house. I was not however, going to don a bathing suit and swim. I don't like wearing next to nothing around pervs-on-the-make like Percy and swimming in his little terrace top pool sort of grossed me out. Percy perv germs, pool slime, eewww! I put on cut-off khaki shorts, an old, blue, Clorox stained, polo shirt and my Jesus sandals and off I went. I parked on

the street, noting that Serenity's little yard patch out front needed
watering, it was brown and her white Range Rover needed a wash and
one hub cap was missing. Darla and Ronnie must really be settling in.
I went down the side path that leads to Percy's front door and there
was Wanda waiting at the front door, decked out in a brown with pink
trim, one-piece swim suit. Her head was covered in a blue and white
flowered old lady's swimming cap. "How did you know I was here?" I
asked as she led the way inside.

"I'm psychic. No, just wait 'till you see what Percy has up here
on his tree-top swimming deck Alex! It is too much. I could hear the
soul satellite station piping in Marvin Gaye's "Sexual Healing"
throughout the house, in and out of doors. We went out on the patio
and went up the stone stairs. On top, Percy was splayed out on a float
in his pool. He looked like a massive white blob wearing a table cloth
sized green paisley print swim suit. Well, at least he had the good sense
not to wear a Speedo; the suit far too many over-middle aged, pot-
bellied, trolls seem to favor. "Percy, Alex wants to know how I knew
he was there." Wanda said as she led me around the pool deck.
"Check this out Alex, Percy has himself a state-of-the-art video
monitoring system. Look at this thing it pops up out of that planter
just like the privacy screens. Makes me feel like I'm visiting James
Bond." Wanda was pointing to a color TV monitor that appeared to
run six video feeds of various parts of Percy's house, one of which was
the front walk and front door. So all along, Percy had been watching
his monitor and he knew when someone arrived and started to walk up

his front walk. Clever and paranoid. Then I noticed one of the feeds appeared to be Serenity's back yard, a wide angle shot.

"Percy, you have had this video feed running all the time I presume. Why do you have a feed on Serenity's back yard?" I asked.

Percy chuckled and paddled over to the side of the pool, "Oh my, well you might as well know. I had that feed installed when Serenity and her ex moved in. I told you Hayes had a chest to die for and well, I just let this puppy run and sure enough I caught him many times out back without his shirt on. Too delicious but I guess it also serves as security too. I have all sides of the house on a feed, I just had the feed for that side put on a wider lens. I didn't want to miss a second of that man when he was out and about!" Well there it was, he was officially a perv. "Percy the Perv" is the correct description. Talk about needing a life, just pathetic in my book. Oh well. Then it hit me, "Percy, how long do you keep the feed tapes before they erase?"

Percy lolled back on his float, "Well, let's see they last for ten days and then auto erase, so that one is due to erase well, tonight. Why? You don't think Hayes is on there anymore? Alex, he moved out ages ago and I haven't caught him or anything remotely hunky on my feeds in months. It's been dreadful."

"Ah, yeah, I'm sure it has been dreadful Percy. No, I am asking because Serenity went missing six days ago. We should at least look at her back yard feed to see if anything unusual occurred. Did you tell the police about this? Have they reviewed this feed?"

Percy sat up, "You know I didn't even mention this to the police and I actually forgot all about it. Why Alex you are right on

263

target. Here help me out, we should go inside and review that feed from last Saturday and see if anything is there!" He starting to flail with excitement and promptly fell off the float into the water. Finally he was pool side and had put on a flowing red terrycloth robe. He led Wanda and me up the ramp to his bedroom balcony. Inside, he led us through his bedroom, which was a white and cyan blue decorator's masterpiece if I do say so. It looked like no one had ever slept in it, much less lived there.

Into a small room off the upstairs hall we went. It looked like a security fortress. Video monitors covered the small end wall, electronic boxes with lights, a little desk top with a computer monitor and keyboard below. All part of Percy's personal security surveillance empire. He cued up the monitor for Serenity's back yard and punched the key board, dialing up last Saturday. He started in the wee morning hours and then selected some kind of fast forward time lapse whereby half hours passed by with main frame shots at a fairly rapid pace. Wanda and I stood over as Percy sat at the keyboard and the shots of Serenity's backyard last Saturday advanced. There was Kali out back, running wild all over the yard, the frames making her appearing to skip and hop in rapid succession. It was hilarious when she was digging in the back, the way her new hole appeared almost immediately. Then late in the morning, there was Serenity in her barely there tank top thing and her Lycra shorts. She appeared to be yelling at Kali and was swatting at her. Kali clearly wanted to play and dropped a stick in front of her feet. Percy typed on the keyboard and the video monitor was now playing the tape in real time, no more time lapse. Serenity picked up the stick, wacked Kali across the face with it. While screaming and ranting, she threw it in the rear of the yard. Kali looked confused but then ran to get the stick. Serenity stomped over to the open septic tank and stood with her arms on her hips, peering down. Then she got down on her knees right on the edge of the large opening, her arms balancing her on either side as she appeared to lower her head down and peer into the huge underground tank. That's when Kali reappeared with the stick in mouth and she promptly head butted Serenity's skinny Lycra-ed ass right over the edge into the septic tank! Kali then went up to the lid's edge and barked, ran around in circles, went back to the tank's open lid and barked. This went on for the next half hour or so. Serenity never reappeared. She had been head butted into the old septic tank and never came out.

We all let out a collective gasp and Wanda said, "Damn shit! Did ya'll see that there? Honey, that dog done knocked her white ass into the tank. I tell you I think she drowned in there, 'cause I sure don't see her coming back out!" Percy was rewinding and replaying it.

I was in shock, "Yes, it does appear Serenity drowned in her septic tank. Who would ever? I mean the old tank is clearly large enough for someone to drown. That tank is at least eight by six feet according to Arnie and when I saw it, I was amazed at how big those old septic tanks are. It was completely full of water and waste, hence the dire need for pumping. I don't think there are any handles or ladders inside. Oh my god, she really did drown in her own septic tank!"

Wanda was shaking her head, "Lord if that don't just beat all! I'm telling you, she was such a bull shitter and here she done drowned in her own shit." God, how is that for poetic justice I thought. Then I said we should hit the speed dial for Detective Davies. That's what we did. Percy burned a CD of the surveillance tape, for backup, while we waited for Davies to arrive. Percy called Arnie and asked her to come over, he wanted her to see the tape and maybe pry the lid off if need be. Once Detective Davies arrived, he was as floored as we were at what the tape showed. Arnie was just as shocked. "We should get over there now and I'll pop that lid so we can take a gander. I got my crow bar in my rig. Damn when I was out here last Saturday afternoon, as you all can see on that tape, I didn't see nothing out of the ordinary. Just Kali sitting in the yard all calm for once. You could see, I put that heavy iron lid back on, rolled out a bit of the sod and that was it."

We all went next door, Ronnie let us in. She and Darla were in yet another TV, fast food marathon, the cigarette smoke almost as thick as the haze at the Wharf Rat. Detective Davies sat them down and explained what we had discovered. Darla started to cry. Then Davies and Arnie went out to the back yard. No real surprise, once Arnie popped the lid, Serenity's body was floating on top inside the tank.

Thirty-seven

The weekend passed by in a haze of its own. By Monday, the coroner had ruled Serenity's death to be a drowning. She had apparently hit her head when Kali knocked her in the tank and then blacked out and drowned. Once again, a media whirl ensued and Katie Katori was really after me for an "exclusive" interview. As if I could really add anything. On Tuesday, I watched at Wanda's house a report Katie did with RG. There she was in her gleaming white men's suit, yellow crew cut and now a black arm band. She appeared somewhat tired. I guess the daily hits of Power Up Serenity drugs were no longer there to give her a boost? "Well, Katie as a star member of Serenity's Winner's Circle, I do have to say her death is a tragedy on all levels for all concerned. As one of Clinton's VIPs I find it especially horrible that Serenity broke the trust of all who believed in her and her cause. I did learn a lot from her, despite her deception and there is still an inner core truth to which she spoke. That's why I've personally formed a Serenity recovery group and we are going to meet every Tuesday evening at Cooper's Hawk Mortgage. Anyone who is interested in attending can get the contact information on their screen. My husband Eddie and I both look forward to helping facilitate this critical healing that survivors of Serenity and TOTAL need and deserve." Katie then said she was going to be there, "Closure is so important for healing." RG quickly interjected, "We will also, of course, have information on various loan products available. You know I have personally found that when I encounter a personal crisis, such as a death of a loved one, a crucial part of closure can involve rearranging or shaking up your finance sector, to encourage the wounds to heal faster and new things to flourish."

Yes, RG the mortgage broker was not missing a beat at her endless self-promotion. I would think the recovery group should be called something like "Imbeciles Who Believed a Lying Twat Like Serenity" or some such. I heard that TOTAL was temporarily shut down; most likely it would remain closed but who really knew until all the legal and police dust settled. Until then, Clinton had an unemployed army of ex high school girls' hockey team coaches to deal with.

Wednesday rolled around and it was Norman's closing day. I had a gift of champagne and chocolates all ready for Norman and Amy. Once the escrow officer called me at 4:00 p.m. and let me know the deed had recorded in Norman's name, I took off to get the keys from the listing agent. Then I picked up Wanda at Safety Mortgage. She wanted to come along to hand off the keys with me. She was curious as to what the house Norman had purchased looks like and she had a nice house plant she wanted to give him for financing his purchase with her. I called Norman to let him know we were heading over to the house and he said he'd be there in a half hour or so. He let me know Amy might get there before he did. Wanda and I drove over to Rosedale. She had on a billowing flower print dress and a large potted plant with a big red bow sat in her lap with the bulk of it hanging out of the passenger side window.

I turned on Norman's street and as I pulled up I noticed a For Sale sign in Tyler and Tammy Matthews' yard. I suppose Tammy was not about to partake in any dance classes or pool parties at Norman's house. I noted it was a Winterfrost sign from my branch. The listing agent was Tiger Conley. "Wanda that must be the new agent Todd was so excited about the other day. Have you ever heard of that agent?" She nodded no as she attempted to get out of the car without the plant falling from her grasp. The For Sale sign was one of our office's generic signs with a listing agent rider placed on its edge. This is usually what new agents use until they are established or until the sign manufacturing company can complete the custom For Sale sign order. This Tiger didn't waste a minute procuring a listing. I'd never heard of her or him but that really didn't mean too much; it's not as if I swim in "A-list" real estate agent circles—god forbid!

We walked up the front walk and I unlocked the door. The sellers had left everything all spic and span. I turned on the kitchen and bathroom lights, opened blinds and we placed our gifts on the empty kitchen counters and then went out the back door. The sellers had allowed Norman to have his pool people come over and stake out the sight where the above ground pool and hot tub was going to go. I also noticed down by the basement's rec. room's sliding glass door were hardware supplies and a gleaming steel pole. Wanda took note, "This must be the stuff to make Amy's dance space. That's a damn big pole they got there, she gonna be doing some serious rehearsing on that there shiny pole." We heard a car door slam and walked around to the front. On the street was a taxicab and next to it was an older woman wearing a cloth, powder blue overcoat and large blue tinted glasses with two huge suitcases next to her. She was paying the cabbie and looking around. I called out, "Hello, may I help you?"

The cab pulled away, "*Oy!* My *tuchis* is killing me from that flight. You must be Alex. Here, come help with my bags dear. I'm Mrs. Ethal Kluntz, Norman's mother. We've already met over the phone. I thought I would fly out here and surprise my son on his big day, he doesn't know I'm here! I feel like you are a son of mine already Alex, even if you are a *goy*. You've done such a good thing, such a good thing, getting my Norman to finally invest his money and buy a house! I told him for years, *Norman you are just flushing your money down the toilet.* I mean literally down the toilet every time he paid that *gozlin* landlord. *Oy vay*, I tell you that boy would not come to see reason. His father Herman Kluntz, gawd rest his soul, was like to die that his only son could be such a *putz* and pay a landlord his good money all these years. Why this house looks just like the photos my Normie sent me. Just like it! Oh, who are you?" She said while pulling down her large bluish glasses which were on a safety chain and looking up at Wanda. "I'm Wanda Billings, I did your son's loan." She said while shaking Ethel's hand.

"Oh, the finance lady, of course Norman told me all about you. *Mazel tov* to you! Such a smart young woman running her own business and making my Norman see why he needs to invest his money in a mortgage not the landlord's retirement fund! So let's get inside, I want to see that kitchen. I brought some of my cleaning supplies with as I know it's going to need a good cleaning. You can help me figure out which bedroom I am going to take, leave those bags at the door for now."

Oh god, did this woman just indicate she is staying over for a while? I don't think Norman has any clue she is coming, does he? "Ah, certainly Mrs. Kluntz, I'll grab these bags for you and please go right in." I nearly fell over trying to lift the huge suitcases, what did she pack in them, bricks? Wanda reached out and stopped me from tumbling over and then helped me lug the bags into the entry way.

"Ohh, so nice, so nice, such a very nice place! Now I just love a split level, I always have. I told Norman's father we should've had a split level but did he listen? Did he ever listen, *oy*! Not Herman Kluntz, gawd rest his soul. Now this kitchen is a nice size, not completely the correct appliance triangle layout I told Norman about mind you but we can make do. *Feh*! Now these yellow curtains over the sink have to go, they need to go right now I tell you! Can you reach them Alex? Just pull that rod right down. I've got my measuring tape somewhere in this purse, I can go ahead and take note of this window. I am going to make new curtains for all of Norman's windows. You know I sold draperies for years? Years I tell you, years! I know quality window coverings when I see them and I tell you these are not, just look they aren't even lined! Yes, that's right just rip them down Alex, toss them in the trash. Oh, look at the view from the sink's window. What's with all those stakes out in the yard Alex? What, are they excavating or something? Normie didn't buy on some landfill now did he? Please tell me my Norman took precautions and read all the deed paperwork. You know I told Norman it was very important that he....”

"Ding-dong, I'm HOME! Normie, it's ME! Come on baby, aren't you gonna come out here and carry me over the threshold?" Oh dear god, Amy had arrived. I quickly glanced over at Wanda and her eyes were bugging out. From the look on Ethel's face, I could tell this visit from Amy was news to her. She walked out of the kitchen into the entry hall and stopped half way to the front door. There in the open doorway stood Amy in all her finery. Today she was wearing a hot pink fish net dress that just barely covered her business. It made Wanda's Angela Davis/Panther vintage mini dress look positively quaint and wholesome. With her ample cleavage spilling out, the dress might as well not have had a top at all. Despite being a crocheted fish net weave her nipples and privates were somehow covered with a flesh colored liner or what? Her long legs were glistening with oil and sparkles and she wore extremely tall see-through acrylic stilettos with hot pink flowers on the toe parts. Her wavy black 1980s Cher hair was extra puffy and glistening with shellac or something. She parted her inflated pink lips and gasped at the sight of Norman's mother. Then she ran towards Ethel squealing, "Ohhh, you must be Mother Normie! It's so cool to meet you!" This she shouted as she engulfed and bear hugged Ethel Kluntz in her arms, actually lifting her off the floor for a few seconds.

Ethel immediately began to squirm and started clawing at Amy, "Let me go you *kurva*! Oh MY gawd, who are YOU? What are you doing in my Norman's house? How do you even KNOW my Norman?"

Amy's inflated lips broke into an enormous smile, "Why you *are* Mother Ethel and surprise, I'm Amy! Norman has been keeping me a big secret from you. Oh this is just too cute! He wanted us to have like a surprise meet-up today. He didn't tell me you were coming out to visit. Now isn't that just like Normie to go and surprise…"

"Visit, EXCUSE me? I am certainly not here on a visit. No, I can tell you this. If it is in fact true, and please gawd tell me it is not, but if it is indeed true that you even remotely know my son then it is clear as bell to me, Norman Kluntz's mother, that I need to be here all the time. *Oyyy*, Alex tell me this is not true!"

"But Mother Ethel, Normie and I are practically married, we've been together for like a year and he's the whole reason I'm now the headliner at Scandals. Wait till I show you the basement where he is having my very own dance rehearsal space built! They were supposed to deliver my pole today, Alex did you happen to notice if there's a shiny pole anywhere out back?"

"NORMIE? Why you common little hussy whore! *Kurva!* My Norman wouldn't a bit more have anything to do with you or your kind. Alex, you tell this stranger she has to leave and right now!"

Before I could reply, we heard a car pull up in the drive and out popped Norman. He came running up the walk with a bouquet of flowers in his hand. Amy turned and ran out the door to greet him. She leapt up into his waiting arms and they did a happy little spin in the front walk. That is until he caught sight of Ethel out of the corner of his eye and then he literally dropped Amy into the grass. Ethel was at the top of the front door stoop and Wanda and I stood a couple of feet behind her looking on in horror.

"WHAT? Norman Anthony Kluntz THIS is how you thank me? You KNOW this *kurva*, this hussy woman? *Oy*! You are killing me Norman, just KILLING me! Quick Wanda, get my purse there's some salts in it, I'm feeling faint. OH MY GAWD, tell me I am dreaming. This IS a dream, right Alex? Please tell me that my only son has not disgraced me and worse, his father too Herman Moishe Kluntz, gawd rest his soul. Ohhh, the pain, the PAIN! I need a seltzer, they're in my purse, Wanda! Ohh, get me a glass of water for my seltzer, oh the agony, the treachery and betrayal of an ungrateful son! And you are not even wearing your *yarmulkah* Normie! Oh, I need that water and seltzer right now, right now I tell you! Is somebody bringing me my salts?"

Wanda had run in the house and was bringing Ethel's sizable black purse out front. Amy had picked herself up and upon hearing the need for a glass of water said, "Now I saw someone next door around the side of the house with a hose, I'll just run over there and fetch a glass of water. I'll be right back!" And off she tottered into Tyler and Tammy's yard.

Ethel Kluntz was now sitting on the front stoop, clutching at her chest and Wanda was digging through Ethel's purse to find the seltzer and salts for her. Norman still stood dead frozen in the center of the front walk looking as if someone had shot him with a stun gun of sorts. Ethel started to wail, "OHH dear GAWD please tell me this

274

is not so! Not my ONLY son. The son his father and I worked so hard to put through Temple mind you. Four years, four years of higher education Alex, that's what we saved and sacrificed to pay for. We even helped out with Normie's grad work too mind you. And this! This is how he chooses to repay his own mother? *Oyyyy*, such a disgrace! Oh, I did not raise this, no! I knew I should never let you move out of Philly, I knew it would not be good. Ohh, the lies, the deceit Norman. You have been having relations with that *goy* hussy, not even a nice gentile mind you but a whore, a *KURVA* Norman! I am so happy your father has passed, I really am. He would just up and die if he saw this here Norman, just up and die. WHAT HAVE I DONE LORD TO DESERVE THIS? And in my golden years no less! Ohh, and to think Mrs. Rosenshine's little Gabriel is all grown now Norman and he has given her three grandchildren. Three, count them! Gabe your best friend and look what he does for his mother. Do I ask too much, tell me DO I? Wanda as a woman, do I ask too much? He thanks me with a *kurva* and one that dances no less! Did you find my bottle of salts, oh mother of gawd pass them over here I'm feeling faint."

As if this dramatic episode were not enough now we heard screaming from next door. It appeared Amy was being chased with a hose by Tammy across the Matthews' yard. I quickly ran over and tried to intervene. Tammy was soaking Amy and Amy was trying to run in her hooker heels while screaming for Norman to help. Norman remained frozen on the front walk, more panicked than ever. Amy ran across the property line and into the back yard. Tammy stopped at the

line, her garden hose still spraying on the grass. "Oh, it's YOU! That
AWFUL real estate agent who sold this house to that man and his
hooker! Well you can see for yourself, the Matthews are not long for
this block! I will NOT have my children live next door to and be
exposed to that, that woman! She has the nerve to come over and ask
ME for a glass of water? You better warn her Mr. Shit Agent, if she
dare sets one toe into my property, just one, I will KILL her, do you
hear me?" Tammy's mom hairdo was completely frayed up on one
side and despite her perky suburban sailor blue and white outfit, she
looked like a psychopath who was quite capable of killing.

I managed to sputter, "I-I-- I'll make sure she knows that and
she stays in her own yard." Tammy glared back at me, "You do that,
you neighborhood wrecker!"

I decided it was time to leave. The wonderful house warming
presents were already inside, the keys on the counter, the family had
gathered to celebrate and break bread. Time to go! Wanda seemed to
psychically catch my thoughts and came down the front stoop. She
patted Norman's arm, "Now baby your mama is bit upset with you
now but don't be too concerned, I'm sure she will come around."

Ethel snapped up, "Come around? Oh, no I am NOT coming
around, especially around here! Wanda, Alex, you put my bags in your
car. I am leaving with you. Norman here has a LOT to think about.
He needs to kick that hussy out of here before I will even begin to
THINK about forgiving him and moving in this house and making it a
proper and respectable home for him." With that she walked over to
my car and got in the back seat. Wanda and I looked at each other

wondering what to do. Ethel reached over and hit my car horn, "Come on already! Get my bags, make haste, we are leaving!"

Wanda and I lugged Ethel Kluntz's bags to my car's trunk and then got in. Norman turned and stared at us in the car, his look still beyond shock and awe. "Drive!" Ethel ordered. And I did. "Now, whose house am I staying at?" Ethel asked as I rolled through a stop sign in surprise. "Better I should stay at Wanda's house I think. You know the whole girl thing and all. I'll just be there until Alex can help me find a nice retirement property to buy. My Norman may be with that hussy for now but mother is moving here and mother will win this battle! Wanda what kind of mattress do you have in your guest room?" Wanda gave me a panicked, wide-eyed look. I smiled and nodded in the rear view mirror. "Well Mrs. Kluntz, Wanda used to date a salesman a few years ago who sold mattresses. That was before her most recent ex, who is a high end appliance salesman. I am quite certain she has the highest quality mattress you can purchase, don't you Wanda? She also has a state-of-the-art kitchen. Her refrigerator even has curtains in it Mrs. Kluntz! Didn't you mention that you once sold curtains? You'll just be amazed at these custom refrigerator draperies.

The following chapters are from the Alex Campbell Real Estate Mystery Novel, <u>No Rest</u>.

1

The scaly and yellow fungus-covered toe nails were really gross! She's gotta be kidding me, a pedicure? Sure enough, the one un-pedicured foot was sitting up on the blue leather ottoman awaiting my attention. Resting on the floor was her other fat foot, completely scale free, oiled and shiny, the five toe nails painted a perfect dark pink. "Here's the pumice stone, I'll start soaking in this tub of water. Be a dear and pour some witch hazel in it for me."

What? "Ah, Mrs. Holzer I came over here to give you my listing presentation, remember today at 12:30 our appointment? It looks like your pedicure person only got one foot taken care of. I can leave and come back another time if this isn't convenient." I was feeling it was time to leave but for some reason I didn't see the door.

"Leave, what? My you must be kidding me! Stewart Vezano was just here from Rockside Realty and look at what a great job he did with my left foot." Mrs. Holzer, pulled her pale blue bath robe open a bit and fanned herself. She was a white haired, well over 75 year old woman. I thought she was interested in listing her house. I had all my comps prepared and was ready to review and tour her house. I still couldn't make out a door anywhere, odd. "Now come on Alex, opportunity knocks. Come over here and take care of my right foot for me, it really needs a good scrub." She patted the sofa cushion with her gnarly liver spotted hand. "Alex I'm waiting. Stewart sure had no problem cleaning up my left foot, now did he? He also gave me a wonderful listing presentation and you know if my right foot isn't taken care of to my satisfaction, I may just have to list with Stewart."

She has got to be kidding me? Was my bank account really in such dire need as to scrub her nasty foot? No, definitely not! It is time to get out of here, let Stewart the major kiss ass whore, have this one. I'm out! But where is the damn door? I can't..."

"Alex! Alex, come on over here now and let's get my foot all nice and pretty...."

Aghhhh! What the? What's that wet slimy thing on my face? Oh god! Whew, that was one awful nightmare, "Get off of me Clyde, you can see I'm awake! No need to try and French kiss me as well." Oh my god what a fucked up nightmare. Jeesh, and I usually don't recall my dreams, much less wake up in a cold sweat from a nightmare. I got out of my bed and stumbled into my small bathroom and proceeded to scrub my face. Time for coffee; definitely coffee. I walked into my open kitchen and living area, pulled up one of the steel and glass garage doors which is also the rear wall of my little cottage. I let Clyde, my reddish brown Benji movie look-a-like dog, run out onto the patio and into the fenced yard to check out his turf while I filled his stainless bowl with kibble. God, things have got to improve I thought as I filled the coffee pot with filtered water. The last listing I had got all screwed up due to a missing owner. (see Volume Two) The real estate market in Clinton is definitely slowing down, still not as bad as the rest of the nation but worrisome enough. Hence the nightmare, eeewe!

I'm Alex Campbell, just over 41 and I have been selling residential real estate in the mid-size city of Clinton going on almost five years now. Some days are better than others and the start to this one was not exactly auspicious. Why would I have a nightmare about some old woman and a listing appointment? No listing appointment like that was on my calendar. I poured my coffee and went to sit outside on my patio. The sound of the gurgling water was nice and soothing. I had finally managed to build a little water fall feature in the small stream that runs through my back yard. My 800 square foot 1919, gutted and rebuilt, arts and crafts bungalow is in an undiscovered/un-named neighborhood just south of downtown Clinton and my lot borders a greenbelt. Clyde was out at the far end of my back yard, scouting for his nemesis, the squirrels, in the large oak tree. I was sitting there contemplating nothing when my cell phone began to ring. I noted it was Wanda's number and picked up.

"Damn, just let that phone ring and ring before you pick up!" She barked in an annoyed tone. "Wake yo' butt up! Alex, you get yourself dressed and get over to my house and take that Ethel Kluntz OUT! And honey, I mean out and you are NOT to come back with her until you have SOLD her something and her moving day is set in stone. I'm telling you the truth, that woman is playing on my VERY last nerve today. You know she took out them curtains I had made for my refrigerator this morning and was starching them? Says, the creases are not sharp enough! Then, sounds like she gonna be emptying out all my kitchen cabinets and cleaning them. She wants to put down that shelf liner crap, talking 'bout how no kitchen can have clean cabinets without no shelf liner paper. Wanting to know if I want plain white liner or one of them patterned liners. I'm telling you Alex this here is no good! Not gonna do no more at all!"

Wanda had taken in Ethel Kluntz as an unexpected house guest almost two weeks ago. Ethel is the mother of my client Norman Kluntz and Wanda was the mortgage broker for his loan. He recently moved into his new split level house in Rosedale that I sold to him, along with his girlfriend Amy. Ethel had flown from Philadelphia to Clinton to surprise her son on his closing day. However, Norman failed to let Ethel know he had a girlfriend or that he was moving in with her. Things did not go well when Ethel discovered what the living situation was. Thus, Wanda inherited Ethel. As it turns out, Ethel has decided she is going to move to Clinton and I guess it has become my job to find her a new place to live. Either that or Wanda commits homicide in her own home. I tried to placate Wanda, "Good morning to you too Wanda. I can tell you are not having a very good morning. You sound as if you are feeling a bit stressed? I can understand that feeling Wanda. I know Ethel may be a bit frustrating but at least you have helped her out and…"

"Frustrating? Have you lost your white-ass mind? Damn fucking pain in my fat black ass is more like it! Oh NO, I ain't hearing none of your new pop shrink/Dr. Phil wanna-be crap. You just do like I say! Get your bony butt dressed and get over to my house and take Ethel out and SELL her a house TODAY! Got it? That is what you still do right, sell houses? Last time I checked that's what your business card had written on it, *real estate agent*. So get moving and sell damn it! Cause unless you get it done and fast, there's gonna be some serious shit going down at *Chateau* Wanda and none of it pretty or fun in a reality TV way neither."

"I hear you Wanda and I understand your frustration. You know I have a tour set up for her today and I'm rolling over there in an hour or so. I'll see what I can do."

"I already told you to cut out that shrink validation crap, now didn't I? You read anymore of them damn pop shrink books and we gonna have blows. Hell, if that boundary assertion book you read wasn't bad enough, and now it sounds like you readin' some phony care bear book. All I can say is bitch better be ready to look her ass off, 'cause she best be buying herself a house today!" With that Wanda hung up. Clearly she was annoyed and honestly I can't say I blame her. Ethel Kluntz is a tad controlling. That said, Ethel was cleaning up Wanda's house, overstepping her boundaries in the process perhaps, but Wanda's house sure was looking shiny and clean these days. Wanda was correct, I had started reading another psychology book. This mass market tome is all about acknowledging others' feelings and validating where they are. Yes, <u>Honoring Me, Honoring You: Creating We Synergy</u> would hopefully help me out as much as the previous book on boundaries I read, <u>Step on My #ick and I'll Slug You!</u>

I finished my coffee and proceeded to get dressed. I wanted to wear my cut-off khaki shorts, a tee shirt and Jesus sandals as Wanda calls them, (a.k.a. Birkenstocks). Especially with the summer just about over, it will not be too much longer that I can roam around in my favorite attire. However, today I had already scheduled a tour for Ethel to see a couple of listings at Seaview, the snotty seniors-only town just south of Clinton. As rigid as Seaview is I am surprised I did not receive a memorandum as to what constitutes acceptable real estate attire when showing a listing at Seaview. They have a rule for absolutely everything. Well, since no memo was received, I had to use my best judgment. I figured blue jeans of any kind would scare the hell out of them, so I opted for stone colored and dry cleaner pressed chinos, socks, which I despise, brown slip-on shoes (slip-on being key when you are a real estate agent), and a brown belt to match, an effort on my part. I found one of my more conservative short sleeve plaid shirts, this one a pale yellow and blue (soothing Swedish flag colors). I then put on my navy summer blazer and called it good. This is as close to proper real estate attire as I could muster. I made sure Clyde was okay in the back yard, shut up my little ranch and went to pick up Ethel at Wanda's house.

anda lives in the Highmont, an old neighborhood that sits
directly north and above downtown Clinton. It is situated on a
very high hill and has some of the best views of downtown and Warner
Sound of any neighborhood in Clinton. The Highmont was developed
in the 1890s and for a brief period it was the premier neighborhood
during Clinton's boom years as a shipping port. However with the
advent of the car in daily life and the removal of the trolley system in
the early 1930s, the Highmont lost its luster. It is now a predominantly
black neighborhood with artists and free spirits thrown in. It was
Clinton's version of Haight Ashbury back in the day and still has a few
active communal living houses and brightly painted Victorians and
clapboards are fairly common. Wanda's house blends right in. It is a
bright turquoise, late 1920s, three bedroom bungalow with two eyelet
windows up top. Wanda frequently repaints her front door when her
moods change and it had recently been repainted a vivid orange.
However, as I pulled up to the curb in my aging, two-door, blue Volvo,
I noticed her front door was now a dark brown. That certainly was
off-character as Wanda lives for bright colors in all parts of her life. I
was about to get out when Ethel shot out the door.

"No need to come in Alex, I am right here. Just a second and
let me lock this door, the paint is still wet so this is a bit tricky." Ethel
called out from the front stoop. Down the front steps she came
dressed in a pink cloth coat, sensible tan lace up shoes, a big black
purse, her oversized blue glasses, secured with a chain, making her eyes
appear a bit bugged. "*Oy*, my feet are already killing me and we haven't

even started our tour." she said while getting in the car. I had learned from the last tour, that despite her over 70 age bracket, she did not like old school open the doors for women protocol. This was fine by me. It reminded me of the sixth grade when we had this new "women's lib" English teacher at our school who was making waves left and right. One of her axes to grind was boys holding or opening any doors for her. She would yell and scream if you did it, going off on some diatribe about how she was a grown woman and could open her own doors thank you very much and how it was her duty to make sure boys like us never babied women, etc.… If she saw you holding the door or helping carry books for a fellow student that happened to be a girl, she'd start to yell and immediately dash over and lecture you about patronizing women, grabbing the books out of your hands and thrusting them into the girl's.

At the time, it was considered good manners to hold the door for any elder, male of female. But for Ms Autri that was not acceptable, "Ms" being her other major point of contention. If you dare said "Mrs." by mistake she'd yell out, "No I am sorry, my mother is not here!" Then if you slurred or made a mistake and said "Miss" all hell broke loose. You were in for a lecture on male chauvinistic pigs and how demeaning that title was; such an odd time period the early 1980s were. Nowadays people are so rude in general that Ms Autri need not worry about anyone patronizing her by holding a door open for her, male or female. I'm sure she's just thrilled with the recent group of 20-something women who seem to favor baby talk, acting like helpless bimbos, and dressing to look like hookers, not to mention plastic surgery out the yin-yang. Yes, I'd love to hear her take on the "sisterhood" today. However, I am sure the sisterhood is now all amiss due to some enormous male conspiracy.

Junior high flashbacks aside, I was driving Ethel Kluntz to Seaview today. She had not liked any of the in-city condos I had previously shown her and then she decided it would be best if she could live in an age restricted community. The few in-city age restricted condos that I showed her, she did not like at all. So, this left us no other choice but the town of Seaview.

Seaview is situated about 30 minutes south of Clinton, actually it is directly south of the greenbelt that is at the back of my house's lot. Well, the old Sutton estate and land preserve lies in between but close enough. Seaview is a legally incorporated town that was built by developers starting in the early 1970s. Only developers could have come up with such an inaccurate town or housing complex name. The "sea" is nowhere close by. The correct name should have been Soundview but the developers probably thought "Sea" sounded more exotic and would boost the sales prices, who knows! It was designed to be an age restricted town. Originally the minimum age was 70 but at some point it was lowered to 62. In the 1960s some retirees had an informal seniors-only mobile home park on the land where Seaview is. From there, the developers entered the picture, smelled money, took over and expanded. There are no mobile homes anywhere near Seaview today.

The first phase was completed in 1973 and that includes the town part and the first two five-story "tower" buildings. Originally they were rental apartments but they converted to condominiums in the late 1970s. These tower condos have actual views of Warner Sound far below. The three other building phases (1984, 1995 and 2000) consist of some bungalow neighborhoods, another grouping of five-story towers (without water views), and a small assisted living condo complex. As long as you have the bank account, from age 62 to death, Seaview has got you covered. Seaview, the town, is legally incorporated and has its own mayor, city council, police force, utilities; it is its own gated fiefdom. It is probably easier to get through the White House's front gate than the front gate at Seaview.

To show a listing at Seaview entails some pre-planning. First, you must contact the listing agent as all units require appointments regardless if they are vacant or owner occupied. They also require the listing agent be present for all showings, a ludicrous stipulation, but one of their rules none-the-less. One could surmise they put this rule in place because they would prefer the owner to list with Seaview Realty which is the town's real estate office and exclusive representative for all units which are owned by the Seaview Care Corporation. That works out to over 70 percent. They allowed a third of the units constructed to be owned in full by the occupant with no legal stipulation to list with Seaview Realty. However, they still retain very strict co-op board control approval of anyone who is going to live in Seaview and even the independently owned units must pay a hefty fee to the Seaview Care Corporation before title is transferred. With two thirds of the units in Seaview, the corporation actually holds title and they are exclusively listed through Seaview Realty. Even with the independently owned units, a listing agent and seller must present the list price to the Board for approval, prior to listing the unit for sale. He or she must also make sure prospective buyers meet all of the rigid income and rule guidelines prior to having the seller sign off on any offers. In addition, once an offer is accepted by an independent seller in Seaview, this offer must be submitted to the Board for further review and final approval. All signed around purchase and sale agreements must also include an addendum which outlines this and several other laborious buyer/seller processes that are unique to Seaview. In short, listing or selling in Seaview is a major pain in the ass for a real estate agent. Hence, the majority of listings and sales go through the Seaview Realty office. They are notorious for treating "outside" agents such as myself with great scorn and seemingly do everything they can to persuade owners not to list with another brokerage besides Seaview Realty. In recent years, there has been pressure by the State Attorney General's office to force Seaview to open up its real estate, lest they be charged with running a monopoly or racketeering I suppose. Therefore, Seaview is now reluctantly more open to agents such as myself representing a buyer or allowing an owner in Seaview to have one of us "outsiders" represent them as sellers.

However, this "openness" can only go so far as one of the state's ex-governors currently resides in Seaview and was preceded by two ex-governors before him who passed away there. And the death turnover rate is exactly what Seaview Care Corporation is all about. They count on deaths and a controlled turnover rate to ensure their profits. Regardless of who sells or buys at Seaview, the Seaview Care Corporation is assured at least a 40 percent share of all profits. And 40 percent is the very least, the norm being somewhere around 60 percent and 100 percent for the actual corporate owned units. The fees they charge as a "citizen" moves from say a bungalow to the assisted living complex are quite steep. And if you make it to "God's final waiting room" (a.k.a. Seaview Sunrise Care) then they empty all of your bank accounts before your last gasp registers on the EKG monitor. Not to worry though, because once you have expired, they'll move you along to the Seaview Mortuary where those kind folks will fleece the remainder of your relatives' pennies to put you up in style in the exclusive Seaview Eternal Slumber Columbarium. Cremation is mandatory in Seaview; I guess bodies take up too much saleable real estate? The Seaview Care Corporation has it all figured out, you never need to leave the gated town. They have their own supermarket, gas station, car wash, dry cleaner, drugstore, hair salons, movie theatres, radio station, local cable access TV station, weekly newspaper, shopping mall, gym, spa, restaurants, clubs, golf course, it's all there and only for residents and their approved guests' use. It is all safe and secure and marked up at least 10 percent over "real world" retail prices.

Once I exited the interstate and pulled onto the Seaview access road, there was the colorful billboard sign all spick and span (per the rules, they probably wash it once a day) complete with drawings of boats bobbing in water and seagulls flying above, *City of Seaview, Where Rest and New Beginnings Await You and Tomorrow Starts Today!* Then in smaller print below the huge shiny logo *Incorporated 1973. All access strictly limited to member residents and their approved guests only.* Who knows, since my last visit a couple of years ago, maybe they've installed iris scans as part of their front gate, security shake down procedure.

3

There is one gate for Seaview residents which has a keycard swipe and personal entry code and then there is the visitor's gate. The guardhouse is built to look like a mini Swiss chalet and the gate is no ordinary wooden slat that slowly moves up and down. No, the gate is a heavy metal affair that moves across tracks and the only thing that could remotely smash through it would be a semi truck.

I pulled up and a guard in the Seaview uniform, green polo shirt and navy slacks, came up to the car. "Dave" as his name badge indicated was somewhere in his early 50s and outfitted with a microphone on his lapel, a stun gun in his belt holster along with an industrial grade flashlight, a ring of formidable looking keys and handcuffs hanging from his belt. He asked for both our i.d.'s and took them in the gate house. After a long wait, he reappeared with a clipboard. He gave me a map directing us to the visitor's parking lot and said the Seaview Realty representative would be waiting at the Visitor's Center to meet us. Dave noted my car's make and license plate number, gave me a laminated card to place on the driver's side of the dashboard and two laminated visitor badges on green lanyards for us to wear. He said we could get our i.d.'s back when we checked out and returned the visitor badges. Dave then gave us a semi frigid smile and said, "You two enjoy your visit to Seaview today. Make sure you obey the 15 mile an hour speed limit at all times until you have safely parked your vehicle in space number six in the visitor's lot. Sir, be sure you only park in that designated space, or you will be towed." With that said, the huge metal gate slowly slid open and we were off.

Why Dave even mentioned the speed limit is beyond me, as they have sizeable speed bumps in the road every 50 feet. It would be a miracle to get your vehicle anywhere over 10 miles per hour before you lurched over the next speed bump. The entry road is windy and extremely well manicured. Vivid green (chemically fed) Bermuda grass lines either side of the two lane road with carefully maintained birch trees planted alongside every 100 feet. Around the curve on the right is the Seaview Gas Company and Car Wash. Directly across on the left is the sign for the Visitor's Center and parking. The lot had about 10 cars in it and there were plenty of open spaces. At least eight of the parked cars were large boats like Wanda's late 1980s Lincoln Town Car. She would appreciate their car choices. I followed Mr. Gate Nazi's orders and made sure I found the space with the large number "6" painted on the shiny clean asphalt in day glow yellow. It appeared each parking space's sizable number was repainted every month and the asphalt was squeaky clean. The Visitor's Center building looks like a Disney version of a Swiss chalet Heidi would live in. And just like Disney, there was a good (I hope) witch waiting at the Center's front doors.

"Well hello there, you must be Alex Campbell with Winterfrost Real Estate and this must be Mrs. Ethel Kluntz?" This, from an immaculately dressed, pressed and coifed woman who was over 70, although it was hard to tell exactly how far over 70 because she had obviously had a face lift or two. Her gray hair was sprayed into an unmovable helmet which was styled to hide her face lift scars no doubt and accent her gold ball ear rings which perfectly covered her ear lobes. She wore a light pink dress with tan hose and matching pumps. Over her dress she was sporting a green blazer with gold buttons. The Seaview crest was sewn on the breast pocket and a small gold name badge was tacked on her blazer's left lapel next to a pinned-on pink rose. "I am Beverly Ann LeFaye, so nice to meet you all!" She said as she smiled a wide frosted pink lipstick smile, while conspicuously winking at both of us. "I am the exclusive Seaview Realty agent, Social Coordinator for Seaview Care Corporation, resident since 2000, and homeowners' association board president going on two years now. Welcome to Seaview! Won't you please come in and let's get better acquainted." This she said in her honey coated voice, as she held the glass door open for us.

She let us in the immaculate lobby which had an empty front desk with a large framed map of Seaview behind it. American, state, and Seaview flags hung limply on metal poles off to the side. She led us into a smaller office with a sofa and coffee table seating area. "I see you are on time for your appointment and that is always a plus mark in my book! I always say it is so important to adhere to one's planned schedule. Please do have a seat and won't you join me in some light refreshment? I just brewed this pot of coffee. I always think coffee is best when served fresh, now don't you agree? The vice president of our refreshment committee, Patti Giffin Lawford, made these delicious coconut macaroons for us to enjoy, so please do help your selves. I don't think one or two will hurt our waistlines too much, now do you Mrs. Kluntz?" She said as she politely tittered and indicated we should sit down on the pale blue upholstered colonial style sofa. "Now Mrs. Kluntz do you take cream or sugar in your coffee?" Beverly asked as

16

we sat down. She picked up the silver tea pot from the silver service tray and started pouring coffee in three bone china cups with matching saucers and silver spoons. The green Seaview emblem was on the side of each cup. I suppose having coffee was mandatory, not that I really wanted a cup thank you very much. But when Mrs. Wholesome quizzed me as to my java preferences, I let her know cream and three lumps of sugar. "Oh my no, Mr. Campbell! I'm afraid three lumps is just too much. Why you wouldn't believe it now, but sugar habits such as those will just make your waistline balloon as you get older dear. How about some nice saccharine, I personally prefer saccharine." I nodded my head no. She sighed just a bit and then picked of the silver tongs and promptly dropped one lump in. "Let's just see how we do with one lump, I think you'll find it is much better that way especially with my fresh coffee." She said as she winked at me and handed me the cup and saucer.

"Oh, aren't these coconut macaroons delicious? I see Patti has perfected my recipe! The secret is to make sure the egg whites are not beaten too stiff. I'm going to tell stories out of school here, but I believe you are from out of the area Mrs. Kluntz? And Alex, you didn't grow up in Clinton, did you? I don't know your family name from around here so I doubt it. Anyway, I used to be the hostess for the much missed ladies show on Channel Four. These macaroons are one of my most popular recipes from way back." She smiled demurely while offering us the plate of coconut macaroons again.

While taking another one, I let her know how good they were and then went for bonus points by asking her to tell us more about her

17

TV career. Beverly coyly tilted her head to the side, her helmeted hair not moving a follicle, while she slowly stirred her coffee, "Oh my, well since you ask, I had the number one locally ranked TV show for years in Clinton. I started way back before you were even a glimmer in your parents' eyes and I was in my 20s. I was already pretty well known in these parts as I was the local and state pageant beauty queen. Gosh darn, I competed in the Miss America pageant but that tricky Miss North Carolina won that year!" she said while setting her cup and saucer down and winking at us. "I did however, gain a lot of knowledge about live TV from the pageant. Anyhow, I was a happily married, young housewife living in Clinton, when the producers at Channel Four just practically twisted my arm and had me fill in as the hostess of the local ladies home show. Of course it didn't hurt that my husband was a local television executive. I was only supposed to be the substitute hostess for a few weeks while Mary Anne Devail took some time off for health reasons. Poor thing wasn't well and it was a darn shame when she passed away. They never did find out exactly what her cause of death was. If you ask me, I always thought Mary Anne was just too enthusiastic and I don't think her poor heart could handle it. Anyhow, I hosted the award winning, *The Ladies Hour with Beverly Ann LeFaye* every weekday from 1964 all the way until 1979. It was so special and such a treat to help all the homemakers out there and learn new fun and interesting things! Of course by the late 1970s, all that women's liberation stuff just changed everything. I am sure you remember that now don't you Mrs. Kluntz? Aghh, anyhow they reformatted the show and changed the name to *Women Are Talking* and moved the time slot to after the soaps. Gone were any helpful tips, crafts or recipes. They wanted me to talk to women guests about politics, world events and business. Oh it was so tedious and no real lady is interested in that sort of thing. By 1981, we were gone and an era ended. Then my dear husband passed away and gosh, I have just been flying solo ever since. I was lucky enough to become a Seaview resident in 2002. My but I have just gone on here!

Now, let's talk about Seaview and first off I will relate this to what we were just talking about. Seaview has its own mini broadcast station here on the grounds and our local cable access channel is piped into every unit here and also available on extended local access in Clinton. Anyhow, everything just comes full circle and I now host a live weekly show every Saturday night right here called, *What's Happening Seaview!* Isn't that a fresh and hip name? We might be gated and secure but we are up on things here at Seaview. We've dialed in the 4-1-1 as the young folks now say! Mrs. Kluntz you may be interested in attending a broadcast once you live here. The shows are taped live and open to Seaview residents and their select guests. I've tried to combine a bit of my old show with some of the old late night TV glamour that we all so sorely miss these days. We always just have a ball doing the show. There's so much local retired talent living right here in Seaview, that we only need to have two outsiders help us with the production. The rest we handle in-house as we like to say here. Well, Mrs. Kluntz, Ethel if I may, why don't you tell me a little about yourself and then we can all go take a look at the lovely units that are for sale. Why you could even start with your last name. That is such an unusual and interesting name." Beverly set her cup and saucer down again and smiled demurely with her frosted pink lips, her left hand patting her shellacked hair making sure it was all still in place, while she stared directly at Ethel.

Ethel set her coffee cup and saucer down and proceeded to fill Beverly in, "My husband, Herman Moishe Kluntz, passed away over 10 years ago; gawd rest his soul. I naturally took his name when we married in 1958. Not like these girls do today Beverly, you know keeping their own names and all. The hyphenated names, I mean what are their kids supposed to do with all of that? Where will it end I ask you? What, their children's children are going to hyphenate too and then we will just have long hyphenated names, *feh*! Not that I'm some orthodox from Philadelphia. I am Jewish Beverly and I like some of the old values but certainly not to the orthodox extreme. Now Alex might have told you about my son, Norman Kluntz, he works at Clinton Chem Labs. He is a well respected chemist there. His father and I worked our *tuchases* off to put him through Temple and then graduate school as well. So I ask you Beverly, how does this only son of mine thank me? He moves away from his widowed mother here to Clinton. And then what? After years of pleading with him to quit throwing away his hard earned money on rent, he finally decides to wise up and buy.

Oh you say, this is good. No! Not good. You know what this disrespectful son of mine goes and does Beverly? He goes and purchases a perfectly lovely split level home, in Rosedale right Alex? He purchases and I come out here to surprise him and what do I find?

What did I find Alex? I find my only son has taken up living in sin with a stripper! A common two-bit, *goyishe*, stripper Beverly! Have you ever? I mean I don't know if my heart can stand it. Clearly now I am not moving in with my Normie but I do feel the call to be nearby. Only his mother can talk sense back into him and I need to be here to do that. I am only thankful that his dear and loving father is no longer here to see what he has done. So we are here today Beverly to tour your units for sale. I am thinking an age restricted community with progressive care facilities is exactly what I need, I mean we aren't getting any younger now are we Beverly."

Beverly shifted in her chair a bit and sat up straighter. "My, Ethel that is quite a story! You know a number of our residents here also have similar problems with their misbehaving adult children. In fact, we even have a support group, Parents of Misbehaving Adult Children Who Should Know Better that meets on Tuesdays in the Meeting and Activities building. Oh and you, *at my age!* My goodness, you are a youngster here in Seaview terms! We are a bit different from other adult communities. Most are restrictive to age 55 and older and if there is a spouse, they need to be 50 or older. Well, Seaview is 62 and older and any spouse has to be 57 or older. We just feel our age policy keeps things, oh just so! Of course, many of the newer adult communities conform to the *Housing for Older Persons Act of 1995* and don't provide any real activities or senior related services. But that has never been the Seaview way. You'll see we have an enormous range of activities for our residents and there is the option to move on to the assisted care complex when the time comes.

Anyway, I heard you mention that you are of the Jewish faith Ethel? That is just wonderful and here at Seaview we are a diverse and accepting community. We have an interfaith chapel on site and each Saturday there is a Rabbi who comes in from Clinton and he does a Jewish service. I should introduce you to Herschel and Harriet Moshberger and let them fill you in on all things Jewish at Seaview. You know, each year, we even put out and light up a large plastic Menorah along with the big Christmas tree in the town square. Oh yes, I think you will find Seaview is quite the diverse and Jew accepting place to be! You strike me as a woman who values diversity Ethel, not like some of those adult communities in our more humid climes which are shall we say, Jewish exclusive. Now *that* would be boring, not to mention petty, don't you agree? I am sure we can find you just the perfect place to call home here and you can start living your new life and who knows, maybe even reform that wayward son of yours! Now, let's go outside and get in the touring cart and take a look at the wonderful homes that are for sale!"

About the Author

Charles Chaplin (no relation) lives on planet earth (for now) and works in residential real estate (for better or worse).

To receive an e-mail notification when the next Alex Campbell Real Estate Mystery Novel, is available for purchase, please e-mail charles@lifeinseattle.com and write "notify me" in the subject header.

Friend Alex at:

Facebook.com/acrealestatemystery